JUVIE

STEVE WATKINS

**WALKER
BOOKS**

First published in Great Britain 2015 by Walker Books Ltd
87 Vauxhall Walk, London SE11 5HJ

2 4 6 8 10 9 7 5 3

Text © 2013 Steve Watkins
Jacket photographs: jail bars © 2013 albund/Veer;
jumpsuit © 2013 maron/Veer;
girl © 2013 moodboard Photography/Veer

This book has been typeset in Warnock Pro

Printed and bound in Great Britain by Clays Ltd, St Ives plc

British Library Cataloguing in Publication Data:
a catalogue record for this book is available from the British Library

ISBN 978-1-4063-5862-9

www.walker.co.uk

For Janet

CHAPTER 1

In which I say good-bye

My three-year-old niece, Lulu, sits alone at the kitchen table, eating a frozen waffle. It is early, barely sunrise, the day I have to turn myself in to juvie.

"Hi, Lulu," I say as I stumble in. I haven't really slept.

"Hi, Aunt Sadie," she says back.

I pour myself a cup of coffee that smells hours old and sit next to where Lulu perches sideways on her booster seat.

"Where's Carla?" I ask.

"Bathroom." Only she pronounces it *baff*room. It kills me how she says that.

Carla is Lulu's mom, my older sister. Lulu and Carla have spent the night so they can say good-bye one last time. Usually it's just me and my mom in the house. Carla and Lulu have an apartment downtown that Carla pays for with child-support money. She's twenty and waitresses at Friendly's, even though most of her coworkers are stoned most of the time and she promised to get another job. Lulu goes to day care. Her dad is twenty-five and apart from the child support is out of the picture.

"What about Moo-Moo?" I ask. That's what Lulu calls my and Carla's mom.

"Bedroom."

"Did Moo-Moo make the coffee, or did you?"

Lulu smiles. "Moo-Moo made it."

"You want some?"

She shakes her head. "Too stinky."

"Oh, yeah," I say. "Like monkey poo."

Lulu laughs at that.

"Aunt Sadie?" she starts. I know what's coming next, because she's already asked me a hundred times. "Where you going again?"

I try a bite of her frozen waffle, which isn't bad. I wonder if they have them in juvie. "It's one of those missions they send me on sometimes," I say. "For national security. Fighting terrorists."

She blinks, waiting for a real answer.

"It's just this place I have to go to because I got in trouble," I say. "It's called juvie. It's kind of like day care for big kids, only I'm not allowed to come home at the end of each day. But I'll be back soon. And I'll think about you every day. I promise. And I'm pretty sure they'll let me talk to you on the phone."

She's quiet for a minute, chewing on her waffle. I'm afraid she's going to cry.

Then she asks if I can bring her back a Happy Meal.

"Yes, Lulu," I say, relieved. "I will bring you back a Happy Meal. It just might be a while."

Carla walks in right when I say that. Her hair is a wreck; she's wearing socks and an oversize T-shirt I haven't seen before. She looks gaunt, her face all sharp edges and shadows. I remember when she used to be so pretty, back before she met Lulu's dad and started hanging out with druggies. She starts crying, which gets Lulu crying, too.

"I'm so, so, so sorry, Sadie," Carla says, also for about the hundredth time, while I try to comfort Lulu, who doesn't even really understand why she's crying.

"You sure have a funny way of showing it." I nod toward the Pop-Tart wrappers strewn across the counter. I'm wondering if maybe Carla smoked something last night after the rest of us went to bed and then raided the cupboard for anything sweet. "You better get rid of those."

But Carla doesn't move fast enough before Mom comes in, looking tired. And angry.

She brushes past Carla without saying anything, then grabs the wrappers and throws them in the trash.

She must have already seen them when she came in earlier to make the coffee. She just wanted to make sure Carla knew.

She gives Lulu a big hug, then turns to me.

"Is that what you're wearing?" she asks. I have on jeans and a sweatshirt.

"Yes, ma'am."

She shakes her head at me this time. "Couldn't you at least put on a dress?"

"Can't," I say, though the last thing I want to do this morning is disappoint Mom. "I'm riding over on the motorcycle, remember?"

She doesn't respond, just pats Lulu on the head. "I'm off to work, Bug," she says. "You be good today, all right?"

"OK, Moo-Moo."

Mom turns to me. "Are you sure you don't want me to drive you over there?" she asks. "I can take you on the bus, before I start my route." Mom drives a school bus in the mornings and afternoons and then works evening shifts at Target.

"No, that's OK," I say.

She sighs hard and then pulls me to her. She smells like cigarettes, which I know better than to comment on.

"You be good, too," she says. "And just, you know, just—"

She can't finish.

"I'll come on visiting day," she says, and kisses me on the forehead. She grabs her purse and brushes past a sniffling Carla without saying a word. The sound of the door slamming makes me jump.

I don't have to show up at juvie at any particular time, so I take Lulu back in the spare bedroom to help her get dressed for day care. I pretend I can't figure out which hole her head goes through in her shirt. "No, Aunt Sadie!" She laughs. "That's for the arm!" I pull Lulu's pants on her next, and *then* her underwear, which cracks her up, too.

Carla is sitting at the kitchen table when we come out, Lulu finally dressed for real. Carla's staring into a cup of coffee, still disheveled, her hair still a wreck. "Could you clean yourself up already?" I say, harsher than I intend. "I have to go, and you have to get Lulu to day care."

I don't wait for an answer, just grab a bag of stuff I've packed. Carla catches me before I reach the door, though – hugs me and kisses me on the cheek and whispers some more about how sorry she is. I pull away.

Lulu follows me outside to where my motorcycle is parked. I bought it used last year when I was sixteen and got my license. I had to have some way to get to work, and Mom couldn't afford a second car. Plus I had wanted a motorcycle since the first time I'd ridden on one, back when Carla was dating this guy with a Harley. I loved the thrill I got when he let me ride on the back. Mom was mad at me at first, but since I used my own money, there wasn't too much she could say.

Carla stands at the back door and waves, still holding her coffee.

Lulu picks up a pebble from the driveway. "For you."

I hold it in my hand. "Pretty heavy. What is it? Gold?"

"No," she says. "A rock."

I hand it back. "You better keep it for me while I'm gone. Will you do that? Keep it someplace special?"

She nods. Her chin quivers. "I love you, Aunt Sadie."

I lift her up on the bike with me and hug her so tight I can feel all her bones.

"Love you, too," I say.

"Love you three."

"Love you four."

"Love you more."

I have one more person to see before I turn myself in to juvie: my dad. He lives half a mile away in a wing of Granny's old house down a gravel road. Granny died three years ago, not long after Lulu was born; one of the last things she ever got to do was hold Lulu. She made Mom the executor of her estate, which wasn't much besides the house, a big wood-frame place with a wraparound porch. Two engineers, a husband and wife, rent the main part of the house. But they spend most of their time commuting to their jobs up in DC, so aren't around much. Dad got what was left, an addition off the side with a separate porch and entrance – enough room for him to do his hoarding thing. He also has access to three large sheds on his end of the property. There isn't any mortgage, so the rent and Dad's disability check cover his expenses. Either

Mom or I bring him groceries and leave them on the porch once a week. If he needs anything else, he leaves us a note in a Tupperware container, also on the porch.

I see right away that the renters haven't been mowing, though I got on them about it a couple of weeks ago. The weeds come halfway up the wheels on my motorcycle, which pisses me off. I make a note to have Mom talk to them about it the next time she comes by.

I wade through the weeds and onto the porch, squeezing past piles of junk. The wind picks up while I stand there by Dad's door, not knocking. It blows gently through the trees that surround the property and shade the house, and is probably my favorite sound in the world. I close my eyes for a minute and listen. It's like a symphony of whispers. I figure this might be the last time I hear it for a while, so I want to capture the sound and keep it with me as long as possible.

The wind dies after a little while and I finally make myself knock. I don't know how many times over the past three years I've done that and then waited and waited on the chance that Dad will actually answer. Floorboards creak inside, which could be him tiptoeing around, but which could also be the settling sounds of an old house.

"Dad," I say, leaning my head against the door. "It's me, Sadie. I just wanted to tell you that I'm going away today. I have to turn myself in to juvie. You remember. I told you all about it – what happened with me and Carla. And Carla, she's OK. She started going to AA and swears she's going to keep it up while I'm gone. I know she's said that before, but I think she means it this time. She was so scared when she thought —" I clear my throat. "Well, anyway, I just thought you should know."

I pause, not sure what else to say. It isn't as if I need anything from Dad, or expect anything, which is good because Dad's not really in a position to help anyone these days, not even himself. But Granny always said that everybody has a purpose, even if you can't see what it is. Her purpose, the last years she was alive, was taking care of Dad. I can't figure out what Dad's purpose is now, except for wandering around pig paths carved in the towering piles of paper and junk he can't stop himself from collecting. But he's my dad, and even if I don't know what his real purpose is, I know that one of mine is to keep coming over here and checking on him, and I guess to be a good daughter, or as good as I know how.

"I have to go now, Dad," I say to the door. "I'll write you letters. Not that you need any more paper or anything." I laugh lamely. "I hope you'll read them. I hope you'll write me back."

I wend my way off the porch and am halfway to my bike when I stop. I change direction and head around the back to the toolshed. I fill the mower with gas and spend the next hour and a half cutting the grass. I do the weedy areas twice to make sure I get everything. Weeds have a way of lying down under a mower and then springing back up once you're past. I get sweaty in my jeans and sweatshirt, but since the only place I'm going is juvie, I figure it doesn't really matter.

It takes me about fifteen minutes to get there – back down the long driveway from Dad's, through a couple of neighborhoods, ten miles north of town up a straight, wide, boring stretch of Route 1, past a trailer park and a couple of used-car lots and a bunch of abandoned businesses and old motels. All that ends after a while, and for the last couple of miles it's all trees and woods except for a lonely 7-Eleven. I try to turn off my brain and just enjoy the ride – the thrill of being on the Kawasaki this one last time, an open highway that's all mine, the high whine of the gears when I downshift going into a curve, the thrumming of the engine when I hit cruising speed, the chill blast of early-autumn wind that always feels like freedom.

I nearly miss the small juvie sign altogether – I'm going too fast to stop when I see it and have to turn back around. And then, half a mile down a narrow access road, there it is: the Rappahannock Regional Youth Correctional Facility. I sit on my bike in the parking lot and just stare at it for a while. It looks like my high school from in front, all red brick and green corrugated roof and tall, narrow windows no wider than my hand. The whole place sits on about five cleared acres surrounded by a thick tangle of central Virginia oaks and pines and brambles and brush.

I get off my bike and walk around. Along the side and at the back there's a thirty-foot chain-link fence topped with barbed wire, and from there juvie looks even *more* like my high school: picnic tables, exercise area; short basketball court with a couple of bent rims; dusty vegetable garden; nobody in sight except the guard and his reflective sunglasses in the guard tower.

I'm glad to see the basketball court, even if it is just packed dirt and even though they don't have any nets. Coach kicked me off my Amateur Athletic Union team a week ago. The other players threatened to walk if he didn't let me back on the team – they said it wasn't fair, since I hadn't been convicted, at least not yet – but that never happened. Most of them called to commiserate with me for the first couple of days, then they texted, then my cell phone just sort of went dead.

I walk back to my bike and grab the bag of stuff I've brought – shaving cream, razor, deodorant, toothbrush, toothpaste, floss, and tampons. They told me I'm not allowed to bring in any personal items, but I assume that means no cell phones or teddy bears or whatever. I leave my helmet on the handlebars and hide the key under the seat of my motorcycle so Mr. Lewandowski, the auto-repair teacher at the high school, can send somebody to get the bike later. He said they'd take good care of it in his classes while I'm away. That's how he said it, too: "While you're away." As if I'm going on vacation.

Mr. Lewandowski and my dad were friends when they were in high school. My dad isn't friends with anybody now, but Mr. Lewandowski still remembers him, and I think he feels bad that he didn't do something to keep me out of all this trouble.

I stand outside the juvie entrance for five minutes, one hand on my bike, the other shielding my eyes from the morning sun. A couple of blue jays are caterwauling from a tree nearby. The sky is cerulean, the air still crisp with this first dose of autumn. I can't breathe in enough of it, though I try and try. I hate the thought of giving it all up – the bike, the sun, the sky, the air. Haven't I already given up enough? Haven't I already paid the price for something I didn't even do?

Screw this. I grab my helmet and jam it back on, slip the key back out from under the seat, throw my leg over, kick-start the engine, and take off, gunning it out of the parking lot and down the access road back to the highway.

I could do it. I could keep on driving and not look back.

If I turn north onto Route 1, I can zip up to Coal Landing Road, then another couple of miles down Coal Landing past a cheap housing development to where the land gets wild again, and in five minutes I'll be at Aquia Creek, a wide tributary to the Potomac River. There is a certain copse of trees I know about with a lot of under-growth that I use all the time to hide my bike.

Once I do that, I can jump from fallen log to fallen log through the marsh, and slog through some places where there aren't any logs, until I make it over to a place called

Government Island. The brush is so thick there that no one can see to the interior no matter how close they come in their boats on their way down Aquia Creek to the wide Potomac. I've been going to Government Island for years, mostly alone, where there's nobody but me and the squirrels and the raccoons and the otters and the ospreys and the herons, and I wish I could go back there now.

But I know I can't do it. I just can't. Not to Mom. Not to Lulu. Not to Dad. Not even to Carla.

So I make a U-turn in the middle of the highway, the tires squealing in protest, and ride back to juvie.

The first thing I see when I pull up is a woman who kind of looks like my mom standing outside the front door, eating an apple.

She watches me as I pull off my helmet. She watches me as I kick down the bike stand. I watch her, too – eating that apple slowly, like a cow chewing cud. She tilts her head to look into that cerulean sky and takes in a deep breath of the early-autumn air, too. Then she cocks her head in a way that makes me think she's listening to those blue jays, back at it again in the top of a nearby pine.

Finally she speaks. "You must be Sadie Windas."

"Yes, ma'am," I say.

"I'm Mrs. Simper." She has a strong southern accent. "The warden."

"Yes, ma'am."

She nods. "I suppose we'd best get you inside."

I don't move from my bike, though. I can't.

Mrs. Simper studies her apple core as if it holds the secret to the universe, or maybe just to make sure she's eaten all there is to eat. Then she tosses it in a trash can.

"Somebody coming to pick up that bike?"

"Yes, ma'am," I say again. "Key's under the seat."

"That a Kawasaki?" she asks.

"Yes, ma'am. Three-fifty cc."

"All righty, then," she says, and I realize she doesn't actually know anything about motorcycles. If I wasn't suspicious of Mrs. Simper before, I sure am now. Anyone trying as hard as her to be nice – you can't trust them. At all.

Mrs. Simper holds the door open and says, "After you, Sadie."

The last thing I hear, right up until the door bangs shut behind us, is those blue jays in that pine tree, going *Caw, caw, caw, caw, ca —*

CHAPTER 2

In which it's a few weeks earlier, Carla
wants to party, and things fall apart

It was three weeks into September, a Saturday. I'd already
gone to basketball practice for three hours in the morning
and worked at the car wash all that afternoon. The tips had
been lousy, my boyfriend, Kevin, was out of town, Mom was
at one of her jobs, and now I was home playing with Lulu.

We started out sitting at the kitchen table, me tossing
Cheerios at Lulu, trying to land them in her wide-open
mouth. Most of them ended up on the floor, a few got
tangled in her hair, and one hit her upper lip and stuck
because she had a runny nose. That got Lulu laughing so
hard, she fell out of her chair.

She grabbed her head, pretending to be hurt, which was this thing she did all the time so I would get her an ice pack out of the freezer. "Poor Lulu," I said, playing my part. "Did you hurt your butt?"

"My *head*!" she yelled.

"Oh," I said, shutting the freezer door. "So it *is* your butt."

"No!" she yelled again. "*Not* my butt."

I pulled her into my lap and handed her the ice pack. "Well, hold this on wherever it is so you don't get a butt lump."

"Not my butt!" she yelled, and then she stuck the ice pack down my shirt, which was what she always did as well. Only this time she somehow managed to slip it inside my sports bra.

I jumped up, dumping her out of my lap. Lulu rolled on the floor laughing, so once I extricated the ice pack, I grabbed her and stuck it down her pants.

That somehow led to her peeing herself, which led to us taking a bath together, which led to us playing with a family of tub ducks she'd had since she was a baby. They were supposed to turn blue on the bottom if the water was too hot. Or maybe they were supposed to turn blue on the bottom once the water was the right temperature. Either way, we just used them as battleships and made giant explosions that soaked the bathroom floor.

That's what we were doing when Carla came in, reeking of Friendly's.

"Hi, Mommy," Lulu said.

"Hey, Carla," I said.

She kissed Lulu on top of her wet head and then started in on me about this party she wanted to go to, and would I go with her?

"Please, Sadie?" she begged me. "We haven't gone out in forever. Girls just gotta have fun, right?" Before I could say no, she coaxed Lulu into singing that song with her, Carla dancing right there in the soggy bathroom, still in her ice-cream-and-ketchup-stained waitress uniform, and Lulu standing up in the tub and dancing her naked little self along with her mom.

Carla pulled a dripping Lulu out of the tub, and they kept singing and dancing together while I slid down in the water and watched. For a minute it was like the old, sweet Carla was suddenly, magically back. I wondered how long that would last.

Carla brought up the party again after I climbed out and we got Lulu dried off and plopped her down in front of the TV. She pulled me into my bedroom and made me open my closet to look at clothes. "Come on, Sadie," she said, holding up this stupid leopard-print blouse that Mom must have stuck in there. "I need you to go with me. Mom'll only babysit Lulu if you agree to be my designated driver. I'll even pay you. Look, here's my tip money from this afternoon."

Carla had been on probation for the past year, first

for pot possession and then, a couple of months later, for shoplifting. She'd stolen a pack of baby wipes, which was understandable, maybe even forgivable, except that she also stole an iPod Shuffle.

Maybe it was her dancing in the bathroom with Lulu. Maybe it was the way she seemed so excited for us to hang out. Maybe it was the fact that Kevin was out of town and I was bored. Whatever the reason, I finally caved. We told Mom we were going out with some people to dinner and a movie. She raised her eyebrows, but I kept my expression straight when she looked at me. Finally she settled back into the couch and told us to have a good time. "Don't be home too late," she said.

So a couple of hours later, past Lulu's bedtime and what should have been mine, we walked into an old run-down Victorian house near the river that looked like it ought to be condemned – weedy yard, slanting porch, missing shingles. It smelled of beer and sweat and pot and something totally out of place, like lavender. Everybody I saw was in their twenties or thirties, most already trashed. I was probably the only one there without a visible tattoo or piercing.

I let out a breath and tried to relax. The last time Carla dragged me to one of these parties, she ended up puking in her lap as I drove home, which was not only disgusting but totally freaked me out, since I'd only had my permit then and wasn't supposed to drive at night or without a sober adult riding shotgun. But that was a couple of years ago, and I had a better sense of how to handle Carla now. Besides, we were driving her car tonight instead of Mom's; if she puked again, she'd have to clean it out herself.

Somebody handed me a cup of beer. I tried to say I didn't want it, but it was impossible to hear anything over the pounding bass. I turned to see if Carla wanted it, even though she usually drank harder stuff, but somehow she'd already slipped away into the raging circus of spinning mirror balls and girls dancing with girls and smoke as thick as ocean fog.

"Carla!" I called, though my voice was drowned out by all the people screaming at one another over the retro music. I fought my way through the crowd, my earlier optimism about the evening already gone. Of course Carla didn't want to hang out with me. All that joking about girls just wanting to have fun was really about *Carla* having fun and Sadie cleaning up the mess afterward.

I finally spotted her on the far side of the living room. Even in the crowd she was hard to miss in her bright-yellow Midas Muffler shirt that she bought at the thrift shop. I pushed my way to her side.

"Hey, Sadie!" she yelled as if we hadn't seen each other in forever. She grabbed my beer, said "Thanks," and drained it as she made her way to the kitchen. I followed her and told her to slow down, but she'd found the keg and was already pouring herself another. She handed me one, too.

"I don't want this," I said, or tried to. "I'm the designated driver —"

"Hey! Kendall!" she hollered right next to my ear at someone behind me. She elbowed her way across the kitchen to a girl who was leaning against the refrigerator, smoking a cigarette and looking bored. Kendall had a bright-red scar on her cheek and I couldn't stop staring.

"This is Kendall!" Carla shouted. "She used to play something when we were in school. I can't remember what. But she was an athlete. I remember that."

"Cross-country," Kendall said.

"Yeah," Carla said. "I knew it was something like that. Anyway, Sadie's a jock, too. So you guys can talk."

She practically shoved us into each other and then started talking to a skuzzy guy who was working the keg.

I angled myself so I could keep an eye on her while I got to know all about Kendall the athlete.

"So you ran cross-country?"

Kendall nodded but didn't say anything. She was already looking past me to see who else was around, smoking her cigarette hard, as if she was mad at it.

"I play basketball," I said. "I'm on an AAU team. And I play at Mountain View."

"What's Mountain View?" Kendall asked dully.

"New high school. Just opened a couple of years ago. You went to Stafford with Carla, right?"

She grunted, which I guessed meant yes. She kept looking past me.

"Hey, check it out," she said. "Carla already made a new friend."

Carla and the scuzzy guy were leaning into each other near the keg. At first I thought they were making out, but then they shifted and I realized that the guy had a joint and was shotgunning a stream of smoke into Carla's mouth. I should have gone over and tried to get her to stop – there was no such thing with Carla as just getting a *little* high – but I was already tired of playing nanny. At least we were still in the same room.

I turned back to Kendall and tried again to start a conversation.

"So where did you get the scar?" I asked, trying to sound flippant or breezy or something.

She touched the raw scar tissue absently. "I went to this party and started asking somebody I didn't know a bunch of nosy-ass questions," she said. "It was the wrong person to be asking."

She pushed herself away from the refrigerator and dropped her cigarette on the linoleum floor, grinding it out under her shoe.

"I got to go see somebody," she said, shoving past me.

"Great," I said. "Whatever."

Carla and Scuzzy had started working their way toward the living room, so I tried to follow them, but a crowd of more people suddenly pushed into the kitchen and made for the keg, pinning me against the counter. One girl stumbled in her heels and spilled her beer on my sleeve. By the time I found a towel to dry it off, Carla was gone again.

I searched the entire house, including the bathrooms, which probably made me some enemies since I didn't bother waiting in line. I checked the driveway; at least the car was still there, though that didn't mean she hadn't left with Scuzzy. All I knew for sure was that I couldn't find her anywhere. I took a sip of beer and told myself to calm down. Carla might be self-centered and irresponsible, but she'd never leave a party with some guy she just met – at least not without telling me first.

I wandered onto the back porch, where a noisy game of beer pong was going on. It was as good a place as any to wait for Carla to show up. At least here the music wasn't deafening, and there was enough breeze to carry away some of the cigarette and pot smoke choking the rest of the house.

A decent-looking guy with blond dreads came over and asked if I wanted to be his beer-pong partner. I eyed the cup of beer I'd been carrying around for a while now and had hardly touched. I shrugged. Why not? I was a pretty good shot, even when I'd been drinking a little. I'd still be able to drive OK.

Dreadlocks, who might have been high, hugged me every time I nailed a cup – nothing creepy, just hugs – which was a lot since I was a good shot, like I said, and because I was easily the soberest person playing. Dreadlocks and I owned the table for a good hour.

Eventually, though, I started to worry too much about Carla and told Dreadlocks I had to go find her.

"I'll go with you," he said. "What's she look like?"

I told him and we scanned the faces of the crowd as we pushed out way back into the living room, which was still jammed with people – freak dancing on one side of the room, slam dancing on the other. The music was some hard-core rap, bass shaking the walls, and I was already getting a headache.

Dreadlocks hooked an arm around my waist and tried to pull me over with the freak dancers.

"What are you doing?" I shouted.

"We should dance!" he shouted back, circling behind and trying to grind against me.

"Knock it off!" I yelled, twisting around. Then, for some reason, I added, "I have a boyfriend!"

"No problem," Dreadlocks yelled back. "I have a girl-friend."

I shoved him away, but the crowd pressed him right back. The next thing I knew, he was trying to kiss me.

I jerked my face away. "You have a girlfriend, remember?"

He blinked and wiped his mouth with the back of his hand. "Did I say that?"

"Yeah," I said, nodding too, in case he couldn't hear me.

He shrugged. "It's OK! She's cool!"

I tried to slide away from him, but he kept his grip on my arm. "Ah, come on, Sally!"

"It's Sadie!" I said. "Anyway, I have to find my sister."

Eventually I made it through the scrum of dancers and into the hall. I was just about to go up and check all the rooms again when someone half stumbled down the stairs. Two people, actually: a scuzzy-looking guy holding up a very drunk girl. The girl was Carla.

"Hey," she said with a wan smile, her yellow shirt half unbuttoned, no shoes, makeup smeared. She draped herself over me and I hugged her back, trying not to think about what she'd just been doing.

I buttoned up her shirt, wiped off her smeared lipstick, and combed my fingers through her hair to get it halfway decent. "Where are your shoes, Carla?" I shouted over the music.

She blinked at me, as if the concept of shoes was foreign to her, or as if she didn't have shoes, had never had shoes. "Forget it!" I said. "I'm taking you home!"

To my surprise, she nodded. "OK. I'm ready."

We nearly made it out of there. We got all the way to the front door. I was turning the knob, fishing in my pocket to double-check that I had the car keys, when Dreadlocks and Scuzzy appeared next to us in a cloud of pot smoke – a couple of stoner ghosts.

"You can't be leaving yet," Dreadlocks said.

"Hey, baby," Scuzzy said to Carla. "We're not done partying, are we?"

I was surprised to see Dreadlocks and Scuzzy together. "You guys know each other?" I asked.

Dreadlocks grinned. "Oh, hell yeah." He didn't elaborate.

I hung on to Carla. "We're leaving," I said.

Scuzzy laughed a cigarette laugh — as much smoke as words. "Hey, that's OK. But Carla promised you girls would give us a ride first. Just over to the 7-Eleven to get some more beer for the party. You remember, baby, right?" he said to Carla. He shrugged a small backpack over his shoulder. "For beer."

Carla nodded hazily. "For beer."

I protested, but what Carla said, even if she was just stupidly repeating the words, gave the guys some sort of forward momentum. They ignored my protests and followed us out of the house and down the street to Carla's car.

"Fine," I said, my shoulder aching from propping Carla upright. "Just make it quick."

Scuzzy tried to convince me to put Carla in the backseat with him. "Don't you and him want to sit together?" he asked, nodding at Dreadlocks.

"No," I said, trying to maneuver a limp Carla into the front seat. She was all deadweight.

"Me and her already hooked up," Scuzzy said. "That counts for something, doesn't it?"

"No," I said, buckling Carla in. "My car, my rules. Boys in the back."

Scuzzy got in and slammed the back door hard, to let me know he wasn't happy. Dreadlocks at least was polite. He even opened and closed the driver's-side door for me.

Carla slumped against the window. Dreadlocks lit a cigarette, but I made him put it out.

"Jesus," Scuzzy muttered to him. "And you wanted to hook up with this ho?"

I clenched my teeth and sped toward the 7-Eleven. Carla hummed to herself, a song that sounded familiar but that I couldn't quite make out, which pretty much summed up Carla these days: somebody who seemed familiar but who I couldn't say I really knew.

There were empty spaces in front of the store, but Dreadlocks told me to park in a dark corner of the lot, out of the light. "It's closer to the bathrooms," he said. I didn't want to argue and figured it wouldn't be the worst thing in the world if no one saw us driving around with these two losers – though it occurred to me that it was the sort of place somebody might park if they were planning on robbing a store.

And besides that – I realized too late, as I watched them disappear into the 7-Eleven – Dreadlocks would have to return the key to the bathroom, and so it didn't save him any time if I parked here.

"Carla, I have a bad feeling about this," I said, trying to keep my eyes on the guys inside the store, which was nearly impossible. Were they at the register? Were they asking for the bathroom key or for all the money in the register? "Carla?"

But Carla didn't seem to hear me, or to care about anything that might be going on. Her head was leaned back on the headrest, and her eyes were closed. She was still humming, only now I recognized the tune: an old Led Zeppelin song called "Going to California." It made me think of Dad, who used to play Zeppelin all the time. And Pink Floyd and the Grateful Dead and all those guys.

I liked "Going to California" a lot – the acoustic guitar, the sweet lyrics about riding a white mare and trying to find a woman who'd never, ever been born, whatever that meant. Dad always played vinyl albums on an old record player when we were growing up. He said he never threw away a single album he ever owned, and I believed him. Once when I was little, I bought him a Led Zeppelin CD for Father's Day, but he never listened to it. I hoped he still played his records now, alone in his wing of Granny's old house, and I hoped they made him happy, at least a little.

The back door of the car opened suddenly. A bearded guy in a knit cap and a heavy gray overcoat slid into the backseat. He smiled an oily smile.

"What are you doing?" I demanded. Carla just looked back at the guy as if it was no big deal, happened all the time.

"You got something for me, right?" he said. "I got the call to meet a girl here." He nodded at something in the backseat. It was a backpack that I only dimly recalled Scuzzy carrying. "That it?"

He handed me a thick envelope and I stupidly took it. It wasn't until I held it up to the dim light from the store that I realized it was stuffed full of money.

"What is this?" I asked the guy in the knit cap, looking around for Scuzzy and Dreadlocks, hoping they would reappear and clear this whole thing up. "Nobody called you. I don't want this—" I tried to give him back the envelope, but he ignored me.

He grabbed Scuzzy's backpack off the floor and pulled out a freezer bag filled with pot. He sniffed it, tasted it for some reason, stuffed it back inside the pack, reached in his pockets, and pulled out a badge and a gun.

"Nice doing business with you, ladies," he said, again with that oily smile. Other men with beards and knit caps and badges and overcoats and guns materialized out of the darkness and surrounded the car, which was suddenly flooded with the light from a dozen flashlights.

"And now you're under arrest."

CHAPTER 3

*In which I get intaked, learn a new
word for vagina, and confess my
violent basketball past*

The door to juvie closes with a solid thud, leaving
behind the sound of those blue jays, leaving behind my
motorcycle, leaving behind everything.

Mrs. Simper takes my bag right away. "You're not
allowed to have this," she says, lifting it with two fingers
and handing it to a guard whose name tag says OFFICER
WALLACE. He's wearing a khaki-and-blue uniform and
blue medical gloves.

"You're not allowed to have anything besides whatever money you'd like to put into your phone account,"
Mrs. Simper adds. "Perhaps they didn't make that clear."

But her tone says that she knows very well that they did make it clear and that I seem to think the rules don't apply to me. Great. I've already gotten on someone's bad side, and all because of a few tampons and a disposable razor.

Officer Wallace tucks my stuff in a garbage bag. "You can have it back when you get out," he says. He has a very flat face. I've never seen one like it before – with a nose that barely casts a shadow.

"Take good care of it," I say.

Officer Wallace lets the bag fall to his side. "In here," he says evenly, "you don't speak unless you have permission. Maybe they didn't make that clear, either."

He starts to say more, but Mrs. Simper puts her hand on my shoulder. "Officer Wallace is our intake supervisor, Sadie," she says. "He'll take over now. I'm going to have to get back to my office, but you and I will have an opportunity to talk later."

She nods at Officer Wallace. "Officer Wallace."

He nods back at her. "Warden."

A door next to where we're standing buzzes and then makes a heavy clicking sound. Mrs. Simper opens it and disappears inside. A lady guard comes out with handcuffs and ankle cuffs and a whole lot of chain. She sees me eyeing them.

"Most inmates come in directly from court, from off the transport van," the lady officer says. Her name is Officer Kohl. "They already have their chains on. It's procedure we got to put them on you before we take you back to intake."

Officer Wallace grabs the ankle cuffs from Officer Kohl. "Legs apart," he says.

He squats in front of me with the ankle cuffs while Officer Kohl does my wrists. Everything locks together, my hands shackled in front of me, my legs hobbled. My arms already ache from holding it all up.

Officer Wallace says something into his walkie-talkie, then there's another buzz and another click and they lead me through another door off the lobby in the opposite direction of Mrs. Simper. I shuffle through the door and down a short, gray hall to yet another door, this one marked INTAKE. It took more time for them to put me in the shackles than it does to walk there.

The hall is bare except for a mop and bucket next to a set of gray double doors at the far end of the hall, which is where I figure they bring kids in off the transport bus.

"What's that doing there?" Officer Wallace snaps. "That's not supposed to be there."

"I'll take care of it," Officer Kohl says. "It isn't my job, though."

"If it's something where it's not supposed to be, then it's your job," Officer Wallace says back.

Officer Kohl wheels the bucket and mop over to a closet, which she unlocks with a key. Officer Wallace unclips his walkie-talkie from his black belt and mutters something, and the by-now familiar buzz and click happens and then the intake-room door opens. Officer Kohl, back with us now, nudges me from behind, and I shuffle through there, too. It's still morning, though it could just as easily be the middle of the night since the only light comes from stuttering fluorescent bulbs high overhead. Suddenly I feel very, very tired.

A row of holding cells lines most of one side of the intake unit. I can see through their small windows: each has a bench bolted to the wall, a stainless-steel toilet with no seat or lid, and a stainless-steel sink, the kind where you push down on a button so water comes out for five seconds – just long enough to wet your hands but never enough to rinse them properly. In the main intake area are a couple of desks, a long shelf with stacks of what look like uniforms, and a row of hooks with enough cuffs and chains hanging from them to stock an entire Inquisition torture chamber. The officers unlock me from my restraints and add them to the Torquemada collection.

At the far end of the cells are two shower stalls. Officer Kohl leads me to the farthest one while Officer Wallace stays back at the computer.

"Take your shoes and socks off right out here," Officer Kohl says. "Then when you go in the shower, you can take off everything else."

A minute later, I'm standing in my underwear and bra while Officer Kohl pulls on blue medical gloves like Officer Wallace's. "I said to strip," she says. "All the way."

I add my underwear and bra to the pile of clothes and cross my arms over my chest while Officer Kohl inspects it all. Then she dumps everything in another garbage bag.

ur mouth," Officer Kohl says, so I do.

n wider.

ook your fingers inside your cheeks, and pull open your mouth wider. Then stick your tongue way out, too."

She shines a flashlight in my mouth for a while, then grunts.

"All right. Now I got to have you bend over and spread your butt cheeks."

I've probably never blushed at anything in my life, but I blush when she says that, and keep blushing as I do it and she aims her flashlight on me.

"Spread wider," she says. I move my feet farther apart, but that's the best I can do. She grunts again.

I think we're finished, but we aren't. "Last thing," she says. "Now I got to look in your business."

"You mean my vagina?"

She shrugs. "Some call it that."

She taps inside my thighs. "Spread wider."

"Can I ask you something, Officer Kohl?" I say, trying to sound calm and composed, though I don't know how successful I am, since I can't stop clenching my teeth. "Do you ever actually find anything when you do these body cavity searches, or is it just a thing you all like to do?"

She frowns. "Like Officer Wallace already told you, how it works in here is you don't ask questions. You get told what to do and you do it."

I don't say anything.

"Can't hear you," she said.

It's a pissing contest, but I know there's no way for me to win, so I lower my eyes the way I figure I'm expected to and say what I figure I'm expected to say: "Yes, Officer Kohl."

"That's a lot better. And since you're brand-new here, I *am* going to answer your question, just this one time. And the answer is you'd be surprised at what we find in them body cavities."

"Like what?"

Officer Kohl laughs. "Like I'm gonna tell you? Give you some ideas? I don't think so. And anyway, we're done."

"Does that mean I don't have to take a shower?"

"Everybody showers," she says. "On the regular schedule, you take one three-minute shower every day. Today's your special day, though, since it's intake. Today you take you a long shower until I decide you're through."

She hands me a white bottle. "This is lice shampoo. You wash your hair and everything with it, including your hair down there."

"You mean my business hair?"

Officer Kohl frowns again, and I shut up. She steps out of the shower stall and shuts the door, but stays at the window.

I hope the hot water will steam it up so she can't see, but that doesn't happen because there isn't a handle to turn it on with, so the water stays freezing. The shock takes my breath away and I lather and rinse as quickly as I can.

Officer Kohl cracks open the door once I'm done.

"Back in," she says. "And do it all over again. Only scrub harder this time, and stay under that shower longer till I say you can come out. You bringing anything in here from outside, it's going down that drain."

Officer Kohl issues me one orange jumpsuit, two pairs of underwear, two pairs of socks, one wireless bra, and one pair of plastic sandals.

"You get clean ones of these every two days. Second-day underwear and socks you keep in your locker. That'll be right outside your cell door. Dirty ones you put in your locker when you get the clean ones out. Change after shower. Sandals you wear until they wear out."

She hands me two blankets and two sheets.

"Once a week you turn them in for washday. You wet the bed, that isn't our problem; it's your problem."

"Do many people wet their beds?" I ask.

"Now, what did I tell you about asking questions?"

"My bad," I say.

"You right it's your bad. And there's another thing: you don't look at the guards unless they tell you you can look at them. You keep your eyes to yourself besides that. And when you're walking in the hall, you stay in line with your unit and you keep your hands behind your back and you don't look anywhere but right in front of you and you don't talk; you don't say one single word. You just go where you're told to go and stop when you're told to stop. Understood?"

"Understood."

I put on the underwear and bra that aren't mine, and the starched orange jumpsuit that isn't mine, and the socks and sandals that aren't mine, and carry the extra underwear and the blankets and sheets that aren't mine back to the intake desk with Officer Wallace and his flat face and his computer.

"Sit down," he says, indicating a chair across from his, positioned so I can't see what's on the screen. "These are questions you're required to answer. We already know the answers to some of them. They're included to see if you're being truthful. You are required to be truthful."

The jumpsuit fits surprisingly well, but it itches, and I shift in the chair to scratch the middle of my back, but then I think that maybe it makes me look nervous or uncomfortable answering questions, so I stop.

"Ready to start?" Officer Wallace says. He doesn't wait for me to respond. "First question: State your full name."

"Sadie Ruth Windas."

"Age?"

"Seventeen."

"U.S. citizen?"

"Yes."

"Race?"

"White. Caucasian, I guess. But part American Indian. One-sixteenth, or thirty-second. I forget. I think my great-great-grandmother was Indian. That's what my granny told me."

"We'll go with white."

"OK."

"I didn't ask you."

"OK."

"Last time you thought about hurting yourself?"

"I've never thought about hurting myself."

"Any suicidal ideation?"

"What's that?"

"That's thoughts about hurting yourself."

"I've never thought about hurting myself."

"Mental-health history?"

"No mental-health history. That is, no mental-health problems."

"Ever been sad?"

"Of course."

"Depressed?"

"I guess. Yeah."

"Ever been diagnosed with clinical depression?"

"No."

"Medications?"

"No medications."

"Violent episodes?"

"No violent episodes."

"Most recent episode."

"No episodes."

"You are required to answer truthfully."

"I haven't had any—" But then I stop. Because there was this one incident recently, during a game, and what if they know about it somehow and this is a test?

"Well?"

I'm suddenly glad for the rule about not looking at officers. I study my hands for a minute. "There was this one thing," I start. "At an AAU basketball game, like a couple of weeks ago. Anyway, the other team's center was beating up on our center, Julie Juggins, and the referees weren't calling it. So I kind of grabbed the girl's ponytail and jerked back on it – harder than I meant to – and she fell on the court and landed on her elbow. I got a technical foul and got kicked out of the game." My gut twists just thinking about it. I'd never done anything like that before, I hated the idea of it being entered into an official file on me.

"Was she injured?"

"Not really. They iced her elbow and then she was back in the game."

"When was this?"

"I already said. It was a couple of weeks ago."

"Charge?"

"From the basketball game?"

"No. We're done with that. From the arrest."

"Don't you already have all that?"

"Answer the question."

"Felony distribution."

"Adjudication?"

I answer that one, too, though he already knows the answer. He knows the answers to the next twenty questions as well, but that doesn't stop him from asking them.

I feel more like a criminal with each one, which must be the point.

Once they're done, and once I'm back in shackles, Officer Kohl takes me on a long walk down a series of gray corridors, all of them wide, all of them deserted. We pass through a couple of locked doors that require radios and requests, more buzzes, more clicks, until we reach my unit. Inside is a common room with cells branching off to the sides, a TV high on a wall, tables and chairs, a bookcase crammed with books and board games, and a short, stout, white female guard whose name tag reads OFFICER EMROCH.

"All yours, Sheila," Officer Kohl says, handing over a file with my name on it.

Officer Emroch laughs a polite laugh. "Start the party."

There's only one other person on the unit – that I can see, anyway: a white girl sitting in a chair, wearing what appears to be a dark-blue quilt with Velcro straps that fits her like a sack with holes cut out for her head and arms. The girl isn't doing anything. Just sitting. She might be sixteen. I doubt she's any older. She doesn't look up when I enter.

Officer Kohl unlocks all the cuffs and chains. I'm still standing there holding a stack of blankets and sheets and underwear.

"That's it, then," she says to me. "You belong to Unit Three now."

Officer Emroch's face falls as she watches Officer Kohl leave. I wonder if she's lonely in here all day, nothing to do but hang out with quiet girls in quilt sacks.

"Windas," Officer Emroch says. "What kind of a name is that, anyway?"

"English, I think."

"Huh," she says. "Not one we've had in here before."

She takes a long look at me, as if trying to figure out if I might have some other ethnic identity I'm trying to hide from her. We're the same height, but she's easily twice my size.

"All the others in Unit Three are at afternoon gym with Officer Killduff," Officer Emroch says. She speaks in the same terse way as all the guards I've met so far. None of them seem to ever smile. "You'll meet him when they come back here for showers, then free hour, then dinner. I'll show you your cell and locker, right over here. You need to go ahead and make up your bed. You know how to do a military tuck? You can come out and sit with me and her after you're done. No TV allowed until free hour, though."

She leads me over to an empty cell – Cell One – and gestures for me to go inside. I stop, though, framed by the door. I can't seem to go any farther. The cell is the same as the intake cells I saw: eight feet by eight feet with dull-green concrete-block walls and a gray concrete floor. A narrow bunk is mounted to the far wall, with a thin mattress that's fatter at one end for a kind of pillow.

A stainless-steel sink sticks out from the wall next to the door, and on the other side of that is a stainless-steel toilet with no seat or lid. And that's it. No table, no chair, no desk, no shelf, no posters, no window except the dirty rectangle of reinforced glass on the door. A fluorescent bulb high overhead crackles and hums and gives off a dull white light.

Officer Emroch looks up at it with me. "That stays on," she says. "Twenty-four/seven."

She nudges me into the cell the way Officer Kohl nudged me into Intake. "Come on, now. That bed isn't going to make up itself, and you don't want Officer Killduff to come back here and see you haven't done it yet. He wouldn't like that, and you don't want to do anything he doesn't like, I promise you."

She turns to leave. I hear her cross the common-room floor, hear the scrape of a chair, hear the creak of hard plastic as she sits down, hear her say something to the girl in the quilt. It's a kinder voice than she used with me, but even so, I don't hear an answer.

I set everything down on the sink so I can rub my eyes, then take inventory again, hoping I've missed something. I haven't, except for a roll of scratchy toilet paper sitting on the floor next to the toilet. I take another step, then another, until I stand next to the bed. At least from there I can see the door, and at least the door is still open. I can't imagine how much more claustrophobic I'll feel at night when they lock me in. Just contemplating it makes me start to sweat even though it's cold in my cell, cold everywhere in juvie.

I make myself think about something else – about Lulu that morning giving me a rock, about how good and scary it felt the first night I rode my motorcycle, about that tournament last month when I had twelve assists and seven steals in the championship game – and slowly I start to feel better. I can handle this. I've spent plenty of nights alone, camping out on Government Island in a tent a lot smaller than this cell. Granny always said it's our job in life to learn from everything that happens to us, so that's what I'll do here.

I busy myself with the sheets and blankets and military tucks and then step outside to put my underwear and socks in the locker. The girl isn't there anymore; I assume she's gone back to her cell. Officer Emroch sits at the guard's desk, writing in a logbook.

I trace the hard plastic number one bolted to the outside of my cell door and take a deep breath. The air tastes stale.

So this is it. So this is home.

CHAPTER 4

In which Mom bails us out and we go back to the scene of the crime

They brought us to the magistrate's office after the arrest, after reading us our Miranda rights, after the pointless interrogation about who the guys were who gave us the drugs.

Carla didn't know their names, either. Not even Scuzzy's.

I wanted to kill her. I wanted to make her tell me what the hell happened back there at the 7-Eleven, and did she know we were going to be part of a drug deal? But I couldn't very well ask her that right now, and I probably couldn't kill her right then, either.

The magistrate's office was in a small, shit-brown, wood-frame house near the train station. They had a couple of holding cells and stuck us in one after we called Mom. Carla was alternately crying and cussing at the officers, which didn't help matters any. I kept telling her to shut up, but she was still so drunk that she tried to hit me. Then she lay down on the floor and fell asleep. There were a couple of other drunks in there with us, but they were passed out as well. I was the only one awake when Mom showed up.

"What the hell's going on, Dave?" Mom demanded when she stormed in the door. She had Lulu with her, wide-eyed but sleepy, still in her pajamas.

The magistrate said, "Hey, Gretchen. Long time no see." I was surprised that they knew each other. He pointed at us on the other side of the room. "They yours?"

Mom turned and just stood there for a minute, glaring. I nudged Carla with my foot and tried my best to look innocent, which should have been easy but wasn't.

Mom turned back to the magistrate, Dave, and said something I couldn't hear. He seemed vaguely familiar, and I thought maybe he was one of the guys Mom went out with for a while after Dad left. She did that for the first year or so, then quit. She never said why.

Dave was kind of heavy, thin on top, walrus mustache. He didn't look anything like Dad.

Mom had put Lulu down in a chair and told her to

stay, but Lulu hopped up when she saw us and pattered over to the holding cell. "Hey, Aunt Sadie. What's wrong with Mommy? Can I come in with you guys?"

"Lulu!" Mom barked. "Over here. Now. Sit back in that chair."

Lulu's bottom lip quivered. She did what Mom told her.

Mom didn't seem in any hurry to speak to me or check on Carla. She sat down at Dave's desk. The cops who arrested us had long gone. A brown-suited deputy sat nearby, talking on his cell phone.

"So what's the deal here, Dave?" Mom asked, loud enough now for me to hear.

Dave tugged on the sides of his mustache. "Drug bust. Undercovers got them at that 7-Eleven off Caroline Street. They sold, like, a kilo or something."

"Pot?" Mom asked.

"Pot," Dave confirmed.

Mom turned and glared again. "Is this true?" she called over to me. Carla was awake and struggling to sit up.

"No," I said. "I mean, yeah, that's what they arrested us for, but we didn't do anything. It wasn't even ours."

Mom lifted her hand. "Stop right there. Don't say anything else. I shouldn't have asked." She glared at Carla. I knew what she was thinking: that whatever happened must have been Carla's fault.

She turned back to Dave. "So what do we need to do to straighten this out?"

Dave shrugged. "Can't do anything tonight, Gretchen. They're supposed to stay right here until tomorrow and then the older one goes to court for arraignment. She's got priors. I'm supposed to send the younger one over to Juvie Detention until they schedule her a hearing at JDR, and they're not in session until Thursday."

"JDR?" Mom asked, obviously exasperated – at him for speaking in acronyms, at us, at the world. Lulu was crying now but not making any noise.

"Juvenile and Domestic Relations Court," Dave said. "JDR."

Mom sat back in her chair. "I'm taking them home with me tonight. I don't want them staying here." She pulled Lulu into her lap. "This one needs her mother."

Carla crawled over to the toilet and vomited.

"Can't do that," Dave said.

Mom leaned forward again. She propped one elbow on his desk so she could lean in even closer. "Yes, you can," she said.

They talked too low for me to hear anything for the next ten minutes. Finally, though, Dave threw up his hands. When he released us and we were filing out of the building, I heard him say to Mom that he was looking forward to their dinner.

We didn't go directly home once we got into the car. Instead Mom drove us to the 7-Eleven on Caroline Street, the place where we'd been arrested. It must have been four in the morning by then.

"This is it?" Mom asked when we got there.

I nodded. I was in the front seat. Carla and Lulu had fallen asleep in the back. I pointed to the corner of the parking lot. "We were over there, actually."

Mom looked. "Why?"

"The guys bugged me to park there. They wouldn't shut up about it, so I did it so they'd hurry up and go buy their beer and we could dump them off back at the party and go home."

Mom kept staring. "You were supposed to be at a movie. Out to dinner."

"I'm sorry," I said. "Carla just wanted to party. You know how she is."

"And what about you?" Mom demanded, still looking at the place where we'd been arrested.

"I messed up," I said. "I didn't think anything would happen. Just a party."

Now she turned to look at me. "You lied to me, Sadie."

I didn't say anything. What could I say? I was supposed to be the good daughter, the responsible one, the one who made her proud, the one who wasn't any trouble, ever.

"Your sister is on probation," Mom said, as if I was to blame for that, too. "Did you forget about that?"

Mom didn't talk to me for the rest of the drive. Not even when we woke Carla up and dragged ourselves into the house. Mom went out on the back porch, where I was pretty sure she smoked a cigarette, even though she was supposed to have quit ages ago. Carla mumbled some stuff that I couldn't understand and went off to her old bedroom and passed out again on her old bed. She didn't bother to take off her clothes, though she was disgusting from the holding-cell floor and the vomit and everything else she'd been up to that night.

Lulu slept with me, although I couldn't say I actually slept. I mostly worried about what was going to happen next. I knew I hadn't done anything wrong except be stupid enough to go out with Carla in the first place. But I had to go to JDR on Thursday. What was I going to tell Kevin? My friends? My coach?

This didn't fit into my plans at all. I was supposed to keep playing basketball, make all-region, maybe even all-state my senior year, study my ass off and crush the SATs, finish school, land a basketball scholarship – at whatever school Kevin ended up going to for soccer. We'd be one of those couples that just worked: him doing his thing, me doing mine, but ending up together no matter what.

And out of this town forever.

I heard Mom come in off the porch. She didn't go to bed, though. She turned on the TV, and I was pretty sure she stayed awake most of the night. So did I, sick with worry that the life I'd been so carefully building these past few years had just crashed and burned.

CHAPTER 5

In which I meet the queens of
Unit Three, find a missing spork,
and have a dark night of the soul

It's late in the afternoon of my first day in juvie. The girl in the quilt has long since gone back inside her cell, and I'm sitting in a hard plastic chair out in the common room, sort of reading but actually just bored, when the rest of the girls come back from gym. They're with a thirty-something white guy with an ex-military buzz cut and a melanoma tan, Officer Killduff. His khaki-and-blue looks a couple of sizes too small, probably on purpose to show off how ripped he is.

There are eight girls in total. Six of them, three white and three black, look like they're around my age. Another white girl appears to be a couple of years younger, middle-school age, and the last of the eight, a tiny Hispanic girl with big watery eyes, could be in elementary school. All wear the same orange juvie jumpsuit as me.

Officer Killduff stands just inside the door with his hands on his hips as the girls shuffle over to the chairs as if they're in shackles, the way I was earlier. Two of the black girls stop in front of me.

"That's my chair," one of them says.

I close my book and look around. There are plenty of empty chairs, all of them the same. My first impulse is to tell her to get another one. I don't let girls push me around on the basketball court. You let that happen and they own you for the rest of the game. Everybody knows it's the same in prison – at least in the movies. Maybe it's the same in juvie.

Or maybe it's not. Maybe the best thing to do in here is just try to get along, no matter what.

So I shift to the next chair.

"Nope," the girl says. "That one's hers." She tilts her head at her friend. They could be sisters – both tall, both heavy, both with their hair in cornrows, both with cheeks so pronounced that their faces look like peaches.

I keep my mouth shut, hard as it is, and get out of that chair, too, keeping my expression as impassive as I can, as if giving up a chair is no big deal to me and I might even be doing it just because I want to.

As I sit down in a third chair, Officer Killduff comes over.

"Problem here, Wanda?" he asks the first girl.

Wanda smiles. "No, sir. Just saying hello to the new girl."

"Nell?" he asks the second girl.

Nell shakes her head.

"All right, then," he says. "You said your hello."

The girls grin at each other and drag their chairs over in front of the TV, right up front. I think Officer Killduff will say something to me, welcome me, maybe, or tell me not to worry about them, but he doesn't. He just walks off. The other girls park their chairs behind Wanda and Nell, and the TV comes on as if it has a mind of its own and has been waiting for everybody to get settled. Out of the corner of my eye, I see the little Hispanic girl turn in her chair to look at me, but when I lift my head from my book, she twists back around.

Officer Killduff stands in the guard station for fifteen minutes talking to Officer Emroch, then crosses the common area and goes into Cell Seven; he stays there for a few minutes and then comes back out with the girl in the quilt, though now that I can see it better, it looks more like a giant oven mitt. She sits in a chair, sort of facing the TV and sort of just staring off at nothing. One of the other white girls, all blond and sunny, as if she's just come back from a beach vacation, gets up and sits next to her. Even though the blond girl doesn't say anything, the oven-mitt girl seems nervous all of a sudden, fidgeting in her chair, tapping her foot, tugging at her limp brown hair so it hides half of her face, glancing around anxiously, anywhere but at the girl beside her. Finally she goes back to her cell. The blond girl laughs and re the seat she was in before.

Wanda, the one who ordered me out of my chair, watches the whole thing unfold and has a sour look on her face. She whispers to her friend Nell and glares over at the sunny blond girl. Then they all go back to watching *Wheel of Fortune*.

Wanda and Nell make a point of sitting on either side of me when the guards wheel in the food cart. All the tables are shoved together, surrounded by our chairs. The oven-mitt girl comes out of her cell but sits alone, an empty chair on either side.

Dinner comes in Styrofoam boxes: some sort of meat cutlet, waxy green beans, a container of applesauce, a container of green Jell-O, and a roll. Officer Emroch sets a spork and a Dixie cup of water next to each of our boxes.

Then Officer Killduff materializes from somewhere, standing over us. "Bow your heads," he says, and everybody bows over their food as he says a rushed grace: "Lord, please bless this food that you have set before us so that it may nourish our bodies so that we may better serve thee. Amen."

My spork bends when I try to cut a bite of the meat.

"You can't eat it that way," says Wanda in an overly helpful voice. "You'll break your spork trying to cut it. You just have to stab it in the middle and lift the whole thing up." She nods at her friend. "Show her, Nell."

Nell shows me.

I take a sporkful of green beans instead, but Wanda interrupts me before I can bring it to my mouth. "You know where the food comes from, don't you?"

"No," I say, my spork suspended over my Styrofoam box. A bean drops.

"The Correctional. That's a mile from here, through the woods. That's the adult jail. They got inmates over there that work in their kitchen. They make all the food, and the guards and the jail trustees drive it over to us in their food truck."

"Interesting," I say.

"Yeah, right?" Wanda says. "And you know what they do to it first. . . ." She trails off.

Nell nods. "I've seen stuff, too," she says. "You don't even want to know." It's the first time I've heard her speak.

I know they're just jerking me around. I *know* it. But still . . . I look hard at my beans, imagine the worst, and dump them back in the box. I pick up the applesauce container; at least it has a sealed lid.

"I'd think about that one, too," Wanda says. "I've seen holes poked in some of those. Especially the applesauce. And the Jell-O, too. And I've seen some things once I opened them up, too, I wished I'd never seen."

"Me too," says Nell.

"How about the water?" I ask.

"Good water here," Wanda says. "I wouldn't worry about that. You drink all the water you want around here.

I think it must come from a well or something. A real deep well."

Nell reaches over with her spork to spear my meat cutlet. She's already eaten hers. "I guess if you're not going to . . ." she says, trailing off again.

Wanda helps herself to my beans. Both check to make sure the guards aren't looking before they dive in for the rest of my food – and half the food in the boxes of a couple of the other girls. Nell gets my applesauce; Wanda takes the Jell-O. I do end up eating the roll but make sure to chew each bite twenty times before I swallow.

One more thing happens – so fast I almost miss it. The sunny blond girl has been sitting on the other side of Wanda during dinner, though they practically have their backs turned on each other the whole time we eat. At one point, while the sunny blond girl is talking to someone, Wanda slips the girl's spork into her lap, then lets it drop quietly to the floor.

Nell breaks into a coughing fit that catches everybody's attention – the oldest, dumbest trick in the world, so of course I fall for it, too. When she stops, I look back down on the floor and the sunny blond girl's spork is gone.

Officer Emroch comes out with a big gray trash bag shortly after that, and one by one we shove our Styrofoam boxes in – everything except our sporks.

The blond girl's eyes widen as she holds her empty Styrofoam box – she looks as frightened as the little

Hispanic girl – and she frantically checks all around, in the box, in her lap, on the floor, under the tables. When Officer Emroch gets to her, she has no choice but to throw away the Styrofoam box, though.

Officer Emroch brings the trash bag over to the guard station and comes back with a Tupperware container. "Spork count," she says.

Wanda drops hers in first and says, "One."

Nell is two, I'm three, and the count continues around the table, though Officer Emroch skips the oven-mitt girl, who was never issued a spork and had to eat with her hands. The sunny blond girl freezes when Officer Emroch gets around to her. She's the last girl. She doesn't look sunny anymore.

"Spork count," Officer Emroch says again.

The girl's lips barely move as she mutters, "Can't find it."

"Say what?" Officer Emroch asks.

"It was just right here," the girl says. "I don't know what happened to it. Can I check back in my box? Maybe it got in there and I missed it. Maybe it's in the trash bag."

"Officer Killduff!" Officer Emroch shouts. "Can you bring over the trash bag?"

Officer Killduff comes out of the guard room and gives her a look that I'm pretty sure means that fetching trash bags is Officer Emroch's job, not his.

Officer Emroch corrects herself. "I mean, can you come over here while I get the trash bag?"

A minute later, Sunny Blond Girl has her arms deep

in the trash, pulling out every Styrofoam box, every Dixie cup, every applesauce container, every Jell-O cup. She feels through the soggy leftovers that spilled out and slid to the bottom of the trash bag. She starts crying. "I know it was right by me. I didn't do anything with it."

Officer Emroch takes away the trash again. Officer Killduff looms over the girl. He seems to have gotten taller, larger.

"I didn't do anything with it!" the girl says, shouting now. "I didn't do anything with it!" She keeps repeating herself, as if saying the same thing enough times will convince the guards.

Officer Killduff grabs the back of her chair and drags it away from the table. "Shut it, Gina," he snarls. He turns to the rest of us. "Grab some floor."

All the girls immediately drop from their chairs and lie facedown on the floor. I follow them.

"Officer Emroch," he says, "take this one to her cell for a full-body search. Once you're done, if she's clean, come back for the next one." As soon as they leave, he pulls a chair to the middle of the room and sits in it, boots planted wide apart, elbows on his knees, glaring.

I keep my cheek on the floor. My stomach rumbles from hunger – I missed lunch, obviously skipped most of dinner, haven't eaten anything all day except that one lousy roll and a bite of Lulu's waffle. I'm lying there, wishing I hadn't fallen for Wanda and Nell's stupid ploy to get my food, and that's when I see the missing spork, several feet away under the game shelf, where Wanda must have kicked it during Nell's phony coughing fit.

"You all know how this works," Officer Killduff says. "Every one of you gets a full-body. That spork doesn't show up, it's lockdown for a week. That's twenty-three out of twenty-four hours a day in your cell, which is fine by me because it means less work for me. I sit in the guard room eating chocolate. You all remember chocolate?"

He stands up again and paces around us. "But I want that spork. And I will have that spork. One of you – Gina in there, in her cell getting the full-body right now, or else one of you – *will* give me that spork."

The Hispanic girl whimpers. Soon she's crying, practically sobbing.

"Officer Killduff," I say.

He stops pacing.

"Who said that?"

I signal with my hand from where I'm lying halfway under a table. "Sadie Windas."

"Windas," he repeats, as if he's surprised there's someone here by that name.

Wanda grabs my arm, digging her chubby fingers into my bicep. I shake her off.

I point. "It's over there. Under the shelf over there."

"And you know this how?" Officer Killduff demands.

"I can see it," I say.

He goes to the game shelf, bends down, and feels around until he finds the dirty spork.

He studies it for what seems like five minutes, as if he's looking for fingerprints.

He shouts at us – "Stand!" – and all the girls jump to their feet, arms behind their backs, eyes down.

"Grab a door!" he shouts again, and the girls all hurry to their cells – walking quickly, careful not to run. Once I'm in my cell, I sit on my bunk and wait, breathless, wondering what's next. But what comes next is the obvious thing: Officer Killduff slowly, deliberately, walking the perimeter of the common area, stopping at every cell and locking every door.

My cell is his last. He doesn't lock me in right away, though. He steps inside and just stands there staring down at me. I'm still sitting on my bunk, back against the wall.

"You saw how that spork got there?"

"No, sir," I say, which is technically true. I have no idea why Wanda took it, or kicked it across the room, other than to get Sunny Blond Girl in trouble, but I'm not about to tell Officer Killduff anything.

I think I'll get a full-on interrogation, but that's it. Officer Killduff leaves without another word.

My cell door makes a doom sound when he slams it shut as he leaves. I know he must be locking me in, too, but I can't hear anything else because of the echo, which goes on for a long, long time.

F. Scott Fitzgerald wrote that it always seems to be three a.m. when you're having a dark night of the soul, and

I guess it's probably true, except that when you're in your juvie cell, you can't ever know what time it is. You've got no watch or cell phone to check, no windows to see the stars or the moon or the sunrise or the sky grow darker or lighter. You don't have any clocks on your wall or your computer or TV or microwave or stove to tell you the time *all* the time. To force you to think about what you're late for or early for, or how little time you have left, or how long you have to wait for something, like 0600, when they finally are supposed to let you out of your cell for breakfast. In juvie you lose all sense of time because you can't sleep and because of your dirty, dull fluorescent light that just keeps stuttering overhead and never ever goes out, ever.

At one point during the lockdown, I start counting to myself and don't stop until I get to ten thousand and it still doesn't seem as if any time has passed. At another point, I hear someone crying in another cell, on and on and on, crying that gets so hard it turns into a wracking cough that also goes on and on and on. Other girls yell at the crying girl to shut up, and keep yelling until a night guard threatens to cut off the air-conditioning. But the girl keeps crying. My heart aches for her. I want to rescue her from her cell and bring her into mine, wrap her in one of my blankets, let her sleep on my floor, or sleep with me, or take my bunk and I'll sit up and watch over her if it will help, if it will stop her grief or loneliness or whatever it is, stop her crying.

And then, finally – who knows when? – she stops.

But now, in the silence, I find myself crying, too – only quietly, tears dampening my blanket until I think I'm going to have to scream, too. I miss my mom so much, and Lulu, and Carla, and Granny, and even Dad, and my boyfriend – my *ex*-boyfriend – my sorry ex-boyfriend, who wouldn't stand up to his parents when they told him we couldn't go out anymore after they found out I got arrested.

Apparently Kevin had never heard of Romeo and Juliet and how his parents trying to keep us apart was supposed to make him want to be with me even more, and how he was supposed to sneak out of his house and come over to mine and throw pebbles at my window and say, "But soft, what light through yonder window breaks? It is the east, and Sadie is the sun. . . ."

I get up. I measure my cell in the number of juvie-issue sandal steps it takes to walk from the bed to the door and from one wall to the other. I wash my face and let it drip-dry because the guards didn't give me a towel and the toilet paper is so thin it shreds as soon as I touch it with my wet hands. I lay my blankets on the floor and do all the yoga poses I can remember from some sessions we had in gym class one time. I do push-ups until I can't lift myself off the floor or feel my arms. I stand flat against one wall and stare at the other to see if I can unfocus my eyes enough to see any patterns in the green concrete blocks. I stare at my arms, wondering if it's the light reflecting off the green walls that makes my skin take on a sickly green pallor.

I lie down on my bunk again and pull my blanket over my head but can't breathe. I try lying on my stomach, but the shape of the mattress with its pillowed end makes that impossible, so I lie the other way. That doesn't work, either. I shut my eyes and pretend I'm in my bedroom at home; or having a sleepover with Lulu, squeezed into bed with her and a dozen stuffed dogs; or in my sleeping bag camping out on Government Island.

You can sit in a room by yourself for hours, but the minute someone tells you you aren't allowed to leave, all you can think about is how badly, how desperately, you want out.

Even worse is that after a while – hours into not sleeping, hours into not being able to turn off your brain – you start playing those videos in your head again from a month ago when everything went wrong. You see a million things you'd do differently if you had the chance, but it's a kind of torture to keep thinking about it, because you're stuck where you are and there's nothing you can do to fix anything now.

My first night in juvie, my dark night of the soul, finally ends after thirteen hours of lockdown. I wake up on the cold concrete floor of my cell, no idea where I am at first, or how long I've been here, or what's happening. There's a lot of noise. Incomprehensible shouting and banging. Then the heavy click of a lock, and the door creaking open, and someone stepping inside, saying, "Well *that* looks comfortable." A new guard is standing over me. She looks vaguely familiar – not a guard I've seen before in juvie, but someone I might know from somewhere else. She can't be more than four or five years older than me. She's about my size, with her hair in tight cornrows like Wanda's and Nell's. Her name tag says C. MILLER. The uniform doesn't fit her very well.

"O-six-hundred," she says. "Breakfast." She drops a small hand towel on the edge of the stainless-steel sink, looks at me hard for a second, as if she maybe recognizes me from somewhere, too, and then leaves.

I drag myself up and can't figure out why my arms are so sore until I remember the shackles, and the push-ups, and Wanda's fingers clamping down on me when I told Officer Killduff where he could find the missing spork.

There's no mirror in the cell, so I just assume I look terrible. Not that it will matter in here. Nobody's wearing makeup, or doing much with their hair, or shaving their legs, or plucking their eyebrows, or getting their nails done.

I tuck my hair behind my ears and pull my fingers through to untangle some of the knots that have probably been in there since the day before. My orange jump-suit is wrinkled; I'll still have to wear it for another day before getting another. I wash and dry my face, stick my hands in my pockets, and shuffle out to meet whatever version of the day they let into juvie at six o'clock in the morning.

The Styrofoam breakfast boxes are already off the

transport cart. A couple of girls, one white, one black, sit together at one end of the mass of tables with their boxes open in front of them; Wanda and Nell sit with theirs at the other end. Some of the other girls are just wandering out of their cells, rubbing their eyes, stretching, coughing, wiping their noses. The little Hispanic girl yawns and looks around dully until Wanda waves her over to sit with them. I don't see the girl in the oven-mitt dress yet, or Gina, the sunny blond girl whose spork Wanda stole.

I grab a breakfast box and take a chair next to the girls who aren't Wanda and Nell.

"I'm Sadie."

The white girl – slight, with red hair, pretty in a washed-out sort of way – nods. "Hey. I'm Good Gina. This is Chantrelle."

"Hey," Chantrelle says, looking annoyed. "You believe this? They're not giving us our sporks on account of yesterday. We got to eat with our hands. I ain't even washed my hands yet. Not with soap."

"Yeah," Good Gina says, though she doesn't seem as bothered. "Sucks, doesn't it?" She lifts some eggs tentatively to her mouth with the tips of her fingers.

"Did you say *Good* Gina?" I ask.

Chantrelle answers for her. "That's what I call her. The other Gina – the one that got in trouble last night about the spork – we call her Bad Gina."

"Yeah," says Good Gina. "Bad Gina's not that bad, though. I don't think."

"Yeah," Chantrelle says. "And you ain't all that good, either."

They both laugh.

I check out the food: a Dixie cup with four desiccated apple slices, burnt scrambled eggs, an undercooked sausage patty, a dry piece of toast, a little plastic container of grape jelly, another Dixie cup with water.

"Any coffee?" I ask. They break out laughing again.

"No coffee in juvie," Chantrelle finally manages to say.

"Yeah," says Good Gina. "No hot anything. They're afraid we'll throw it on somebody and burn them."

I rub my temples, sure I'll be suffering even more of a headache later as I go through caffeine withdrawal.

"I know, right?" Good Gina says. "I used to measure time in my day from latte to latte."

"I don't drink coffee," Chantrelle says. "Don't like it. I like a Red Bull first thing in the morning, though." She shakes her head as she chews on a tough apple slice. "I do miss my Red Bulls."

I drink the water, pile my sausage and eggs on the toast, then ask if they know who was crying last night.

Good Gina nods. "Same one as every night since I've been here." She points to Cell Seven, where the new guard, C. Miller, is just walking in, carrying a breakfast box. "Annie or Angela or Angelina Jolie or something. Can't remember her name. Everybody just calls her Cell Seven. That thing she wears, they call that a suicide pad. They make you wear one if you try to hurt yourself. Can't tear it apart. Can't hang yourself with it. She doesn't even get to have any underwear – no bra, no T-shirt, nothing."

"What happened?"

Chantrelle answers. "Cut her arm. Got a little piece of metal from somewhere. But it wasn't a real cut, like for a real suicide. She did it the wrong way. She wasn't here when I come on the unit. I heard they sent her to where they send the mentals, but just for a couple days. She just come back."

Annie or Angela or Angelina still hasn't come out of her cell.

Good Gina leans close to me. "You know you better kind of watch out – like watch your back and all?" she asks.

"Because?"

"I'm not exactly sure," she says. "But there's something going on between the Jelly Sisters and Bad Gina. You finding that spork – I could tell that made the Jelly Sisters mad."

"Jelly Sisters?"

Chantrelle nods toward the other end of the tables. "Big girls over there with the cornrows. Wanda and Nell. That's the Jelly Sisters. They're not really sisters, though. I think they're maybe cousins. They don't like that Bad Gina. And that Bad Gina don't like them, either. And neither does that friend of Bad Gina's."

"Why do you call them that?"

"Jelly Sisters?" Chantrelle says. "On account of how much they love these little jellies the Correctionals give us at breakfast. Girls that used to be in here, they was calling them that already when I got in."

Good Gina giggles. "The Jelly Sisters are jelly jonesing any morning the Correctionals don't send them their jellies. They don't even spread it on toast. Just eat it like candy. Or like Jell-O shots."

"What are they in for?" I ask.

"Writing checks," said Chantrelle. "But I didn't hear it from them."

"I didn't know it was illegal to write checks."

"Is when it's your teacher's checkbook," Chantrelle says.

"True dat," Good Gina adds.

Chantrelle gives her a dismissive look. "Listen to you – all street talk and everything. You been in juvie, what, a whole week?"

"True dat." Good Gina grins. Chantrelle rolls her eyes.

We eat quietly for a minute, low buzzing conversations going on around the tables. Bad Gina comes out and sits with a big white girl, who I assume is the friend Good Gina and Chantrelle were talking about.

Good Gina finishes eating and closes her Styrofoam box. "What about you, Sadie?"

"What about me *what*?"

"Why're you in?"

"Drugs," I say, hoping that will be enough.

"Just possession?" she asks.

"Distribution."

"Dang, girl. Weed or pills?"

"Weed."

"So you were dealing weed?" she asks.

"Not really." I shrug. "It was a package somebody left in my car."

Good Gina and Chantrelle smile at each other. I probably wouldn't believe me, either.

Chantrelle has more questions. "What offense?"

I don't know what she's asking. "What do you mean, 'What offense'?"

"I mean first offense, second offense, like that."

"Oh," I say. "First."

"Dang, girl," she says, echoing Good Gina. "Nobody gets juvie for first offense anything that's not violent."

"They wanted me to give up some names."

"Why didn't you?"

"It was complicated."

"I'da named them in a heartbeat," Chantrelle says. "They out there running around while you do the time? I don't think so. I don't care about complicated."

"Same here," Good Gina says. "I'da named names out of the phone book if they'd wanted to hear some names."

Chantrelle snorts. "What you know about the life of crime, Good Gina? Or maybe I ought to call you Killer?"

Good Gina ducks her head and grins again.

Chantrelle thumps the table. "Good Gina here shot her boyfriend. Didn't actually kill him, though. Hardly even shot him. Just in his hand."

Good Gina turns red. "I'm probably goi... pay for his surgery and all the medical bills," she...

Chantrelle isn't through. "At least tell me y... him in his business hand. The one he use for chokin... ...s chicken?"

"I guess," Good Gina mutters.

"Why'd you shoot him?" I ask.

"The usual," she says.

"He was cheating on you?" I guess.

"Yeah. And it was the other girl's gun, too. I found it in her purse."

"Should've shot *her*," Chantrelle says.

Good Gina's face turns nearly purple, past embarrassment into anger.

Chantrelle pats her arm. "Well, never mind them," she says gently to Good Gina. "She's just a ho and he's just a pimp. A pimp is a magnet for hos. It's like a natural law. Nothing you can do about it. Ain't even about you, really."

Good Gina shakes her head. "It's not like that. He made a mistake. I made a mistake. People make mistakes. You know."

She looks at me. "I talk to him all the time," she says. "When they let us use the phones. I call him. He likes it when I call him."

Chantrelle shakes her head. Good Gina doesn't see her, though.

I don't know what to say. The whole conversation seems fictional. I've never met anyone who shot anyone.

m not sure I even know anyone who owns a handgun. "How long are you in for?" I ask.

"Don't know yet," Good Gina says. "Still have to go back to court."

"Me too," says Chantrelle. "Grand-theft auto, just like the video game. Wasn't me, though. It was a different Chantrelle. I be home with my mom and my sisters in no time, eating real pie off a real plate with a real knife and fork. Maybe y'all will get you your sporks back by then."

"God, I hope so," says Good Gina. "This sucks."

I wonder how much of what they told me I can believe – about why they're in juvie, about the Jelly Sisters, about me needing to watch my back.

C. Miller approaches the tables and opens a garbage bag. "Here you go, ladies. Trash."

All the girls stand up immediately, though the Jelly Sisters are a heartbeat slower than everyone else, like they're making a point, though I can't guess about what. Everyone stands in line to dump their Styrofoam boxes, then stays in line, waiting. Officer Killduff, who had been sitting at the guard desk drinking a cup of coffee, rouses himself. He unlocks a cabinet, then brings out a plastic container full of toothbrushes, each one labeled with a cell number. I take mine and wait for C. Miller to squeeze toothpaste on it – a job that seems to be beneath Officer Killduff – then we all go to our cells to brush our teeth. We drop our toothbrushes back off, and Officer Killduff orders us to line up again at the door to go to morning classes, though we end up just standing there for a good five minutes while he sits at the guard station writing in a logbook. C. Miller walks around the unit, looking into all the cells.

She stops when she gets to mine. "Windas!" she whispers. I stiffen and hold my breath. I have no idea what's coming next.

She waves me over.

"You didn't make your bunk, girl," she says. "Hurry and do it."

But it's too late. Officer Killduff sees what's going on and comes over.

"That's not how it's done in here, Officer Miller."

"Sir?" she says.

He ignores her and turns to me.

"Sorry," I say. "I'll take care of it."

I start toward my cell, but he stops me. "I didn't hear you ask could you go."

I fight the urge to look at his face – to make eye contact. I study the tops of my feet instead. I clench my jaw. "Can I go?"

He grunts.

When I return to my place in line, which is now last, Officer Killduff gets close to my face. I struggle once again to keep my gaze on my feet.

"That just cost you three days of phone privileges," he says.

CHAPTER 6

In which Carla needs me to save her.
Again.

Mom hit me with chores all morning on Sunday, the day after the arrest, and only let me leave the house to go to work that afternoon at the car wash. She kept asking me what really happened, but I just kept saying the same thing: that we didn't know there were drugs in the car, that we'd just given the guys a ride and that was all. Mom said if it turned out Carla had anything to do with the drugs, she would go to jail for sure.

Kevin came by during my break, but I couldn't even tell him I'd been arrested. I couldn't tell anybody. He left thinking I was mad at him for something, and then I really did get mad at him – for taking off so quickly, for not sticking around to try to find out what was wrong. Mom took away my cell phone for a couple of days, so I couldn't talk to him that night or text him. Every time I tried to apologize, hoping she'd give it back, and maybe ease up on my restrictions, she said she didn't want to hear it until I was ready to tell her the truth.

Monday she took me to see a lawyer, somebody she knew from back in high school. His name was Vance. He looked more like a biker than a lawyer, with his long hair and handlebar mustache. I wondered what was up with Mom and guys with mustaches. Dad never had a mustache.

"Lemme cut right to the chase here," Vance said after I told him about the events leading up to the arrest. I left out the parts about me drinking a beer, and Dreadlocks hitting on me, and Carla hooking up with Scuzzy and initiating the whole thing. I also left out the part about me wondering what Carla knew.

"You've never been in any kind of trouble," he said, "plus you're an upstanding girl, play on the basketball team, hold down a job, make good grades, all that kind of stuff. What that likely means is you get probation. Community service. So you spend your Saturdays working at the food bank or whatever. And you have early curfew. That sort of thing."

Mom relaxed back in her chair.

"But I can still play basketball, right?" I asked. "And

I can travel with the team to away games?"

Vance tugged on his mustache. "Depends. We'll have to wait and see on that. It's still gonna be a serious charge. That was a lot of pot."

He spoke in a growly biker voice that had me looking around his small, cluttered office for a motorcycle helmet or a leather jacket hanging up somewhere or sitting on top of one of his piles of law books. He didn't have either, though – or any shelves, which seemed odd for a lawyer.

"There's another possibility," he added. "Which is you cooperate with the police and give them the names of the guys. That's something you have that could help us here."

I looked down at the floor. My foot seemed to have started this nervous tapping and I had a hard time making it stop.

"What?" Mom demanded. "Out with it."

I said I didn't know their names. Mom practically shot up out of her chair.

"You went off in the car with two men, two *older* men, two *drug dealers*, and you didn't even know their names?"

I couldn't look at her. "Yes, ma'am. It was stupid. I know."

Mom fumed. "Stupid doesn't begin to describe it."

"Yes, ma'am," I said again.

Vance didn't say anything. I was sure he'd heard this sort of thing before, and probably a lot worse.

"What about Carla?" Mom asked him.

He looked at her for a minute, then out the window at the downtown traffic. The building he was in, and his office, were so close to the street that he could practically reach out the window and touch the passing cars.

"She's got two strikes on her, right?"

Mom nodded. "Possession when she was eighteen. And shoplifting last year. She's on probation."

"I hate to say it – and she needs to see her own lawyer, Gretchen, so you can't take what I tell you as anything but my opinion – but if she's involved in this in any way, she's looking at doing time."

"What kind of time?"

He drummed his fingers on the window. Somebody out on the sidewalk waved up to him, and he waved back.

"Real time. For starters, there's the time they suspended on her before."

"It was a year," Mom said.

"A year, then," Vance said. "Plus at least the minimum mandatory sentence for felony distribution, which is three years last time I checked."

Mom's face was pale. "And when was that?"

Vance studied the surface of his desk. "I do criminal law, which is mostly drug cases. So that was, like, last week."

"So four years?" Mom asked, her whole body sagging.

"Minimum," Vance said.

* * *

I stayed home the rest of the day but still didn't have my cell phone. Kevin could have left me a hundred messages by then, but Mom wouldn't let me check. She wouldn't let me go to basketball practice, either, but at least let me use her phone to call Coach and tell him I was sick.

I was in my room doing homework I was supposed to have done over the weekend when Carla came in. Lulu must have been in the living room with Mom. I knew Carla had gone to court that afternoon for the arraignment, but she hadn't called to say what happened.

She collapsed on my bed next to me. When we were younger and she did that, I was supposed to rub her head, brush her hair, braid it, that sort of thing. Play massage parlor and beauty salon.

She smelled like cigarettes and restaurant grease. She must have gone to work after court. I scooted away.

"So how did it go?"

Carla sighed. "They read the charges. The judge continued the recognizance bond and they assigned me a court-appointed lawyer. That was about it."

She started in on the apologies again, and I understood why Mom had told me she didn't want to hear it, because I didn't, either. Those "I'm sorry's" were nails on a chalkboard.

"Never mind about all that," I snapped. "Just tell me one thing. Did you know?"

Carla stiffened. "About the drugs? God, no. Of course not. I was so out of it. I must have had four or five beers, and some bong hits. And you know what a lightweight I am —"

"Whatever," I interrupted. "Just tell me what you want from me. I have work to do."

Carla got that hurt expression she is so good at. It didn't work, though. I had a feeling it might never work on me again.

"OK," she said. "I deserve that. I know I do." She pulled a flattened pack of cigarettes out of the back pocket of her jeans. She threw a couple of broken cigarettes in the trash can – which I would have to empty before Mom saw – and tried to straighten and reshape one that was still intact.

"You mind?" she asked.

I did mind but didn't want a fight. "Whatever."

She lifted the window and then the screen, leaning outside to light her cigarette and holding it out there when she wasn't puffing on it. She made sure to blow her smoke outside, too. If I wasn't suspicious of her before, I sure as hell was now. It wasn't at all like Carla to be thoughtful like that.

"So?" I asked.

"So," she said. "So I'm going to jail." She stopped to wipe her eyes, but the tears were already pouring down her cheeks, leaving tracks in her makeup.

"God damn it, Carla." I yanked a tissue out of the box beside my bed and handed it to her. "What about Lulu?"

"Either Mom takes her in or Social Services takes her."

She shook her head, took another long, wet drag on her cigarette, and blew it out.

"Of course Mom will take her," I said, my insides going cold at the alternative.

Carla nodded and flicked ash out the window. "That's what she said."

We were quiet for a long time. I couldn't believe this was happening – not to us. Not to me.

Then Carla sniffled. "She'll be seven when I get out, you know. I won't be there when she starts kindergarten. I'll miss all those birthdays and Christmases. And it's going to kill Mom. How can she handle two jobs and taking care of Lulu all at the same time?" Now she was sobbing. "And it's not fair to you, either. I know that. I feel terrible." She couldn't talk anymore from crying so hard.

I handed her a fistful of tissues this time. "There's nothing else they can do? To keep you out of jail, I mean?"

She shook her head again. Then she stared at the lit end of her cigarette. "Well, the lawyer did say there was one other option."

"What?" I asked, wondering why she was being so cagey. "Carla, whatever it is, you have to do it. Lulu needs you."

"It's not that," she said. "I mean, it's not something *I* can do." She took a deep drag on her cigarette and blew out a stream of words along with her smoke. "Look, I'm not asking you to do this, OK? I'm just telling you what the lawyer said. He's, like, a court-appointed lawyer, so he probably doesn't give a shit – about me or my case or anything. But it's just what he told me."

"Which was what?" I was back to being suspicious.

"Which was you confess. You say the guys put you up to it, and I didn't have anything to do with anything. I just happened to be in the car. And since you're a juvenile, and since you haven't been in trouble before . . ."

I stood up so fast, it made me dizzy. "You want me to what? Are you out of your stupid mind? I'll have a record! I'll go to juvie!"

"Not for a first offense," she said weakly. "Anyway, I'm not asking it. I'm just telling you what the lawyer said. That's all." She flicked her cigarette out the window and fished another from her flattened pack.

My mind was reeling, trying to make sense of everything, of just what, exactly, Carla was asking me to do. "Carla," I said, grabbing her sleeve, making her drop the cigarettes. "Did you know what was going on? That they had drugs? That we were their cover or whatever?"

Carla shook her head. "No. Maybe. I mean, I was drunk! They just said they needed a ride to the 7-Eleven. They wanted to get more beer. . . ."

"And?" I pressed.

"And they had to get something to a guy and it wouldn't take but a minute. But that was all. They didn't say anything about drugs, I promise. I'm pretty sure they didn't. I thought we were just doing them a favor."

She stopped to light her second cigarette, but I

grabbed her hand, peeled her fingers off the lighter, and threw it out the window.

"What'd you do that for?" she asked.

"Just get out, Carla."

"But what about—?"

"Leave," I said. "Now."

She dragged herself off the bed. "Don't tell Mom."

I felt dazed, as if I was drunk, or maybe high. "Don't tell her what? That you're a world-class screwup? That I'm such an idiot? She already knows. Believe me."

"Any of it," Carla said. "Don't tell her any of it. Not yet. She's so mad at me, she won't speak to me."

"Can you blame her?"

She shook her head and turned to go, but stopped at the door. "Think about it? Please? I can't lose Lulu. I'll promise you anything."

"Great," I said. "Promise me you'll make all this go away. Promise me you'll make it so none of it ever happened in the first place."

She retreated down the hallway. I slammed the door behind her.

Kevin came over that night, but Mom wouldn't let me see him. He drove off but just parked his car down the road and walked back and tapped on my bedroom window. It was a little after ten. I told him to wait in his car and I'd be there as soon as Mom went to bed.

Fifteen minutes later, we were making out in his

backseat on a dark side street a block from my house. We barely even said hello when I got there, just kind of jumped on each other. I hadn't realized I wanted him that bad. Or maybe I just wanted anything that would take my mind off what Carla wanted me to do.

Kevin pulled my T-shirt over my head and was tugging at my jeans before I finally stopped him – stopped both of us. The windows were so steamy, we couldn't see outside, which was no surprise, as hard as we were breathing.

"Wow," Kevin said, brushing his blond hair out of his sweaty face. "Where did that come from?"

I shrugged, pulled my jeans back up, and retrieved my shirt from the backseat floor. "I must have missed you, I guess," I said.

He grinned, grabbed the T-shirt away, and pressed himself back on top of me. I was tempted to pull his shirt off as well, but I stopped us again, struggling to sit back up.

"I have to get back to the house," I said.

Kevin pouted. Actually pouted. "How come? You're already here. I mean look at us."

"Yeah," I said, "but Mom could wake up or something. She'd freak out if she saw I was gone."

Kevin crossed his arms and kept pouting until I leaned in and kissed him long and hard. "Next time," I said. "I have to go. I'll get in trouble."

He threw up his hands, the way you would in a game to convince a referee you hadn't actually fouled somebody you were pretty sure you had – you were just hoping to get away with it. Sometimes it worked. Usually it didn't.

"So how come you've been so weird, Sadie? You hardly talked to me at the car wash, you didn't answer my messages, you don't want to, you know, keep going tonight. It's not like we haven't done it before."

"I got in trouble, OK?" I snapped. "I went with Carla to this party, and Mom busted me. She put me on restrictions and took my phone. It's like I'm in middle school." I pulled my shirt on. "There. Are you satisfied?"

I still couldn't tell him the rest. I was hoping that maybe there was a way to get out of all this without the whole world finding out. Especially Kevin.

"Were you doing drugs?" he asked quietly. Kevin hated drugs. He had an uncle who died from an overdose, or a car crash, or something having to do with drugs.

"No way," I said. "There were a few people smoking pot and stuff, but I just had beer. And barely any of that. Even when I played beer pong."

"Hunh," he said.

"What do you mean, 'Hunh'?" I said, annoyed again. "It was just stupid beer pong."

Kevin got all quiet. "You want me to drive you home?" he asked through his clenched jaw, which was stupid. We were just a block from my house.

"Don't be that way," I said, hating how quickly things had blown up. One minute we were practically doing it in the backseat of his car, now this. "I'm just saying I don't need you to give me a hard time, too. I'm getting enough of that from my mom."

"Yeah," he said. "Whatever." He was back to pouting. I hated it when he did that. It made me angry, but it also made me feel guilty for disappointing him, for speaking harshly, for hurting his feelings. I wished I could just explain about everything: the 7-Eleven, getting arrested, how none of it was my fault, how I didn't even know what was going on until it was too late. How now Carla wanted me to confess to everything so she wouldn't have to go to jail and risk losing Lulu.

But I couldn't tell him. As much as I loved him, and as much as I was pretty sure he loved me, I wasn't entirely sure he'd believe me. I wasn't sure anybody would.

I just wanted to keep my life the way it was.

So I slid back down on the seat, pulling Kevin down with me.

"You're not mad at me, are you?" I whispered in his ear.

He shook his head, which I knew was a lie.

I asked if he had a condom, and he nodded.

"Are you sure?" he asked, which was just like him – pouting and selfish one minute, sweet and caring the next.

"Yeah, I'm sure," I whispered, though that was a lie, too.

CHAPTER 7

In which I get interrogated by Bad Gina about that spork and the Jelly Sisters break my nose

Here's how we walk down the hall to classes my second day in Unit Three: the Jelly Sisters in front next to the guard, C. Miller, followed by the Hispanic girl and the middle-school girl, whose names I still don't know. Chantrelle and Good Gina come next, and then Bad Gina and a large girl who seems to be her friend. I'm behind the large friend and can't see past her, not that I'm supposed to, anyway. We all have our hands behind our backs, heads bowed, mouths shut.

Forty feet down the long, gray hall, C. Miller says, "Halt." I don't stop fast enough, though – the way we're marching, I think we'll be going a lot farther – and so stumble into Bad Gina's large friend. She keeps her arms behind her but shoves me back so hard with her hip that I actually fall down.

Next thing I know, Officer Killduff, who's been trailing the line, is standing over me.

"Off the floor," he snarls.

I scramble to my feet. Several of the girls in line laugh, or that's what it looks like from behind: their shoulders shaking but no noise.

"Eyes down," he barks at me before muttering into his radio. A door opens and we enter the classroom.

A heavy, bright-faced man, his seriously receding hair pulled back in a tight ponytail, stands behind a teacher's desk, fanning himself with the front of his sweat-stained polo shirt, though it feels cold to me here, like everywhere else in juvie.

We sit around four long tables that have been shoved together to form a big one in the center of the room, surrounded by bookcases with stacks of musty textbooks and workbooks and old maps and boxes of who knows what. A whiteboard that doesn't appear to have been properly cleaned since it was installed is mounted to the wall. There's so much up there written on top of so much else that you can't read a word.

Officer Killduff leaves. C. Miller stands next to the whiteboard, crosses her arms, and stares straight ahead. The teacher, a Mr. Pettigrew according to his ID badge, doesn't say anything. He just hands out workbooks and big fat black markers. The girls bend over their workbooks, though Bad Gina's large friend, who sits on one side of me, draws pictures of horses in hers. The Hispanic girl, two chairs away on the other side, just makes dots all over hers, giving each page a bad case of chicken pox.

Mr. Pettigrew plops down in the empty chair between me and the Hispanic girl and drums his fingers on a manila folder. Bad Gina's large friend flips the horse page in her workbook and pretends to work on something else, though he doesn't even glance over her way.

"Hello," he says to me.

"Hi," I say back.

"You're Sadie."

I nod. "I'm Sadie."

"Junior? Mountain View High School?"

I nod again. "Junior. Mountain View."

It's his turn to nod. "Very good. Well. The older girls are working on GED prep. The younger girls are just doing lessons. We'll get you started on GED prep."

That catches me by surprise. "I was still planning on getting a regular diploma," I say. I just assumed I would continue some version of my junior year while I was in juvie, and then start next fall back at my high school as a senior, sort of pretend nothing ever happened, as if I'd just transferred away for a while and then transferred back.

Mr. Pettigrew shrugs. "Whatever." He tugs a bandanna out of his back pocket and drags it across his sweaty face, then hands me a workbook.

"This is yours," Mr. Pettigrew says. "Language arts."

"What else is there?" I ask.

"Social studies, science, reading, math," he says. "You'll also do your reading review in this class. You'll do the others in your other classes. Let me know if you have any questions or if you need any help."

He pushes his chair back and stands. "You do read, don't you?"

I look up. He has three chins. "You mean books?"

"I mean do you *read* read?"

"Do I read at all?"

He nods. "Sixth-grade level?"

I say yes, I do know how to read at a sixth-grade level.

"And I'm getting a regular degree," I say, not that he cares. "I'm graduating with my class next year."

He shrugs again.

Once he leaves, Bad Gina's large friend goes back to her drawing. My language-arts workbook turns out to be my reading-comprehension workbook instead, which makes me wonder if Mr. Pettigrew is the one with the reading problem. None of the other girls are talking, and all keep their heads bent over their workbooks, whether they're drawing, sleeping, or actually working, so I do the same and spend the next half hour reading dry paragraphs on First Ladies, Machu Picchu, potatoes, Cambodian refugees, busy beavers, and how to hang the American flag.

*　*　*

At some point, halfway through the hour, the total quiet gives way to low conversations until just about all the girls are talking to whoever is sitting next to them – Bad Gina and her large friend on one side of me, Good Gina and Chantrelle next to them, with the middle-school girl occasionally whispering in, Wanda and Nell opposite from me at the far end of the table. The only ones not saying anything are the little Hispanic girl and me.

Officer C. Miller's eyes droop shut, though she still stands in the same spot against the wall that she's been at since we came in. Mr. Pettigrew sits at his desk nearby, his meaty hands working a cell phone or something else with a keypad and a tiny screen.

Bad Gina's large friend raps on the table in front of her, then raises her hand.

Mr. Pettigrew looks up.

"Permission to use the bathroom," the girl says in a much higher voice than I expect.

Mr. Pettigrew nods. C. Miller opens her eyes and nods, too, and Bad Gina's large friend crosses the room to a small door I didn't realize was even there next to the crowded bookcases.

Bad Gina raises her hand next.

"Permission to change seats by the new girl."

"What for?" Mr. Pettigrew asks. All the other girls lift their heads to watch the exchange.

"She asked me to help her with something in her workbook."

Mr. Pettigrew and C. Miller do their nodding thing again, and Bad Gina slides into the seat next to mine.

"So," she says with a broad, toothy smile. "What did you need help with?" She grabs my workbook. "Oh, yeah. Here we go. This one is about the American flag. So what it says you do, to hang it the right way, is you send a million American soldiers to Iraq, stomp their Iraq asses, and then you get to hang up the American flag. So the right answer here is D, none of the above."

"Got it," I say, taking the workbook back. "Thanks for your help."

She flashes another smile with her blindingly white teeth. The light actually seems to reflect off them. I feel like I need sunglasses to look at her.

She leans in closer and the smile vanishes. "I know you saw who took the spork last night. It was one of the Jellies, wasn't it? Wanda Jelly. I know it was. Either that bitch or that bitch's friend. But it had to be her. She was the closest."

"I didn't see anybody take anything," I lie. I'm not about to get in the middle of whatever is going on between Bad Gina and the Jelly Sisters – any more than I already have, that is. "I just saw it when we were on the floor. Probably it just fell."

"Then how did it end up ten feet away under the bookshelf?" she asks, somehow managing to sound sweet and vaguely threatening at the same time.

C. Miller stirs from the wall where she's been sleeping

standing up – or that's how it appears. "Problem over there?" she asks.

Bad Gina's blinding smile returns. "Sorry. Were we being too loud? We were just excited because the new girl figured out this problem in her workbook."

C. Miller relaxes against the wall again. "Just keep it down. You know the rules."

"Yes, sir," Bad Gina says. I'm surprised C. Miller doesn't get mad about Bad Gina calling her "sir." Maybe that's what you're supposed to call all the guards, male or female. Maybe it's just the way Bad Gina says it that makes it OK.

She slides my workbook back in front of her on the table and points at nothing in particular so it will look as if we've moved on to another problem. "So?" she says. "How did it end up there?"

"Are we still talking about the spork?" I ask.

"Yes, we're still talking about the spork," she says evenly, as if it takes some effort to keep the threatening tone out of her voice.

"I don't know," I say, lying again. "Maybe you dropped it. Maybe it accidentally got kicked there. I don't know. I wasn't on spork duty."

Bad Gina glances at me sharply, just for a second, eyes like knives, but then softens just as quickly. She laughs softly, too. "You weren't on spork duty. That's a good one."

It really isn't a good one. It's dumb. But I definitely

prefer Bad Gina's smile, and her laugh, to that other look she has – the knife eyes.

She lays a warm hand on my arm. "Sorry I kind of went off on you. It's just really, really hard in here, and I know those Jelly Sisters are out to get me. I don't even know why. They just are. They think they own the place, and I guess I don't exactly like doing stuff just because somebody tells me I have to. We get enough of that from the guards, right?"

"Yeah," I say cautiously. "I guess so."

Bad Gina's large friend comes back from the restroom then and sits where Bad Gina was sitting earlier.

Bad Gina doesn't turn to look, just cocks her head in her friend's direction. "This is Weeze," she says. "Her real name is Louise, but everybody calls her Weeze."

Weeze grins. "Just since I've been in here," she says. Her teeth are the polar opposite of Bad Gina's: crooked and stained. She has a broad nose that lists to one side of her face. I can't see much of her eyes because she has a bowl cut and her bangs are too long.

Mr. Pettigrew stands up suddenly from his desk, as if he's just remembered something important.

"Time," he says.

And that's the end of class.

The Jelly Sisters glare at me from their end of the table as we pass up our notebooks and fat markers.

"Watch out for them," Bad Gina whispers. "Looks like you're on their shit list now, too."

* * *

And that's pretty much how it goes for the next couple of days: boring classes, boring TV, boring meals in Styrofoam boxes, boring interminable nights in our green-walled cells with Cell Seven sobbing until everybody wants to kill her – until, just as suddenly as she starts, she stops.

Every night is a dark night of the soul, every morning a nervous awakening to this palpable tension between the Jelly Sisters and Bad Gina. The rest of us try to stay out of it, but that's hard, especially for me, since Bad Gina seems to have decided we're pals, and seeks me out so often to talk that I can tell Weeze is jealous, and so now I probably have to worry about her, too.

I decide it's a bad idea to tell anybody too much of the truth about why I'm in – or about anything else – so when Bad Gina asks, I tell her I stole a car and shot my boy-friend. Bad Gina looks over at Good Gina and Chantrelle, then back at me.

"In the hand, right?" she asks sarcastically. "Like her?"

I shake my head. "I wish. It was just in the foot, though. I didn't know the gun was loaded."

She knows I'm lying, but I guess it's a good enough lie, or a dumb enough lie, that she decides to let it go for now.

Officer Killduff and Officer Miller march us down to the gymnasium after classes on Thursday. Officer Killduff has been on me since Tuesday if I so much as think about an infraction of any of the juvie rules, and there seem to be rules for everything. C. Miller is a lot nicer, not that we actually talk or anything, but it's obvious that she's just trying to do her job and treat us like we're actual human beings, which is a lot more than I can say for Officer Killduff or any of the other guards I've seen so far.

There's a full basketball court in the gym, the ceiling so low that the rafters seem to barely clear the top of the backboards. A row of chairs is set up at the center line facing an open half-court, while various bins and equipment bags and torn, duct-taped tumbling mats litter the other half behind the chairs.

Officer Killduff grabs a couple of basketballs from a sack and tosses them to the open side of the court – the first time that's happened. I scoop one up, happy for the first time all week, and launch a three-pointer. It has too much arc and nearly hits the rafters, then clangs off the rim. I have to chase the ball myself because the other girls mostly just stand around, waiting for orders or something. Chantrelle follows me over after a few minutes and takes a couple of weak shots that barely graze the backboard, then she and Good Gina break into a slow jog around the perimeter of the gym, in anticipation of what they know is coming next.

"Drop the balls and give me ten laps!" Officer Killduff barks. The rest of the girls groan and then plod after Chantrelle and Good Gina, more shuffling than running. I park both basketballs under the goal and quickly catch up. It's hard running so slow, so I decide to pick it up a little.

"Slow down and run with us," Good Gina calls after me.

"Can't," I say.

It feels good to stretch my legs and fill my lungs and let myself fly around the perimeter of the gym the way I've done thousands of times at thousands of basketball practices, and I pretty quickly catch up to the slow-moving herd of girls before they're even halfway around the gym.

Bad Gina pretends she's going to trip me as I run past. I slide around her in my juvie sandals, which don't have much traction and make corners difficult.

Chantrelle calls after me this time as I pass them, though not so loud that the officers can hear: "Slow down, girl. You're making everybody look bad."

I ignore her and keep running, picking up the pace a little more, and pass them all again just as they're starting their second lap.

Bad Gina jumps in and runs alongside me, her blond ponytail whipping behind her.

"Damn, girl," she says. "You got the need for speed or what?"

She elbows me and I lose my stride, but just for a second.

"No," I say. "Just feel like running."

"You know you're just running circles, right?" she says. She doesn't seem to be having any trouble keeping up. "It's not like you're going to get anywhere."

I don't reply, and Bad Gina doesn't say anything else,

just grins for the next couple of laps until I pick up the pace a little more, to see how it feels and to see how she'll do. She responds by cutting inside and making me work harder at the corners. We keep running hard for several more laps and keep passing the other girls, neither of us stopping when we get to ten.

After several more laps, Bad Gina sprints out ahead. I strain to keep up with her. Sprinting is even harder with the sandals on. We skid every time we round the corners. My breathing turns ragged, but at least hers does, too.

I've almost forgotten the guards are there until we hit what's probably lap twenty and Officer Killduff yells at us, "Last lap! Winner gets double time in the shower!"

"Game on," Bad Gina rasps, pulling more speed from out of somewhere. I respond the best I can, though my legs feel like lead and I'm running seriously low on oxygen. Bad Gina stays two steps ahead through most of the final lap, but I keep pressing, hanging on at her shoulder and she knows it. Then we round the last corner, and she nearly loses control. One of her sandals flies off and she skids in her sock, giving me just enough opportunity to pass her — until she grabs the back of my jumpsuit.

She jerks me back hard and whips ahead, just beating me past Officer Killduff.

"And we have a winner," he says, even though he must have seen Bad Gina cheat.

I grab my knees when I stop, and so does she.

"Double shower time," Bad Gina rasps. "That's six

sweet minutes of hot water. I'd kill my own grandmother for that."

I suppose I should count myself lucky, then. The rest of the girls crowd around us, except for the Jelly Sisters, who keep their distance. Weeze gives Bad Gina a high five, and there's a chorus of "You go, girls" until Officer Killduff breaks up the party.

"Ten more laps for dogging it the first time," he says. "Except for these two." He points to Bad Gina and me. "And if I don't see real running, we'll have to find out how you ladies like doing wind sprints the whole rest of gym class."

"Damn it, Sadie," Chantrelle mutters, out of earshot of Officer Killduff. She looks genuinely dismayed. "I told you to slow it down. Now look what you done."

"Sorry," I say.

"Yeah, sorry," Bad Gina adds. Weeze gives her another high five as she jogs off, but a weak one this time, and with a pained look on her pink face, either from the running she's already done or the extra laps she now has to do.

The Jelly Sisters bring up the rear, jogging shoulder to shoulder, not stopping for anything or anybody. I have to jump back to avoid getting run over.

Bad Gina and I shoot baskets for the next few minutes as the girls plod around the gym. Officer C. Miller snags a long rebound when I miss a three-pointer that hits the back of the rim and bounces practically to midcourt.

She dribbles a couple of times and launches a three-pointer of her own that banks in. I pick up the ball and stare at her for a second. She smiles and shrugs and sits back down next to Officer Killduff.

Bad Gina and I shoot some more. She says she played some before, in middle school. She knows how to dribble, and she can at least hit the backboard from the free-throw line, even if she only makes one in ten.

Finally, when the girls finish their run, Officer Killduff orders us into teams – me, Bad Gina, Weeze, and the young girl, who everybody calls Middle-School Karen, on one; the Jelly Sisters, Chantrelle, Good Gina, and the little Hispanic girl – Officer Killduff calls her Fefu – on the other.

"Hey, no fair," Bad Gina whines – not to Officer Killduff directly but more to the gym in general. "That's our four against their five."

Officer Killduff looks right at her. "Everybody plays," he says, then he throws the ball at her. I step in front and catch it.

"Ball in," he says, and we start.

It isn't much of a game. The Jelly Sisters mostly just stand under the basket and collect rebounds. Weeze does the same for our team. Chantrelle parks in the lane and picks at her cuticles, even though Bad Gina keeps yelling at her that she's violating the three-second rule. Nobody else seems to know what that is, though – I'm surprised Bad Gina does – and Chantrelle ignores her.

Good Gina also knows how to play, at least a little, so she dribbles around for their team, shoots badly when I let her get off a shot, and occasionally tries to pass the ball inside to the Jellies or Chantrelle. Every now and then she passes to Fefu on the perimeter, but Fefu just looks at the ball as if it's an exotic fruit maybe and then passes it back.

Weeze on our team stumbles into the Jelly Sisters a couple of times, not exactly fighting for rebounds, but just sort of mildly contesting them. I mostly hold on to the ball when our team has possession, which is most of the game. There's no driving the lane with the Jellies and Weeze and Chantrelle clogging everything up in there, so Bad Gina and I stay outside and pass the ball to each other. We would include Middle-School Karen, but she's too busy staying out of the way and chewing on her straw-colored hair.

Good Gina wears herself out running between Bad Gina and me as we keep swinging the ball back and forth waiting for an open shot, which I mostly take. It's like shooting free throws since Good Gina can't keep up with our passes and nobody else comes out to contest anything.

Ten minutes into the game, our team is up nine to two, counting buckets by ones. I score eight of our nine, but the game is boring and I finally say so.

"This would be more interesting if we played man-to-man," I say.

"Yeah," Bad Gina chimes in. "Man-to-man."

Good Gina sits down on the court. "I'm tired. I'm the only one running out here. This sucks."

She bounces the ball to Fefu, who doesn't even bother catching it this time, just stares at it as it bounces past.

Wanda comes out from under the goal a couple of steps. Nell follows her. "Just shut up and play," she says to me. "You done enough new-girl bullshit for one day."

"Yeah," Nell echoes. "Just shut up and play."

"Fine, then," I snap. "And screw you." Seeing my opening with the two of them finally out of position, I grab the ball from the floor near Fefu, dribble around them with my quick first step, and drive the baseline for a reverse layup. It feels good going up, but I haven't counted on how quickly the Jelly Sisters can move when they want to.

They suddenly materialize *right there* under me as I come down and they sandwich me hard, almost as if they've been waiting for the opportunity, maybe even baiting me into the baseline move. One or the other of them, or both, knock the breath out of me, and I drop like a sack of rocks to the floor. My face hits somebody's knee on the way down – or somebody's knee hits my face. Either way I feel an explosion of blood out of my nose, showering the court where I fall. I hold my face and know my nose must be broken, as the spray of blood continues with each pounding beat of my heart. I feel dizzy and curl into a ball and fight the urge to vomit.

Everything is frozen for the next few seconds as

I guess everybody realizes what has just happened, though my eyes are too tightly clenched shut for me to know. Then I hear Officer Killduff's booming voice: "Grab some God damn floor!"

Eight bodies sprawl around me, as if they've been hit by a bomb.

Next thing I know, Officer C. Miller is kneeling next to me, pulling on blue latex gloves. Then she holds the back of my head up with one hand and a cloth on my nose with the other. "Just don't move yet, Sadie," she says.

"Officer Miller!" Officer Killduff barks again. "Radio for backup. Take Windas to the infirmary. The rest of these are going on lockdown."

"You know Tarzan?"

That's the first thing the nurse asks when C. Miller delivers me to the infirmary.

She looks about ninety, wears a faded, flower-print smock, and has a chain-smoker's raspy voice. Her ID says BATCH. She scowls down at my face.

"Who?" I ask. It hurts to speak. I'm lying on an exam table, the only one they have in the cramped exam room.

"Tarzan of the jungle," Nurse Batch says.

She shifts her examination light closer and studies up inside my nose. When she pokes at the septum, I nearly dive off the table.

"Reason I asked," she wheezes, "is the actor that played Tarzan in the movies, long time ago, he was always falling off his vines in the middle of swinging through the jungle and kept breaking his nose. So after a while he got tired of going to the hospital every time and he would just take ahold and straighten his nose back out himself."

I look at her to make sure she doesn't have any ideas of doing that to me.

"It's just cartilage," she says. "Not like he was setting bone."

C. Miller steps up beside Nurse Batch and peers down at me, then shudders and looks away. "It does look like it's a little sideways, doesn't it?" she asks.

Nurse Batch nods. "Kind of," she says, poking. I flinch.

"Well, don't worry," she says to me. "I'm going to put this ice pack on to help with the swelling and the bruising, and then we can take a closer look."

She holds up one of those crush-packs of dry ice and squeezes it several different ways to release the cold. Then just before she applies it, so quickly that I don't realize what's happening until it's too late, she pinches the bridge of my nose and yanks it straight.

I howl and clap my hands over my face, blind from the pain, ten times worse than when I got hit in the face by the Jelly Sisters. I let out a string of curse words and Nurse Batch yells back at me to watch my garbage mouth. Then she shoves the ice pack at me, but I push it away, roll onto my side, and finally throw up.

"What'd you do that for?" Nurse Batch yells. "Did you want a crooked nose the rest of your life? You ought to be thanking me, not horking all over my floor."

I can't answer. I haven't ever heard that word before
– *horking* – but that doesn't stop me from hanging off the
side of the exam table and doing it again.

I lie on the table for half an hour while Nurse Batch calls
for a janitor to come clean up the mess, my head pounding with every little movement.

Twice I hear C. Miller ask Nurse Batch if she's going
to give me anything for pain, and twice Nurse Batch says
she'll get to it when she has time – though she doesn't
seem to be doing much of anything besides talking in a low
voice with the janitor once he shows up.

"Hang in there," C. Miller says to me.

My face hurts too much for me to say anything
back. Besides, my voice sounds too strange with these
cotton balls sprayed with Afrin shoved up in my nostrils, which Nurse Batch put in after she straightened the
cartilage.

The janitor finally starts mopping the floor, while
Nurse Batch unlocks a cabinet and shakes a couple of pills
out of a large white bottle.

"My shift's over in an hour, and there won't be nobody
in the infirmary to watch you overnight," Nurse Batch says
when she comes back over to the examination table. "You'll
have to go back to your unit. There's a shower through
that door there. You can shower off all that blood and
change your clothes first. And you can take one of these.

The officer will give you another later, about midnight."

She hands me a white pill and a Dixie cup of water. I look at her dully.

"It's for the pain," she says. "You *are* in pain, aren't you? The guard said you were."

I nod, wanting to ask her why she didn't give it to me an hour earlier, when I first came in, but probably I've already asked more questions than you can usually get away with in juvie. Plus I don't want to make her mad and have her change her mind about the painkillers.

C. Miller helps me over to the shower. "It's on a three-minute timer," she says. A steady river of blood washes off my face and swirls down the half-blocked drain. It mixes with my tears. I don't know whether they're from the pain or from the ordeal of the past hour. C. Miller takes pity on me when the water cuts off and turns it back on for another three minutes. I pull the cotton balls out of my nostrils and shudder to see the trail of thick, black-red slime that comes with them.

When I get out and towel off, I catch sight of my reflection for the first time — and burst into more tears. Already my face is puffy, my nose is green and purple, and I have the start of two black eyes. I know the swelling will go away and the bruises will fade over time, but the longer I stare in the mirror, the more I think that even if they suddenly let me out of juvie, even if this was a giant mistake, a big misunderstanding, even if Carla confesses and I could go back to high school tomorrow and see

Kevin – even if all that happened, he would probably take one look at me and run the other way.

I crumple against the sink below the mirror, sobbing and feeling sorry for myself, until Nurse Batch grabs my arm and pulls me away and tells me to knock it off. She shoves a pile of clean clothes at me and says, "Give it a rest already. You think you're the first girl to get her nose broken in here? Don't worry. It'll grow back straight. Probably."

"I know you," C. Miller says as we walk back to Unit Three. "From before here. I just figured it out."

"How?" I ask, surprised that she's speaking to me. Guards aren't supposed to speak to inmates. Not like this, anyway.

"You went to Mountain View, right? Played basketball? Started when you were like maybe a freshman, three or four years ago?"

I look at C. Miller again. My face still hurts so bad I don't want to talk, even with the painkiller. I make myself anyway. "Eighth grade," I say. "They let me play even though I was still in middle school."

"I played against you one time," she says. "When I was a senior at Brooke Point. You guys killed us. Y'all had this tall, skinny girl playing center. I remember you had about fifty assists, feeding it to her under the basket. She camped out all night."

"That was Julie Juggins," I say. "She was eighth grade, too. We had a good team that year. The rest were juniors and seniors. Two of them are playing college ball now."

C. Miller pauses to say something in her walkie-talkie. A door buzzes and clicks and swings open, and we keep walking down the corridor that connects the administrative offices with the incarceration units, neither of us in a particular hurry.

"Coach had me playing point guard," she says, picking up where she left off. "But really I should have been shooting guard. I never got enough shots. We could have been a lot better if we'd had a natural point guard and Coach had let me shoot more. Bet I could have got on somebody's radar, got a scholarship."

"That sucks," I say.

We reach another door and stop. C. Miller lifts her walkie-talkie again but doesn't press the talk button right away. She looks at me in my orange jumpsuit and handcuffs, with my swollen nose and black eyes and rat's nest hair. Then she sighs and says, "Sometimes I wish I was still in high school."

I try to smile along with her, but my head is somewhere else, stuck a minute earlier in the conversation, wondering if I might still be able to play college ball or if any chance of that happening vanished when I got sent to juvie.

"Yeah," I say at last. "Me too."

By the time we get to Unit Three, the painkiller is kicking in and I can barely walk. Officer Miller leads me to my cell. She tries joking with me on the way. "Thanks for getting me the overtime," she says. "I need the money."

I don't say anything in response, and she pats me sympathetically on the back. I collapse on my bunk without eating anything, without brushing my teeth or my hair, without speaking to anybody, not that there's anybody to speak to, anyway.

One of the night-shift officers comes around what must be hours later to check on me and give me another painkiller. I sit up long enough to swallow it, then collapse back onto my bunk. The last thing I hear, just before I slip under, is Cell Seven, wailing again, crying and crying, begging someone to please, please, come get her.

The drugs quit working sometime during the night – it's impossible to say when. My eyelids flutter open, and the first thing I see, the only thing for a while, is the fluorescent bulb stuttering overhead, bathing my cell in the same eerie green as the night before. My face hurts too much for me to keep lying down, so I force myself into a seated position, cross-legged on my bunk. I pull the scratchy gray blanket around my shoulders and lean the back of my head against the cool concrete wall. I touch my swollen nose and my puffy face but can't tell if anything has changed. I don't have a mirror, but I'm not sure I want one, anyway. My vision turns blurry – maybe from the throbbing pain, maybe because I'm tearing up – and the walls seem to expand and contract, as if the cell itself is breathing. I wonder if I might also be suffering from a concussion.

The fuzziness clears after a while.

In school, in Mr. Turner's biology class, w
this famous terrible experiment from the 1950s
a scientist named Harry Harlow put infant monk
cages by themselves except for two fake mothers. They
called them surrogates. One surrogate was made out of
wire in the shape of an adult monkey. That one had a milk
bottle attached. The other surrogate mom was made out
of cloth but didn't have a bottle. The baby monkeys went
to the wire moms and drank the milk, but then went to
the cloth moms and clung to them, desperate for any
sort of warmth and physical contact. It wasn't enough,
though. They all grew up weird and withdrawn. Some of
them died of loneliness. Even when the monkeys were put
in cages where they could see, smell, and hear – but not
touch – other monkeys, they started acting autistic, with-
drawing from everything, holding on to themselves, and
rocking and rocking and rocking.

Mr. Turner, who was an expert in making everybody
feel like shit, also told us about these babies in Romania,
the ones raised in orphanages where nobody was allowed
to hold them or play with them from the time they were
infants. This went on for years, during the Cold War back
in the fifties and sixties and seventies and eighties. Mr.
Turner said the babies grew up just like Harlow's monkeys. They didn't know how to express affection. They
weren't able to have what Mr. Turner called "permanent
attachments." He said a lot of them were homeless when
they grew up.

So is that how it's going to be with me? With all of us in juvie? I can't see that they're trying to rehabilitate anybody in here with these cold cells, and all the single-file marching we do, with our eyes on the floor, heads down, hands behind our backs. And having to ask permission to so much as go to the bathroom. And no touching unless you're getting your ass kicked and your nose broken.

Or maybe this is all specific to me. Maybe it isn't anything deliberate even. Maybe it's genetic, and I'm turning into a recluse like my dad. I've spent countless nights camping by myself on Government Island, happy to be there alone. Maybe I've always had this tendency, just like Dad, but I've been able to ignore it until I got to juvie and they put me in this cell.

I wrap my arms around myself and hang on tighter, frightened about what might happen to me if I let go.

The unit is deathly quiet. The only sounds I hear are any I make myself, and I'm not moving. Cell Seven must have fallen asleep hours earlier, while I was passed out. Maybe the guards are asleep as well. Maybe I'm the only person awake in the entire juvie, or maybe every girl in every cell is sitting up on her bunk, rocking back and forth, the same as me.

CHAPTER 8

In which everybody begs for what they
think they need

Carla asked around, but nobody knew where to find
Scuzzy and Dreadlocks.

"Their real names might be Walter and Lee," she told
me on Wednesday. "But somebody else said that wasn't
them. They said their names were, like, Reilly and something. And they haven't been here that long. They came
from Charlotte. Or maybe Charleston. And nobody's seen
them since the party."

I didn't know how much of Carla's story to believe.
Were these guys really so impossible to track down, or did
she half-ass her search the way she half-assed most things

in her life? It occurred to me that she might not actually want to be able to find them. If the police interrogated them, and they said Carla knew about the drugs, she'd be going to prison for sure.

She'd gotten off work early for another meeting with her lawyer. It was after school, and I was getting ready for basketball practice. Mom had let up on my restrictions for that and said I could ride my motorcycle to the gym, since she was working at Target that afternoon.

"Don't you need to get Lulu from day care?" I asked Carla to keep myself from saying something else – like accusing her of lying.

"In a minute. Look, Sadie, I know you're going to hate me for telling you this. But just listen first, OK? I'm trying to get us out of this. I told my lawyer, I asked him for more details – what happens if you tell them you sort of knew about it but I didn't. That I was just in the car but didn't know there were drugs or a drug deal or anything. And he said he would talk to the prosecutor's office about that, but that probably they would just drop the charge against me. And he said the same thing again, that since you're a juvie and all, and don't have a prior record or anything, nothing will happen to you. Or nothing very much. But you would have to sign something, a statement or something. He doesn't think they'll believe that neither of us knew anything about the drugs, which is stupid, since it's the truth. But then when you go to juvie court, they would give your statement to the juvie judge. And that's that."

I pulled a white T-shirt over my sports bra, and my practice jersey over that.

Carla was wringing her hands the whole time. "Well?" she asked, leaning closer on the bed. "What do you think?"

I fished through my drawer to find some socks without holes in them. I'd barely slept the past couple of nights, trying to figure out the right thing to do. Make Carla tell the truth whatever it might turn out to be? Let her go to jail no matter what? The problem with that was they could still find me guilty, too. I was the one who took the money, after all. If Carla swore that I didn't know what was happening, though, I would definitely get off. Or mostly get off, anyway. But that meant Lulu wouldn't have Carla for the next three or four years. It meant either Mom raised Lulu – Mom and me – or Social Services took her. It meant everybody suffered, mostly Lulu, and I couldn't bear the thought of that. I'd rather spend the next ten years in jail myself than let that happen.

I sat on the bed and pulled Carla down next to me, squeezing her hands so hard it made her wince. She tried to pull them away, but I wouldn't let her.

I looked hard into her eyes until she dropped her head. I took a deep breath and said, "OK."

She looked back up at me. "What?"

"I said OK. I'll do it." It sounded like someone else speaking, a bad actor reading from a script.

"Oh, my God, Sadie. Thank you —"

I cut her off.

"But first we make sure that having this on my record won't stop me from going to college or getting a scholarship," I said. "And in return you'll do whatever I say, right?"

She nodded.

"You'll go to AA, or NA, or whatever, to stop drinking and smoking pot and everything. You're done with all that shit."

She opened her mouth to say something, but then just nodded again.

"And you'll spend more time with Lulu. Not just turn on the TV when you're home with her and let her watch stuff she shouldn't be watching."

Her face reddened, and I could tell it was killing her not to argue with me, even though she knew it was all true.

"And quit the Friendly's job," I continued. "Get a new job where your coworkers don't all look like heroin addicts."

I knew I was pushing it, but after what she'd gotten us into, and what she was asking me to do, I didn't care.

"And take some classes at the community college. I don't even care what. Just start back to school and do something with that GED. You can't work these lousy jobs forever and raise Lulu right. You want her to be proud of you."

I couldn't believe how much I sounded like Mom. I also couldn't believe I was agreeing to what Carla had asked. How many chances had we given Carla over the years to get her life together? And did I really think this time would be any different?

She whispered a final yes and wiped away some tears, and I knew all I could do was hope maybe this time really would be different. It was the closest Carla had ever come to actual jail time, to losing Lulu. If that wasn't enough to scare her straight, nothing was.

Julie Juggins, who I'd been friends with for as long as I'd played basketball, cornered me after practice. "What the hell's going on with you?" she asked.

"Nothing," I said as I unlaced my shoes. We were the last ones in the locker room. I'd spent an extra half hour by myself practicing free throws and three-pointers. She must have taken a long shower to still be there, her hair still wet.

"Something's going on," she said. "You were way too intense out there today – like maybe you thought it was the play-offs and not just running drills."

My laces got knotted, and I had to work to get them loose. I reminded myself that Julie was about the only person I knew who I was pretty sure wouldn't get on her phone as soon as she left and text the whole rest of the world about what had happened. Plus her dad used to drink.

So I told her – about the party, the arrest, even the plan for me to take the blame.

She didn't hesitate before telling me straight up that

it was a bad idea. "You can't save her," Julie said. "Nobody can. You can't make that deal with Carla. It's just going to mess up your life, too."

"But she's my sister," I said. My voice seemed to echo in the empty locker room. "She'll go to jail."

Julie shook her head. "*You* might go to jail," she said. "Where you should go is to Al-Anon. That's where my mom took me and my brother, to help us when dad got so bad. You remember when we had to live in that trailer? At Al-Anon, they tell you you have to look after yourself, and your dad or whoever has to hit bottom and then put his life back together himself, but you can't do it for him. You can't do it for Carla. Only Carla can."

Julie sounded like she was making an Al-Anon commercial, which got on my nerves. I understood what she was saying, but it wasn't like Carla was a drug addict or an alcoholic. She wasn't a falling-down drunk like Julie's dad had been. She just partied too much and got into trouble – and now she'd gotten me into trouble, too. It wasn't at all the same as Julie's dad.

"I got her to promise to go to AA and stuff," I said. "She's serious about making herself better."

Julie shook her head again, only harder this time. "She's just saying what she thinks you want to hear."

Then she looked at me funny. "Have you told anybody else? Have you told Kevin?"

I said no. "He would flip if he knew."

"But he's your boyfriend," Julie said. "Don't you sort

of have to tell him? Isn't that in the boyfriend-girlfriend contract?"

"I don't remember signing anything," I said.

Julie shrugged her gym bag over her shoulder. "Well, good luck with that."

Kevin was waiting outside in his car, next to my motorcycle. I climbed in the front seat next to him. He handed me a box. It wasn't wrapped. "For our anniversary," he said.

"It's our anniversary?"

"Yeah," he said, grinning. "What? You forgot? We started going out five months and five days ago. So it's like our five-month–five-day anniversary."

I tapped him on the forehead with the box before I kissed him. "God, Kevin," I said, smiling. "You're such a girl sometimes."

"Yeah, I know," he said. "So open it already."

It was a scarf. The whole time we'd known each other, I'd never worn a scarf. I hated anything like that around my neck, plus I was pretty sure I'd seen his mom wearing one just like it.

I thanked him, though, and let him drape it over my neck and pull me to him again. We made out for a while until I was ready to crawl over into the backseat with him right then and there. I was actually panting. And then he stopped. It was the reverse of the other night by my house.

"I have to go," he said. "Sorry."

"No, no," I said, or panted. "You can't. Not yet. Just

a little longer." I started to pull my T-shirt off, but he stopped me.

"You know how my dad is," he said. "I told him I was going to the library after soccer practice, but it's closed soon. He'll make me sit out my next game. Sorry, Sadie."

Now I was pissed. When Kevin wanted to fool around, I was right there for him. But when I was the one feeling desperate, suddenly it was all about him and his damn curfews.

I almost blurted out what I'd been keeping from him for the past four days: *Can't you see what's going on here? For God's sake, Kevin, we have to jump on the opportunity while we can, because who knows what's going to happen when you find out, or how your uptight parents are going to react? Carpe diem, you jerk.*

Mom came into my bedroom late that night, after she got home from a double shift at Target. I was dead asleep, but she turned on the light anyway and woke me up.

"You don't have to do this," she said, as if we'd already been in the middle of a conversation. Carla must have called her and filled her in on my grand sacrifice. She rubbed her temples and combed her fingers through her hair.

"I'm not even sure I'll allow it," she continued when I didn't say anything or do anything except blink. She pressed her cool hand against my cheek, just kind of cupping my face and looking into my eyes. It was the tenderest thing she'd done in a long time, since long before the arrest even.

Then she pulled her hand away abruptly, as if she'd just remembered she was supposed to still be mad.

"I got a message from Vance at work," she said. "They pushed back your hearing by a week. They had a heavy docket or something."

I pulled myself up in bed, and drew my knees up under my chin, relieved, but not very. "What about Carla's thing?"

"Her preliminary hearing?"

"Yeah." Carla hadn't said as much, but I kind of had the feeling that if I was going to confess, I had to do it before her preliminary hearing. "What is that, anyway?"

Mom smoothed out my bedspread. "It's just where the prosecutor tells the judge he thinks they have enough evidence to go forward with the case. He says what the evidence is. The judge decides. Usually he goes along with the prosecutor. Carla's lawyer won't make his case until the real trial, which is set for later on. If there is one."

I was impressed that Mom knew so much about the court system. I wondered how much of that came from Carla's previous arrests and how much came from quality time with Vance, or with Dave the magistrate, who said he'd be calling her about dinner.

Mom was quiet, still smoothing out imaginary wrinkles in my bedspread.

"Is there something you're not telling me, Mom?" I asked.

She looked up at me and then quickly looked away.

"If they don't drop the charges against her at the pre-liminary hearing, the judge will most likely revoke her probation pending trial."

"Wait." I sat up straight. "She would go to jail already?"

Mom nodded.

"When?" I asked.

Mom kept nodding. "It's next week, too. The prelim-inary hearing. Unless the prosecutor decides to drop the charges before then. They would have to work that out – Carla's court-appointed lawyer and the prosecutor."

"You mean they'd have to have me sign a statement about the drugs and that Carla didn't know anything. She was like an innocent bystander or whatever?"

Mom nodded again, then looked hard into my eyes.

"Was she?" Mom asked.

I hesitated. "She was really drunk, Mom. And high, too, I think. I don't know what the guys told her, but what-ever it was, she was way too out of it to know what was going on."

Mom didn't take her eyes off mine. "Did *you* know?"

"About the drug deal?"

"Yes. Did you?"

I shook my head so hard it practically made my brain rattle, though I wondered if it would ever be hard enough to make her believe me.

CHAPTER 9

In which the Jelly Sisters have
a few things to say and I consider
the difference between a labyrinth
and a maze

I'm the first one out when they unlock the cell doors at 0600 the morning after the Jelly Sisters break my nose. I've long since forced myself out of bed and made my bunk, washed my face – slowly and carefully – and raked my matted hair back as best I could. God, what I wouldn't give for a little concealer to at least try to hide all the bruising and swelling.

The Jelly Sisters are the next girls out of their cells, and I flinch when I see them. I flinch again when they grab chairs next to me at the tables, just as they did my first night on Unit Three, but I try to play it off as though I'm just cold.

Wanda, predictably, speaks first. "You look like shit."

Nell grunts. "Like *ass*."

"Yeah," I say, determined not to let them intimidate me. "I know. Can't do a thing with my hair in this humidity." I look left at Wanda, then right at Nell. "Y'all sure look pretty, though. Nice outfits. Whose idea was it to go with the matching jumpers?"

I lean back in my chair so I can see both of them at the same time. Wanda glowers as if she might hit me. Nell glances furtively at Wanda, calibrating how she's supposed to react to my sarcasm.

Wanda clears her throat. "You know it's possible for you to keep on having accidents in here," she says. Nell nods.

I shrug. "Look," I say, mostly confident that if they're going to hurt me, they won't be stupid enough to do it here and be so obvious about it. "I don't know what set us off on the wrong foot, but I'm not looking for any trouble. I just want to do whatever I'm supposed to do and then get out of here as soon as I can, and that's all."

"Then how come you taking up with that Gina bitch soon as you move onto the unit?" Wanda asks. "How come you saving her ass from the spork?"

The other girls have come out of their cells by now, including Bad Gina, and all of them give us as wide a berth as possible. Bad Gina does her best to not seem to be staring at my face, or watching what's going on between me and the Jelly Sisters.

Two new guards roll in the breakfast cart and toss Styrofoam containers in the middle of the tables. Still no sporks. Wanda and Nell peel open their jelly containers first thing and toss them back just like Chantrelle said – like Jell-O shots.

I open my breakfast box and force myself to eat. Not that I'm very hungry; I'm just damned if I'm going to let the Jelly Sisters touch another bite of my food.

"Well?" Wanda says, waggling a glob of scrambled eggs in her fingers. "I asked you a question."

"Two questions," Nell chimes in through a mouthful of toast and eggs.

I take a long drink from my orange juice cup. A bite of potato patty. "Look, I didn't do it to protect Gina. I haven't taken up with her or whatever. We would all have gotten in trouble if they didn't find the spork. You heard what Officer Killduff said." I force down some slimy eggs. "I don't know about you girls, but the one cavity search at Intake was enough for me."

"That was just bluffing, to scare us in case Gina was innocent," Wanda said.

"She *was* innocent," I say. "I don't know why you took her spork, but —"

"I didn't take nothing," Wanda snarls. "You ever say otherwise and you'll wish the only thing wrong with you was your swole-up nose."

I shrug again. "Like I said, I don't want any trouble. But I'm also not about to go through another cavity search just because you have a problem against some girl."

"That bitch deserve to be in trouble," Wanda says. "And this here is the only warning you're gonna get: anything else happens and you try to protect her ass, then your ass is the one getting it instead."

I can practically feel Bad Gina straining to hear the conversation from the other side of the tables. Nobody else seems to be talking. The night-shift guards are busy at their desk, writing down stuff and drinking coffee.

"Fine," I say. "Whatever." I finish my potato patty. "What do you have against Gina, anyway?"

Wanda waves her toast at Nell. "You can tell her."

"OK," Nell says. "She was the one that gave Cell Seven what she cut herself with, some kind of a sharp metal that that Gina trash got hold of from somewhere. She was always whispering stuff to Cell Seven, probably talking her into it or something, getting her worked up. Cell Seven already got mental problems, depression and stuff, from when she first come on the unit."

"How do you know all this?" I ask.

Wanda takes over. "How we know? How we *know*?" She knocks her toast against the edge of my Styrofoam box. "Because we *know*, that's how we know."

"Of course," I say. "So why did she do it – give Cell Seven the metal or whatever?"

"Because she's a evil bitch," Nell says.

"That's it?" I ask.

"Isn't that enough?" Wanda says.

"An evil bitch," I repeat.

"Evil *and* a bitch," Nell chimes in, as if she needs to correct my phrasing. "Plus she been doing Killduff, or didn't you notice?"

"Oh, really," I say, wondering just how anyone would go about that in here, when we're watched like lab rats.

"Yeah, really," says Nell.

I'm all but certain that they are making this all up, but I know better than to say it. "What's Gina doing Officer Killduff have to do with Cell Seven?"

"Got nothing to do with it," says Wanda. "Just the kind of a bitch she is, the kind that will do anything. Even do Killduff."

I know I should just let the whole thing go, but I kind of want to see how this will play out. "How does she get away with it? Or how does *he*?"

"The other guards are scared of Killduff," Nell says. "And the guy they got doing shifts in the control room, monitoring all them cameras, is a buddy of Killduff's. That's what I heard."

I shake my head. "But Gina *did* get in trouble for the spork," I say. "Killduff was the one that ordered Officer Emroch to do a full-body search on her. And they put us all on lockdown."

"Yeah, but think about it, dummy," Wanda says. "Even Killduff had to do something for Gina losing her spork – or trying to hide it – and getting caught right in front of everybody. But I guess you didn't notice she didn't lose phone privileges or visitation, and she didn't get no extra lockdown. And wouldn't surprise me if Killduff gave her a little visit while everybody on lockdown and Emroch in the bathroom or whatever and his buddy on control-room duty."

One of the night-shift guards yells, "Time!" and then, "Spork count!"

We all just sit there, confused. We don't have any sporks.

The guard laughs once she realizes. "Oh, yeah," she says. "Never mind."

She tosses a garbage bag on the tables. It lands right in front of me and the Jelly Sisters. Neither of them moves, so I end up having the honors.

The guards herd us down to the phones that night after dinner – very dry chicken breast, congealed gravy, flaky mashed potatoes that clearly came from a box, green beans so mushy they probably came from baby-food jars, stale roll, juice box, and Jell-O cup. Still no spork.

There are three phones mounted to a green wall across a small room from the control center, which is a reinforced glass booth where a guard monitors the surveillance cameras and I guess controls all the electronic door locks.

It's my first night with phone privileges, and I can't wait to call Mom, even though she's probably out at bingo and I hate interrupting her there. It's about the only fun thing she does for herself, plus she usually makes at least a little money playing.

"Sadie!" she practically shouts my name when she answers, and I can hear bingo people laughing in the background. "Is everything OK?" she asks in a quieter voice. "Hold on." She muffles the phone for a minute. "There. That's better. I've got somebody working my cards. Let me duck out to the lobby."

Friday night bingo is in a fire station meeting hall a mile from our house. Every now and then things get a little crazy when there's a fire and the sirens wail and the trucks race off. The bingo people don't get distracted, though – including Mom. They have great concentration. I'm actually a little surprised that she took my call so quickly.

"So how is everything?" she asks. "I thought you'd call earlier in the week." She doesn't sound angry, just worried.

"I lost my phone privileges because I forgot to make up my bed," I explain. "They're really strict in here. But it's OK."

Mom says to just remember to do whatever I'm supposed to do, and I assure her I will from now on. I should probably go ahead and explain about getting my nose broken, but she'll just worry and I'd rather tell her in person on Sunday during visiting hours. So I make up a bunch of stuff instead. I tell her how great everything is going, how nice everybody is, how I'm keeping up with schoolwork and getting plenty of sleep and exercise, how it's practically like being away at summer camp, or what I imagine summer camp to be if you're the kind of family who can afford it.

"How are things at home?" I ask. What I really want to know is if Carla is going to AA and if she's quit her job at Friendly's. But I'm afraid of the answers.

"Oh, fine," Mom says. She tells me that Lulu has been sleeping with a picture of me under her pillow, plus a pair of my high-top basketball shoes.

"Carla wasn't going to let her, but Lulu got hysterical and your sister caved in the way she always does," Mom says. "I told Carla to at least put them in a plastic grocery bag since they're so dirty and smelly. Lulu doesn't seem to mind, though. I'm going to wash them next time she's over here."

"Why don't you give her one of my jerseys?" I ask. "I bet she'd like something like that, and it would be more comfortable. And wouldn't smell as bad."

We talk like that for a while, about nothing, since I can't tell her what's really going on with me and since she probably can't tell me what's really going on with her or Carla or Lulu.

Good Gina takes my phone when I hang up. Chantrelle and Nell are still chatting away on the other two phones, and the other girls, including Cell Seven in her suicide pad, are waiting their turns. The only empty seat is at a table with Bad Gina and Weeze, about the last place I want to sit, but I don't have a choice. I take my time walking over, hoping another seat opens up at another table.

"First call home?" Bad Gina asks.

I nod, surprised she noticed.

"Sucks," she says. "First time I got to call home, I bawled worse than Cell Seven. Girls were threatening to beat *me* up if I didn't stop. I got so homesick, I threw up in my cell. Guards made me clean it up myself."

"Lovely," I say.

She grins her sunny grin. "I know, right?"

Somebody slams a handset down on its phone hook, and we all turn to look. Good Gina is banging her forehead against the wall next to one of the phones, crying.

"You know why she's crying, don't you?" Bad Gina asks.

I shake my head.

"It's pretty sad," she says with an odd laugh that isn't quite a laugh. "She keeps calling her boyfriend, but he won't accept the charges. I guess she doesn't have any money in her phone account, so she has to call collect. I've heard her before, begging him to take the call, but he never does. He's got another girlfriend. I can't really blame him."

Weeze gets up from the table then and walks over to Good Gina's phone. Good Gina doesn't leave, though. She picks up the receiver before Weeze gets there and dials again and speaks to somebody. She hangs up again after about a minute. She keeps trying. Weeze keeps waiting.

Bad Gina keeps talking to me. "This one time, I was at

the phone next to hers and I heard her calling and nobody accepting the call, and so she pretended she was talking to her boyfriend anyway, about how she couldn't wait to see him again, and how everything was going to be better this time, and how she loved him so, so much. But she was holding the hook down the whole time. She wasn't even trying to pretend she wasn't. It was pretty pathetic. I felt sorry for her."

Good Gina finally gives up the phone to Weeze. Chantrelle is still talking on another phone, so Good Gina slumps into Weeze's seat at the table with Bad Gina and me.

"You OK?" I ask.

She looks at me blankly for a second, nods, then lays her head on the table.

Bad Gina scoots her chair close to mine, far enough from Good Gina to talk privately.

"So how come you've been avoiding me all day, anyway?" she asks. "I kind of thought we were friends."

I shrug. "I haven't. I've just been busy. All these appointments. So much to do."

"Bullshit," Bad Gina says, though she doesn't sound angry. "You got cornered by the Jelly Sisters at breakfast, even though they broke your nose yesterday, but you talked to them anyway."

I lay my hands on the table in front of me and study them for a minute.

"Look, Gina," I say, finally. "You seem like a nice girl

and all, but I'm not interested in getting in the middle of anything going on between you and Wanda and Nell. It's none of my business. They see me talking to you, they think I'm on your side or whatever. You see me talking to them, you're all over me about it."

Bad Gina narrows her eyes and frowns. "If that's how you feel, then I guess that's how you feel," she says. "But you need friends in here. Those girls are capable of some very bad shit."

"Yeah. And they say the same thing about you. They said you helped Cell Seven hurt herself. They said you were hooking up with Officer Killduff."

She draws back. "They *said* that? They actually *said* that?"

"I don't believe them," I say quickly. "I don't have any reason to. But I also don't have any reason to believe you – no offense."

"None taken," she says, heavy on the sarcasm.

"I just don't want to get involved," I say again. "Hell, they're staring at us right now because we're talking." And they are – Nell from her phone, Wanda from two tables over. For all I know, they're planning how they're going to kick our asses, or break Bad Gina's nose, too.

One of the officers comes over and stands behind us. "You making a call tonight or what?" she asks Bad Gina.

Her face changes in a flash, from angry and defensive to bright and smiling. "Yes, thanks, Officer." She doesn't look at me again as she leaves to make her call and passes Weeze, who is on her way back to our table. They fist-bump.

Weeze is smiling, too, but hers seems sincere – her fleshy face all pink, close to radiant even.

"Good phone call?" I ask.

She nods. Weeze isn't much taller than me, just a few inches, but she probably outweighs me by thirty pounds, making her look larger than she really is. "I got to talk to my dad and my little sister," she gushes. "They're both coming to see me tomorrow."

"That's great," I say. "What about your mom?"

Her face darkens. "She's kind of still having problems with me being arrested and in juvie and everything."

"Sorry," I say.

"Yeah," she says, then she brightens again. "But Dad said she's writing me a letter. She just hasn't finished it yet. But he said she's going to send me a really long letter. So maybe he'll bring that with him."

She seems like a sweet girl, but it's hard to tell what kind of person anybody really is here. I figure Bad Gina has chosen to hang out with Weeze because of her size – as protection from the Jelly Sisters. I'm not as sure about why Weeze is hanging out with Bad Gina. It could be that Weeze has a crush on her. It could be that she's just lonely, and when you're lonely, you grab on to whoever will have you.

* * *

That night in my cell feels like the hundredth and not just my fifth. The minute I'm locked in, I start pacing. I count laps for a while – if you can even call them that – but the numbers pile up too fast and it makes me depressed. I try slowing down so each turn lasts longer than the one before, and that works better. After a few hundred, it feels as if I'm moving in slow motion, or walking underwater, and it reminds me of this time Dad took me to a hippie solstice party at a farm way out somewhere on the Northern Neck. They had a roaring campfire and a torchlit Frisbee golf course and a drum circle that went on all night. They'd also set up a labyrinth, with carefully arranged stones marking a twisting, winding path that kept folding back in on itself, with circles inside circles and more circles inside those circles, all somehow connected and yet never crossing over itself, either, and eventually leading to a tiny open space in the middle about the size of a dog curled up and sleeping.

I asked Dad what the maze was for, but he said it wasn't a maze; it was a labyrinth. A maze was something you got lost in and had to find your way out of. But a labyrinth was different. He said you were never lost in a labyrinth. He said a labyrinth was where you went to find yourself.

I didn't exactly know what he was talking about – though later, when he got so lost inside his own head and retreated to his wing of Granny's house and started collecting everything and piling it all up just so, I remembered what he said about the labyrinth and sort of understood.

I try for a while to make my laps around the cell feel like some kind of labyrinth, to let my mind wander, but either I'm so lost that there's no finding myself or an eight-by-eight cell in juvie is too poor an excuse for a labyrinth. All that happens is that I feel dizzy, and very, very sad.

I climb onto my bunk, wrap a blanket around my shoulders, and lean against the wall, feeling homesick all of a sudden, as if somebody has flicked on a switch – desperately missing everybody: Dad, Mom, Carla, Lulu, Julie Juggins, even Kevin.

I lie under my blanket and try to think about something else, anything that can lift my spirits. I think about Government Island and the times I spent camping out there by myself, how it felt like I was the only person left in the whole world and how peaceful that made me feel. I think about the couple of times I brought Kevin out there and how nice it was to *not* be the only person in the world then. I think about the other things I always go back to when I need cheering up: my team and winning regionals last year and getting runner-up for MVP. I think about my motorcycle and flying down two-lane roads in the middle of nowhere, where you can go as fast as you want and never see any cops. I think about Lulu handing me that rock and how sweet that was, and how sweet she is.

And I think about Kevin some more. Being in juvie, even just these five days, has taken the jagged edge off how angry I am at him, how let down and betrayed. Though

I still don't think I can ever really forgive him, even if I have the chance. But I don't want to think about that anymore tonight. Tonight I just want to remember the good stuff, like watching him on the soccer field with his long dirty-blond hair and his face streaked with sweat and that certain grin he gets that means he is so far into the game that nothing outside it exists, except, sometimes, me when he scores a goal and spreads his arms and tears around the field in celebration and does a knee slide near the sideline and looks up for me cheering in the stands. And how he is a kind and decent person who volunteers at the food bank and wants to join the Peace Corps after college and live in Africa. And how he bought me this really expensive motorcycle helmet because he was so worried about anything happening to me on my bike. And how he came over to Mom's house a couple of times when I was stuck at home babysitting Lulu, even though he could have gone out with his friends. And what a good kisser he is and how he'd pull me into this little space next to our lockers at school and we'd make out like crazy between classes. And all the sweet and dirty stuff we used to do together that always left me so weak in the knees, literally weak in the knees, which I'd never believed was an actual thing.

I wrap myself tighter inside my blanket, glance at the little window in my cell door to make sure nobody is checking in on me, and then clench my eyes shut and scoot down in my bed and pretend I'm with Kevin, and we're a couple again, and we're wrapped around each other on a cold autumn night inside my sleeping bag on Government Island, nothing separating us but skin and barely that.

I shudder – hot and flushed.

And then I stop. Maybe I hear something. Or maybe I'm just worried that one of the guards will look in. There's nobody at the door, but there's also no way of knowing when there might be.

Once my mind gets racing, it won't quit. I start thinking about Harry Harlow's monkeys again, and this thing I read on the Internet after Mr. Turner's depressing lecture. It was about how some of the monkeys just sat and masturbated for hours because it was the only stimulation they had, and about how they got addicted to it and kept at it even when it was clear it wasn't giving them any pleasure, but they just couldn't seem to control themselves, so they kept going at it until their hands and arms would sometimes even cramp up and they'd be practically paralyzed, those poor, sad, hapless monkeys.

I pull my hands out from under the blanket and swear it's the last time I'm ever doing anything like that again in juvie.

CHAPTER 10

In which I meet with the detectives,
take Lulu to the Bug Box, and deliver
my last box of groceries

They wouldn't let Mom sit in the interrogation room with us, but I figured she was watching through the two-way mirror, and maybe listening in, too. It was just like on TV: a long metal table, hard chairs, two police detectives, and me and my court-appointed lawyer, a kind of washed-out guy named Mr. Ferrell. One of the detectives even asked if I wanted a soda. The older one, Detective Feagles, was white; he had silver hair and a rumpled suit. The younger one, Detective Boldin, was black; he had an earring and a police-department windbreaker.

Mr. Ferrell mostly just sat there and took notes.

I wished it was Mom's friend Vance, not because he seemed especially amazing as a lawyer or anything, but because I figured he probably cared what happened to me, at least a little. But we couldn't afford him after that one free consultation, and he didn't offer to take on my case pro bono.

Detective Feagles turned on a tape recorder and fiddled with some dials. Detective Boldin asked most of the questions.

"Full name?"

"Sadie Ruth Windas."

"Address?"

"Fourteen-oh-eight Clearview Drive, Stafford, Virginia."

"Age?"

"Seventeen."

"Birth date?"

"June the nineteenth."

"Social Security number?"

I had a brain freeze. He finally gave up and said we could ask my mom later.

My heart raced wildly the whole time, and I was sweating like crazy. Mom had made me get dressed up like I was going to a funeral, with tights and uncomfortable shoes and everything.

"Now, Sadie," said Detective Boldin, "I want you to take us through the events of that night. And I want you to include the names of everybody you can think of who you met at the party."

"I didn't catch any names," I said. "It was pretty loud, and it's not like people were introducing themselves or wearing name tags or anything." I wasn't trying to be a smart-ass, but it was like these guys had never been to a party before.

"You sure?"

I racked my brain, then suddenly remembered. "There was this one girl. Kendall. I didn't get her last name, though. But she had a bright-red scar on her cheek, and she went to Stafford High with my sister, Carla."

Detective Boldin scribbled on his notepad. Good. Maybe she'd get in some kind of trouble for being at the party. "And did she have anything to do with the drugs?"

"No, sir," I admitted. "She was just somebody I met at the party. But we didn't talk for very long."

"Anybody else?"

"No, sir."

"What about the two men you say had the drugs?"

I opened my hands on the table. "I didn't catch their names, like I said. They might have mentioned them, but it was so loud I didn't hear. I just made up names for them."

"What were they?"

"Dreadlocks and Scuzzy. Because one had dreadlocks, and the other guy just seemed really scuzzy."

Detective Boldin wrote that down as well. My lawyer did, too.

"Color?"

"They were white guys."

"Ages?"

"Twenty-something. I'd say mid to late."

"Identifying characteristics?"

"Well, the one guy had dreadlocks. He was pretty tall, maybe six two. The other guy was just real scuzzy-looking. Scraggly beard, greasy hair, that sort of thing. He had dark hair, but Dreadlocks was blond," I added.

"Had you ever seen them before anywhere?"

"No, sir."

"Seen them since?"

"No, sir."

"Would you recognize them again?"

"Maybe. I mean, I guess so. It was pretty dark at the party, and in the car, but I think so."

"And your sister?"

"I don't think she'd recognize them. She was really drunk that night." As soon as I said that, I wished I hadn't, since Carla was twenty, so not legal age. But they let it go.

"Where was she during the party?"

"Not sure. Just hanging out with people, I guess. I was outside playing beer pong."

Detective Boldin looked at me. "Beer pong?"

"Yes, sir, but I didn't drink."

"Right," he said.

"Maybe a couple of sips," I quickly added, since it was clear he didn't believe me.

"Right," he said again. "And you said that was where you met this Dreadlocks?"

"Yes, sir. I just sort of ended up with him as my doubles partner. And then later on, he asked me to take him and his friend to the store. He said they wanted to buy some beer. . . ."

"Is that all?" the detective asked.

I looked at my lawyer. He nodded, which I took to mean he wanted me to just go on and get the rest out.

I stared at my hands, unable to look at the detectives as I continued. "No, sir. He also said they had a package they had to deliver to somebody. They said they would pay me if I took them." I watched the detectives scribble down my lie, making it a permanent part of my story.

"What happened next?" Detective Boldin asked.

"I went and got Carla. She was pretty out of it and practically passed out in the car. The guys got out at the 7-Eleven and left the package in the backseat. And that's when the police came and arrested us."

"And you're saying Carla didn't know anything about what was going on?" Detective Boldin asked.

"No, sir. And I didn't know much, either. They just asked me for the ride, like I said."

"And you didn't ask what was in the package or who was picking it up?"

I couldn't look at him. "No, sir. I guess I wasn't thinking."

"Were you drunk? Had you been drinking? Or doing any drugs yourself?"

"No, sir. Just the couple of sips when we were playing beer pong. We're in season."

"In season?"

"For basketball. In AAU, we have summer and fall ball."

"And what did you know about the arrangement for the drug deal?"

"I didn't know anything about that. Like about how they set it up or anything. I didn't even know it was a drug deal until we got arrested."

"What did you think was in the package, then?"

I wished I'd thought through this line of questioning and had an answer ready, but I hadn't and I didn't.

"I don't know," I said.

Detective Boldin leaned in closer. "You have to tell us the truth, Sadie," he said. "Because it's hard to believe what you're telling us right now – that you just agreed to drive these guys to a drug deal out of the goodness of your heart and your desire to make a few easy bucks. And that you knew they were delivering a package, but it never occurred to you what was in that package. One of you girls – you or your sister – had to know what was going on. You say she was passed out and nobody told her anything. So that leaves just you."

I nodded slowly, dying inside as I realized what I was going to have to say to keep Carla out of jail.

"They might have mentioned it was drugs." My voice was a whisper.

"You're gonna have to repeat that," Detective Boldin said. "The tape recorder might not have gotten what you just said."

"Yes," I said. "They might have mentioned the drugs. To me. Not to Carla."

"Right," Detective Boldin said abruptly. "OK. Well, Detective Feagles has a few questions for you now, but before we get started with him, can I get you another soda?"

"Yes. Thank you, sir. Officer."

Detective Feagles asked me all the same questions, though he phrased them differently. Once he finished, Detective Boldin went over everything yet again, fishing for more details. I was there for three hours. I drank four Pepsis and had to go to the bathroom four times, though once was just to try to stop shaking so much.

Afterward we waited while they typed up a statement and gave it to me to sign. My hand trembled so badly it looked like I hadn't yet mastered the art of cursive writing.

But in the end it was good enough to save Carla. Or at least to keep her out of jail.

I decided to skip the rest of school and take Lulu to the Bug Box. Mom said it was OK and let me borrow her car, since Lulu wasn't allowed to ride on the back of my motorcycle. I was surprised Mom agreed to it, and surprised that she didn't say anything about the interrogation. Maybe she was like me, just hoping and praying that we could make this thing go away and get back to our lives the way they were.

Lulu loved the Bug Box, this strange little bug museum that a local exterminator guy opened up next to his exterminator business south of town. I guess they took kids there on field trips or something, and he got donations that way, for educational tours. Otherwise I wasn't sure how the Bug Box stayed open. It was really just a big room with dozens of terrariums filled with all sorts of spiders and bugs and pests. Wolf spiders, black widows, tarantulas. Lots of cockroaches, which swarmed all over one another and seemed to multiply while you were looking at them. You needed a magnifying glass to see the bedbugs and fleas and termites. They had a couple of ant farms mounted to one wall so you could check out the tunnels and nests and stuff. There was also a big fire-ant hill in this one big case, with the Latin name that I always remembered for some reason: *Solenopsis invicta.* I looked it up, and *invicta* means "the unvanquished."

The Bug Box might have been Lulu's favorite place in the world. Most kids are afraid of bugs, but not her. She especially loved the daddy longlegs and the praying mantises. The proprietor guy let her hold them, and Lulu laughed and laughed and laughed while the daddy longlegs crawled all over her.

Afterward, on the way to the grocery store to pick up some food to take to my dad's, Lulu and I sang this daddy longlegs song that Granny taught me when I was little.

There were a bunch of different verses about him being on your knee, and your shirt, and your chin, and finally your hair. By the time we got to the grocery store, Lulu was practically shouting the words, which was how she sang when she got excited, and I was practically shouting them with her.

I used my car-wash money to buy that week's groceries for Dad. Mom never asked me to; I just sort of started doing it every other week when I realized Mom was skipping lunches because we didn't have enough to go around.

I was pretty sure Dad was out in one of his sheds when we drove up to Granny's, because a door slammed back there, and then another that I recognized as the back door to Dad's wing of the house.

Lulu heard it, too. "Is that Granpa?" she asked.

"Yeah. Pretty sure it is."

She pulled a box of spaghetti out of one of the grocery bags. Lulu always liked to help, but she was too little to carry much. She grabbed a pomegranate, too. I didn't know why I bought that. Or the avocado. I wasn't even sure he ate stuff like that. I just hated the idea of him sitting in that drab house all day, eating nothing but drab food. He should have something beautiful and exotic around, like a pomegranate or an avocado, even if he never ate a bite.

"Can we see him?" Lulu asked.

"Probably not," I said. "You remember how we talked about Granpa, how he has a hard time being around other people?"

She nodded, but I could tell she didn't understand. She was three years old. Of course she didn't understand. I was seventeen, and I didn't, either.

We left the food on the porch the way we always did. Lulu ran off to pick dandelions, and I knocked on the door and waited. Not that I expected Dad to answer. It was just the routine. Then I told him – or told the door – about what had happened with Carla and me and the drug bust. I told him about meeting with the detectives that morning, and agreeing to take the blame, and Carla's promise to straighten out her life. I told Dad I loved him and I missed him and I wished I could see him. I pressed my palm to the door for a minute, pretending I could feel him doing the same from the other side, feel the heat of his hand through the wood. Then I left to collect Lulu and go pick up Mom from work and get ready for basketball practice.

But when I got to the bottom of the steps, I stopped for some reason and turned back around. Something was lying on the porch where I'd just been standing. Dad must have slid it out under the door. I went back to pick it up: a picture of him when he was a lot younger, standing in his swim trunks in shallow waves at the ocean, cradling a little baby with one arm, a shy look on his face but still managing to smile at the camera. A little girl was clinging to his leg and looking up at him, as if wishing he would pick her up, too. That was Carla. The baby was me.

CHAPTER 11

In which I get a visit from Mom,
talk to a dog murderer, and make
a stupid phone call

Mom looks tired when she comes that first Sunday afternoon during visiting hours, which is really just a visiting
half hour because that's all we're allowed. She's already
there waiting when the guard brings me in. I keep my head
down as I take my seat, hoping that my hair mostly covers
my face for now. We sit in facing cubicles separated by
a Plexiglas divider that runs from the floor to the ceiling
and have to talk on telephones though we're only inches
apart. I put my hand on one side of the Plexiglas, and she
puts hers on the other. I can't feel her, of course. It's just as
close as we can get to touching. She starts off smiling, but

a look of horror takes over when I raise my head and push back my hair.

She skips the preliminaries. "What happened?"

I touch my nose and imagine what she sees: the swelling, the bruises, the black eyes.

"Nothing," I say. "We were playing basketball and it got a little rough. I'm OK. It looks worse than it is."

"Tell me the truth."

"I am telling the truth," I say. "I tried to drive the lane when I should have passed off and got sandwiched between two girls. It happens. Really, Mom, there's nothing to worry about. Everything's fine. I'm fine. Like I told you."

"You didn't tell me about this. We just talked on the phone two nights ago."

I take the phone away from my ear and tap myself on the forehead with the receiver. "I'm sorry," I say when I bring it back down. "You were at bingo. I didn't want to bother you about it. So how are things, anyway?" I ask, trying to change the subject. "What about Carla and Lulu? Why didn't Carla come?"

Mom doesn't answer. "Turn your face to the side," she says, and I do. "Now the other way," she says, and I do that, too.

"Is it broken?" she asks.

"No," I lie. "Just sore."

"What about the black eyes?"

"The nurse said that's just the way the bruising spreads.

I didn't get attacked or anything. It was an accident. Honest."

"Well," she says, "I'm going to speak to whoever's in charge."

"No, Mom," I say. "Don't do that. I don't want to call any attention to myself in here. You're supposed to just keep your head down and do what you're told to do. Please. Don't make a big deal out of this."

Mom still fumes. I lie some more and tell her the nurse came down and checked up on me several times after it happened, and the guards did, too. That seems to placate her, and she finally gets around to filling me in on Carla and Lulu, though there isn't much to tell. Carla says she's gone to AA again. She says she put in a couple of job applications and got the community-college spring catalog. I want to believe in Carla, but figure there's only about a fifty-fifty chance that what she told Mom is true. But maybe part of it is.

The conversation shifts back over to me way too soon, but I have to leave so much out about what has been going on in juvie that I quickly run out of things to talk about. We're both ready to say good-bye when the time is up.

I don't start missing her until about two seconds after she leaves.

I avoid Bad Gina, and the Jelly Sisters, and pretty much everybody for the next couple of days. The trick is to sit close to the teachers during GED classes and pretend to be fascinated by such mind-numbing trivia as the fact that Virginia has a state drink (milk), a state shell (oyster), and the distinction of being one of a handful of states that isn't just a state (but also a commonwealth).

I can't hide during gym, though, and on Wednesday Officer Killduff orders everybody to run wind sprints – even me. I don't try to race, just keep up with the others until half of them drop out, exhausted, gasping like fish. Then I go down, too. I'm pissed off that I have to do it with my broken nose, which still aches, but manage to keep my mouth shut.

Officer Killduff stands over us as we sprawl there on the court, grinning his sour grin. He nudges Bad Gina's friend Weeze with his boot. She's lying flat on her back, heaving with every breath. "Looks like we got us a beached whale here," he says. "Whole school of them."

"You mean 'pod,'" someone squeaks. We all look up, surprised. Nobody talks back to Officer Killduff, even I know that. It's Karen, the middle-school girl. I don't think I've heard her speak the whole time I've been in juvie.

He steps over to where she's sitting cross-legged on the floor. I can see her staring at his black, spit-shined boots. Maybe she's looking at her reflection, at her long brown hair hanging straight down her cheeks like curtains.

Officer Killduff taps his boot. "Say again?"

She lifts her gaze to his knees. All the other girls just keep staring, eyes wide.

"Pod," she says, squeaky voice rising higher. "A pod of whales. You can call it a school, too, but usually you call it a pod of whales."

"A pod," Officer Killduff repeats, his face twisted in a strange way, as if he's stepped in gum, or shit, and hasn't figured out how to get it off his shoe. "Well, aren't you just the little encyclopedia."

"Yes, sir," Karen says. "It's from Trivial Pursuit. We used to play it. At my house."

Officer Killduff squats. She lowers her head so the curtains of hair close in front of her.

"Well, that's just by God fascinating," he says. "Thank you for setting me straight."

"You're welcome," Karen squeaks from behind her hair.

"'You're welcome,'" Officer Killduff repeats, looking over at Officer C. Miller. "You hear that? 'You're welcome.' Now, how polite is that?"

C. Miller seems reluctant to play along. "It's polite, all right."

"What a polite little princess," Officer Killduff says. He seems to go deep into thought for a minute, stroking his chin, furrowing his brow, the works. Then he speaks again to Officer C. Miller, though really it's to all of us.

"And for a reward for all that politeness, and all that fascinating information about the whales, how about we let this one pick the next activity?" He thumps the floor with his knuckles in front of Karen. "How about that?"

"I guess she earned it," Officer Miller says.

Officer Killduff nods. "I guess she did earn it," he says. "So there you go. What's it going to be, Encyclopedia Brown? Dodgeball? Jump rope? More wind sprints?"

"Really?" Karen asks, as if she actually thinks getting to choose is going to end up being a good thing. "I really get to say?"

"Really," Officer Killduff says.

"Well, can we go outside?" Karen asks. "Like for recess?"

Officer Killduff laughs so hard I think he'll fall over. Why can't she just keep quiet? I figure we'll be running wind sprints for the rest of the gym hour once Officer Killduff finishes making fun of her.

He keeps laughing his sardonic laugh and shaking his buzz-cut head, as if he still can't believe what she said, or that she spoke at all. Finally he stands up. "Well, why the hell not?" he says. "Let's all go outside for recess. Officer Miller, if you'd be so kind as to radio to control. And ladies, if you'd be so good as to get up off the floor and get in a nice line over there by the door."

We do what he says, everybody bewildered. I take my now-customary place in the back of the line, behind Karen, but Officer Killduff has other plans. "No, no," he says to Karen. "This was your idea. I'd like you to lead our little pod out to sea. Why don't you swim on up to the front of the line, if that's what you'd call it – a line of whales?"

Karen says, "OK," and "I guess so," and slides up ahead of the Jelly Sisters, who nearly always lead. I haven't seen the sky in nine days. Even lined up at the door to the yard, I still can't see it. None of us can. There aren't any windows in our part of juvie, none even in the gym. It's all I can do to keep from lifting my gaze from the floor, to catch the first glimpse of the outside world once the door opens. I can't wait to be out, even surrounded by a thirty-foot fence – to breathe fresh air, to feel the sun on my face, to hear blue jays squawking and the wind in the trees.

Officer C. Miller speaks into her radio, and the door buzzes and clicks and swings open to the yard.

Where it's pouring down rain.

All the girls huddle under the eave, pressed against the dirty concrete wall to escape the rain. There doesn't seem to be a gutter on the roof, so if you don't stay close, water drips on your head. Everybody is cursing Karen under their breath, just loud enough for her to hear. I'm pretty sure even Fefu is doing it, too, in Spanish.

"Putita estupida."

Officer Killduff and Officer C. Miller stand outside the door under an awning, just out of earshot. Officer Killduff lights a cigarette, which surprises me since he's so buff, the kind of fitness freak you just know spends hours a day in the weight room. C. Miller waves the smoke away from her face and edges away.

Karen starts crying after a few minutes, standing as far away as she can from the huddle of girls. The only one farther away is me. Finally I guess Karen can't take it anymore, pushing herself away from the wall even though the rain is still coming down. She wanders toward the outdoor basketball court, which is just an uneven patch of hard-packed dirt with a couple of hoops but no nets, then she negotiates her way around what looks like deep mud puddles toward the fence farthest from the building. Once she gets there, she leans against it and stays.

"Good," Chantrelle says. "Serves her right. I hope her ass melts out there."

"I know, right?" Good Gina says. They're standing closest to me now, so I still have a buffer between me and the Jelly Sisters and Bad Gina and Weeze, just not enough of one. "I mean, what was she thinking talking like that to Killduff?"

"Yeah," says Chantrelle. "He was playing with her, like a cat and a mouse. She too dumb to even see that. Probably thought she made her a new friend in juvie. Probably can't wait to get her phone call this evening. 'Hi, Mommy, I made me a new friend. Officer Killduff. He so nice, let me play out in the rain and I didn't even have to have me an umbrella.'"

I don't want to stick around to hear any more. The poor girl is just eleven or twelve; how could she have known any better? Plus I don't want Bad Gina or the Jelly Sisters to have a chance to come over next to me and maybe start up a conversation, or interrogation. So I step away from the wall and into the rain, too. It drips down my neck and down my back, soaking me quicker than I anticipate, but I lower my head and keep walking, following Karen to the back fence and away from the other girls.

"Hey," I say when I get there. She's sniffling.

"Hey," she says, wiping her nose. "You're not going to be mean to me, too, are you?"

I smile. "No. Just got bored standing over there. Thought I'd come stand over here for a while. It's such a great view."

We stare together out at an empty parking lot, and a dirt field beyond that, and then a desultory stand of skinny pines and scrub brush and a heavy gray sky.

"What grade are you in?" I ask, casting around for a way to start a conversation, maybe make her feel a little better about things.

"Seventh," she says.

"What school?"

She tells me. It's in one of the counties west of town.

"How long have you been in here?"

"Just two weeks," she says. "I was the last one to come in before you. I have my second court hearing tomorrow, I think."

"Are you nervous?"

"A little, but not too much. My mom says they're going to let me out. She says my lawyer thinks just a couple of weeks of juvie is enough for the judge. I hate it in here. Everybody is so mean. Everybody gets mad at you and makes fun of you if you say anything. Those two black girls, I think they're sisters, they keep taking my dessert every night. They practically got in a fight over my Jell-O one time." She pushes her wet sheets of hair behind her ears. "Don't you think everybody is so mean?"

"I don't know," I say. "Maybe."

She studies my face. "Well, look what those girls did to you – to your nose. Don't you think that was mean?"

"It was probably an accident," I say, lying because I don't feel like getting into it. "That's all. Another week and you won't even be able to tell it happened."

"I don't know," Karen says. "It looks terrible. It's all purple and black around your eyes, and your nose is all swollen up, and your face is kind of green. I mean, if that ever happened to me, I wouldn't even leave my room for like about a month. I wouldn't go to school or anything. If anybody ever saw you looking like that, they'd take pictures on their cell phones, and that would be the picture they used for whenever you called them or texted or whatever."

I'm starting to regret coming over.

"So why are you in here, anyway?" I ask to change the subject.

She laces her fingers through the chain-link fence. I glance at the barbed wire; I imagine it would shred your hands if you ever tried to climb over.

"It was like this misunderstanding," she says.

"About what?"

"About these silver dollars this girl had. She had about a hundred of them she kept in a jar, from her pop-pop or something. Her grandfather. I can't remember. But that's real money, anyway, even though you never really see coin dollars very often."

"I think I've heard that," I say.

"So anyway," she continues, "what happened was I didn't think she would ever use them or anything, so I thought I would take them when I found out you can actually spend them like real money. There were some clothes I wanted to buy at Justice. I really love Justice. They have a store at the mall. Have you ever been there? Do girls your age still go there, to Justice?"

"How old do you think I am?" I ask. I probably haven't been to Justice since third grade.

"I don't know," she says. "College?"

"Close enough. And no, girls my age don't shop at Justice."

"So anyway," she repeats – apparently that's the way she starts most of her sentences – "what happened was she got mad that I took them, even though she didn't have any proof it was me, but they found them in my room, so I got in trouble for that."

I have a hard time believing they put a seventh grader in juvie for stealing silver dollars, even a hundred of them, and say so.

"Yeah," she says. "So anyway, they were just going

to make me give them back and pay her back the ones I already used. But we were mad at her, me and my other friends, so we kind of killed her dog by accident. And that's why they put me in juvie. But I'm getting out next week, at my hearing. Did I already tell you that? I think I did. My mom said."

"You did tell me," I say, shivering as the wind picks up and I go from being just wet to being cold and wet. Karen doesn't seem to notice. She shakes the fence, spraying more water on us. I put my hand on top of hers to make her stop.

"So what about the dog?" I ask.

"Oh. That." She giggles. "We didn't mean for it to die or anything. What we did was we got a box of Ex-Lax and mixed it up with a can of dog food and put it out for him to eat. We thought it would be funny when he pooped all over Emily's house, but we might have used too much Ex-Lax because what happened was the dog ended up pooping himself to death." She giggles harder. "I know I shouldn't laugh about that. It's really sad and all. But it's kind of funny, too. But my mom told me I'm not supposed to laugh when I go to court. That's the one thing. I have to let the judge know how sad I am that the dog died, and that it was an accident, and that I really love dogs."

I'm nearly speechless. "You poisoned your friend's dog?"

"Yeah." She keeps on giggling. "His name was Pepper. He shouldn't have died, actually. Even though we gave him the whole box. That's what this veterinarian said. I guess Pepper was just really old or something, and he couldn't handle all that pooping." She giggles some more. "And then my friends, they all said it was my idea, so I was the one to get in all the trouble. I hate them. They're going to be so dead when I get out of here."

I step back to take a good look at Karen, her hair now plastered to her temples and cheeks, water dripping off the tip of her nose, talking as if the subject is new clothes for her Barbie and not some poor dog she murdered.

"Whose idea *was* it?" I ask.

"Well, mine, I guess. Technically." She rolls her eyes. "But they didn't have to tell everybody. God."

I shake the rain off my own face. "Don't you feel bad about it?"

She looks down again, trying to appear contrite, maybe practicing for court, but struggling to keep the grin off her face.

"Right," I say, pushing away from the fence without waiting any longer for an answer. "Well, I'm going back over there now." I point to the building where the rest of the girls are still bunched under the dripping eave. Officer Killduff flicks a cigarette out into the yard with the practiced ease of a chain-smoker, probably getting ready to call everyone into line to go to whatever is scheduled next.

I splash across the basketball court in my wet sandals and socks.

Karen squeaks out after me, "Hey, don't tell anybody any of that stuff I told you. I just remembered I'm not supposed to talk about it."

I wave but don't turn around. I'm busy wishing I had somewhere else to go than back to Bad Gina and the Jelly Sisters and the rest of Unit Three.

Before I get there, the Jelly Sisters take care of things for me. There's an exchange I can't hear between them and Bad Gina and Weeze, and then Nell Jelly gets pushed out into the yard, so hard she slips in the mud. Wanda is going after Weeze when the officers intervene and we're all on lockdown for the rest of the day, and that night, too; phone privileges canceled for everybody. I'm sure my mom will worry, but it's the most relaxed I've been since I got here.

I get a letter from Dad the next day – a soiled white envelope with spidery handwriting that I recognize right away. I tear it open, but there's no letter inside, just a yellowing piece of wide-ruled elementary-school paper with a crayon drawing of a girl, her arms tight to her sides, flying with birds and clouds and an airplane high over a city. I remember drawing it when I was in second grade. There's even a gold star on it from my teacher, Mrs. Delany. The caption reads, "I dreamd I was flying over Lost Vegas. It was for the big meeting."

Dad has probably saved every paper, every test, every picture, every project I've ever brought home from school since kindergarten. Carla's, too. Why he chose this one to send me in juvie, with no letter or even a note – no anything – I have no idea. I can't remember why I drew a picture of me flying over Vegas, either. I've never even been to Vegas – Las or Lost.

I don't get the chance to study the picture for very long and try to figure out whatever hidden message Dad might have meant for me to find. Mail call only lasts fifteen minutes, and before I know it, the guards come around to collect all the letters and stuff them into folders. They say we'll get everything back when we're released. As if that will make any difference.

That evening at phone hour, I blow it. I mean to call Mom, or Carla and Lulu, or maybe even Julie Juggins. But instead I dial Kevin's number. I tell myself to stop, and twice I hang up before it starts ringing. I remind myself that I am as done with him as he and his parents clearly are with me. But then I dial his number a third time because I just can't help myself.

"Sadie?" he asks before I even get to say hello.

"Yeah," I say. "Hey, Kevin. It's me."

"Whoa. I saw this 'Rapp Area Juve' on my phone. So I wondered if it was you."

"Sounds like a song or something," I say. "'Rapp Area Juve.' Maybe we could name a band that."

"Yeah," he says. "I guess so."

The conversation stops for a second as I try to figure

out why I've called and as he probably wonders about that, too.

"So are you doing anything?" I ask. "I mean, am I interrupting anything?"

"No, no, nothing," he says, a little too quickly. "I was just doing some homework, listening to some tunes, checking e-mail, stuff like that."

Suddenly, now that I have him on the phone, I don't know what to say, and I worry that he's already just biding his time, waiting for me to hang up so he can go back to his homework, or his e-mail, or another girl. Probably another girl.

"So, Sadie," he starts, "what's it like in there and all? I mean, are you doing OK?"

"Well, I've never been to Club Med or on one of those Caribbean cruises or whatever," I say, recovering, sort of. "But I'm pretty sure they're like juvie. You've got your gourmet chefs, and your massages, and your Jacuzzis. I'm taking ballroom dancing. Can you believe that? Me? Ballroom dancing? One girl in here, she got on *Dancing with the Stars*. You might have seen her. She wore her orange juvie jumpsuit, and she did a dance to 'Jailhouse Rock.' So funny—"

"Yeah," Kevin interrupts. "So, Sadie . . ."

He's only said it twice but I'm already sick of "So, Sadie." He's never started a sentence like that the whole time I've known him.

He wants to get off the phone. And so do I.

"Look, Kevin, it was great of you to call," I say. "Great catching up and everything. You're doing all right, right? Everything's good with you? Great."

I should have hung up on him immediately because when I pause, he says the last thing I want to hear, ever again, from him or anybody.

"Sadie, I'm so sorry. I just wanted to tell you that, and —"

I hang up before he can say anything else. For a long minute, I just stare at the wall, wishing I could take back the last few minutes of my life.

Then I notice Bad Gina at the next phone, not talking to anybody, just standing there looking at me.

"Broke down and called the ex, right?" she says. "Nothing a guy likes as much as a desperate, pathetic girl calling him up from juvie. Tough girl like you, I'd have thought you'd hold out for at least another week. But hey – now you know, right?"

I can't speak. I can't move. I can't even look away. I seethe.

I am really, really starting to hate this Bad Gina.

Dear Kevin,

I must have just dialed the wrong number when I accidentally called, so don't worry, it won't happen again. Anyway, I've got a lot going on, obviously, and so I'm afraid I don't have time for a relationship, or even a friendship, really. But there is one thing I did want to ask you. A favor, I guess. I told you a lot of private stuff about me and my family when you and I were dating and I would appreciate it if you wouldn't repeat it to anybody. That's really the only thing I wanted to say. Oh, and that place I took you to – Government Island – I would also appreciate it if you wouldn't go there or tell anybody about it, either. And, OK, I miss you sometimes, I admit, but I'm sure I'll get over it. It's just that being in here makes everything so much harder. Like if I was at school or basketball practice and wanted some Mentos, I might not have them right away but I would know I could always go to the 7-Eleven and buy some later. In here if I wanted some Mentos, it's the same as if I wanted a slice of moon cheese; I'm not going to get it. I guess tonight I was just trying to have a slice of moon cheese. Sorry.

Dear Dad,
Thanks for the picture. I guess it was probably hard for you to let it go. I wish I could remember what I was thinking about when I drew it. Anyway, I've been wondering about you a lot, how you're doing and everything. And thinking that my life is sort of like yours now, which is kind of funny. I spend about ten hours every night in my cell, and longer if we're on lockdown, with just my own thoughts to keep me company. I guess the difference between you and

me is I'd leave here in a heartbeat if I could.

I remember one time Mom told me and Carla that your brain worked in a different way than most people's and that's why you had such a hard time throwing stuff away and why you eventually had to move into Granny's house. She didn't want us to resent you for being the way you are. But really Carla and I had kind of figured that out already on our own. We saw you getting more and more that way as we got older. You hid in your bedroom if our friends came over, and you started working from home, and you wouldn't throw away any of your newspapers. You had that one room in the house where you kept stacks and stacks of paper, different stacks for whether it had writing on it or was blank, colored or plain. Remember? We had fourteen bikes for a while that you found at yard sales or in people's recycling and you kept them in the shed even though none of them worked. You collected flat tires, too. Remember that? You said you never knew when you might need all that rubber for something, and Carla and I thought we could start a slingshot business and sell them to all the kids in the neighborhood. Only you didn't want to give up any of your tires or inner tubes for us to make the slingshots with. So I guess in that way I'm the opposite of you now. You have all your stuff that you collect, all your newspapers and bikes and flat tires, that makes you who you are. But in here, in juvie, they won't let me have anything. Not anything at all. Which I guess makes me nothing, too.

CHAPTER 12

In which I hurt that girl, get no
sympathy from Kevin, and retreat
to Government Island

The second week after the arrest was worse than the first. Carla was in the clear but hadn't gotten around to quitting her job at Friendly's or going to any AA meetings or spending more time with Lulu that I could see.

When I confronted her about it, the next time she came over to the house, she had a hundred excuses. "I'm trying, Sadie. I swear. But I can't quit until I have another job lined up, and that takes time. I've got a bunch of applications. I just need to fill them out. And I can't just go to an AA meeting. It's like they're all scheduled for when Mom's at work and you're at work, too, or at basketball practice, or when I have to work. I can show you the schedule. I even printed it out. Probably this Sunday I can go. And ask Lulu about all the stories I've been reading to her at bedtime. I even got her early one day from day care so we could run errands together. I couldn't help it if she fell asleep in the car."

I knew it was 90 percent crap. I wanted to scream at her.

"Just do what you said you'd do, Carla," I snapped, cutting her off. "I'm going to court this Thursday, in case you forgot."

Carla got quiet, even quieter when I reminded her that I was going to have to confess all over again to shit I didn't do. My lawyer had worked out an arrangement with the prosecutor for me to do community service, but I still had to stand up in court and admit that I knew about the drugs – and that Carla didn't know a thing.

She said she had to go, and I said, "Great. Call me when you get your shit together."

I hated all of it. I hated Carla not keeping up her end of the deal, at least not so far. I hated the waiting. And the worrying that somebody was going to find out. And having to keep this dark secret from Kevin, who knew something was the matter though I wouldn't say what.

Then they canceled court again. Mom and I were standing in the foyer, wearing dresses, worried that the lawyer hadn't shown up yet. My case was first on the docket since it had gotten bumped back from the week before, but when the bailiff opened the doors, instead of calling my case, he said the judge had gotten sick. Sorry.

Mom made me go to school late and didn't even let me change, and all day at school people kept asking me what was up with the dress. I got an actual headache from all the lying I had to do.

It was the next night, a Friday, when I yanked that girl down by her ponytail during the AAU game and got a technical and got ejected. I'd never done anything like that before, and I was as shocked as everybody else when I did it. The girl had swung an elbow grabbing a rebound early in the game and had given Julie Juggins a bloody lip. Then she'd stomped on Julie's foot so hard Coach had to pull Julie out for five minutes so she could ice it. That girl had Julie so cowed during the whole first half that we couldn't get anything going on offense, and our defense kept breaking down. We were getting our asses kicked, literally. Julie should have stood up to the girl herself – she was six two, while the girl was maybe five ten – not left it to me, her five-four point guard, to do something about it. But she didn't, and so I was the one that got tossed, and got yelled at by Coach, and had to spend the rest of the game sulking at the end of the bench.

When I met up with Kevin after the game, he gave me grief, too. As if I didn't already feel bad enough. I'd never gotten so much as a technical before that night.

"I don't know, Sadie," he said. We were in his little Ford Fiesta, and I'd just finished ranting about how unfair my ejection had been. "That was kind of uncalled-for."

"Are you kidding me?" I said, though deep down I knew there wasn't any excuse for what I'd done. "Did you not see the way she was beating on Julie all night?"

He opened a can of beer between his legs and handed me one from the six-pack. "Not really. She kept getting position on Julie under the basket. She was pretty much schooling Julie until you did what you did."

"Yeah, but at least Julie turned it around after that," I said.

"Sure," Kevin said. "But the girl was hurt. And probably scared that somebody else on your team was going to do something to her."

I crossed my arms over my chest and sat back stiffly. I hated it when Kevin, who'd been red-carded more than anybody I knew, turned into Mr. Reasonable. And I hated it that he was right.

But I wasn't about to say any of that to him. "Take me back to the gym," I said. I'd left my motorcycle there. We'd been planning for him to drive me back to pick it up later, after we went out. I was supposed to spend the night at Julie's house, but that probably wasn't going to happen, either.

"Come on, Sadie," he whined. "I take it all back, OK? You should have kneecapped the girl. She deserved what she got. Is that what you want to hear?"

I also hated it when Kevin whined. And I hated it that he was so good-looking, and that he knew it, and I hated it that he could be such a jerk but then turn ridiculously sweet just when I decided I'd had enough, and I hated it that when he kissed me, I went all weak and helpless and ended up doing stuff that I told myself I wouldn't do again, only it felt so good that once we got started, I didn't have it in me to say no.

"Just take me back to the gym," I said again, in a voice that didn't give him any room to negotiate, or whine, or try to kiss me, or do any of the things that usually worked for him.

I should have gone home, hung out with Mom, watched some TV, gone to bed early. I had to work at the car wash at eight the next morning. But once I got on my motorcycle, I just wanted to ride, feel that great rush of wind and speed, and leave everything behind – my temper getting the better of me in a way that had never happened before, and hurting that girl, and the stupid technical, and getting benched, and pissing off Coach. And Kevin lecturing me and then whining when he realized we wouldn't be fooling around any that night. And court. And my confession. And Carla.

I rode up Route 1 to Coal Landing Road, and then down Coal Landing Road, faster than I should, leaning into every hairpin curve, until it dead-ended at Aquia Creek. I stashed my bike there and hiked through the marsh, grateful the moon hung full over the trees, a perfect Government Island night-light, helping me pick out the way and keep to where it was driest.

I had to wade through a ten-yard expanse of creek, just a couple of feet deep, so I pulled off my shoes and rolled up my pants as high as they would go. Once I reached the bank, I scrambled up to an old cart path that ran around the edge of the island and then another that bisected it through the middle, over to the channel side of Aquia Creek. They'd used those paths back in colonial days to haul out freestone from the quarry sites, and they used the freestone to build the foundations for the White House and the Capitol. The first time Dad took me and Carla to Government Island, he carried us up Aquia Creek on his johnboat and told us it was Virginia slaves who did most of the quarry work. He said they did the hauling and the loading onto barges for the trip down the deep, wide part of the creek and onto ships to go up the Potomac River to Washington, DC, forty miles north.

All that history was mostly forgotten now. The island was overgrown and wild again, though you could still find the old quarry sites if you knew where to look.

I ended up staying all night there, even though I hadn't thought to bring my sleeping bag or anything to eat or drink. At first I just sat on a freestone outcropping over the black water and let my mind wander wherever it wanted: to how I could make up to Julie Juggins and the team for what I'd done; to my complicated relationship with Kevin, who could make me so frustrated one minute and make me love him until I thought I would melt the next; to conversations I'd had with Granny when she was alive; to happy times with Mom and Dad when Carla and I were little, before Dad retreated into himself and Mom had to start caring for all of us on her own.

It was a warm October night, and when the mosquitoes started biting, I slid down to the water's edge and smeared river mud on my neck and face and the backs of my hands and anything else that was exposed. The mud dried and caked and itched some but did keep the mosquitoes away. I climbed back up to my lookout perch, a wide slab of flat rock thirty feet above the water, and must have fallen asleep at some point.

I woke up just before sunrise. Once my head cleared, I quietly made my way in the dim predawn light to some brush near a certain tree at the water's edge where I happened to know there was a blue heron nest. I waited there, hidden, camouflaged, trying not to move or make a sound until the precise moment the red sun showed itself just over the tops of the trees on the other side of the widest expanse of the creek, and then I rustled the brush and saw what I was hoping to see: the blue heron rising suddenly from her nest with one great beat of her wings, catching a thermal that spiraled up, so that just for a second she was framed, backlit by the rising sun, and then disappeared off into the sky.

When I left the island and returned to my bike, I turned my cell phone on and saw I had a couple of messages. The first was a voice mail from home.

"Sadie, it's Mom. Just wanted to remind you you have work in the morning. Hope the game went OK. Say hi to Julie and her mom for me."

I texted her back: *on way 2 wrk now.*

Kevin had left a text, too – *u ok?* – but that was it. One lousy text. And the minimum number of characters possible. The jerk.

I kick-started the bike and rode back to town and to the car wash, where I spent the next eight hours Windexing and vacuuming and towel-drying an endless parade of cars and trucks and SUVs – and not texting Kevin.

CHAPTER 13

In which I win a spelling bee, meet a girl
who killed her mom, and finally see Carla

It's Friday of my second week in juvie, and I wake up
scratching my legs. I haven't shaved my legs since I've been
here, and for some reason that makes me as depressed as
anything that's happened – or maybe it's just that it's *on
top of* everything that's happened. My armpits are sprout-
ing hair, too. I guess everybody is going through the same
thing except maybe Fefu, who is too little. The rest of us,
though – God.

Nobody has said anything about shaving; we'll probably just get hairier and hairier until we look like apes. Or
guys. For once I'm thankful for the juvie-issue jumpsuits

177 ‖

and shirts, which keep us from noticing how hairy we're all getting. But I shudder to think what I'll look like when they finally let me out of here.

The reading specialist, a little round woman named Mrs. Blanchard, comes later that day, so there's a break in the routine, not that it ends up being much of a break. Mrs. Blanchard decides we'll have a spelling bee. Middle-School Karen gets called out for court right when we're getting started. "Good-bye, everybody," she says as she leaves, sounding as if she thinks she'll never see us again.

The spelling bee doesn't go over very well, since almost everybody goes out in the first round, probably deliberately, though I guess the words might be kind of hard: *quantum, duchess, flummox*. I win on *quadrilateral*, but everybody acts so bored the whole time, I'm not even sure Mrs. Blanchard notices. There isn't a prize.

Next she says we're going to write character sketches.

"About who?" Wanda asks.

"About yourselves."

Wanda shakes her head. "I don't think so."

Nell says, "Me either," though neither speaks loud enough for the guard, Officer C. Miller, to hear.

"I know what you're thinking," Mrs. Blanchard says. "But this will be different from the last time we tried this exercise. This time I brought something."

She pats a machine sitting on the desk. It's a paper shredder.

"I know last time everyone was worried about who might read their essays and that it might cause them trouble or embarrassment. But this time nobody will see what you write. It really is just an exercise. You can shred it as soon as you're finished. I won't even see it. Unless you want me to. I want you all to think of our classroom as a safe haven for expressing your thoughts."

"Then what's the point if nobody's going to read it?" Bad Gina asks. "And, like, how will you grade it or whatever?"

"It's called freewriting," Mrs. Blanchard says. "It's a way to warm up to other essays we'll be writing later on. Kind of like the stretching you might do before you run in a big race."

"We gonna have to race again?" Wanda asks. "Like we already did in gym?"

Mrs. Blanchard looks frustrated. "No. Not a real race. I was just using an analogy to explain."

She passes out paper and markers. Fefu goes right back to coloring in polka dots. Weeze draws more horses. Wanda Jelly plays tic-tac-toe by herself. I can't tell what Nell is up to. Probably writing death threats to Bad Gina. Bad Gina wraps her free arm protectively around her sheet of paper so I can't see what she's doing, either, but it looks as if she's actually writing her essay.

I eye the shredder, look at Bad Gina scribbling away, and decide to give it a try.

SADIE WINDAS

Is kind of popular in school, blond, athletic, pretty
enough before she got her nose broken and hope-
fully will be again. She gets good grades and is
captain of the basketball team and gets invited to
plenty of parties. She's got a cool soccer boyfriend,
or used to. She fits in, but everybody knows there's
kind of an edge to her, too, like an independent
streak. She has a motorcycle. She doesn't wear much
makeup. She doesn't gossip. She's pretty private
about stuff. Like getting arrested. And why her dad
and mom no longer live together.

She's the kind of girl who can sneak off to
Government Island to camp out by herself, and
a couple of times with her boyfriend, and tell her
mom she's sleeping over at Julie Juggins's house –
because her mom is too tired and worn down to
check up on her, and because Sadie is the easy sister,
not the strung-out teen mom sister. Not that Sadie's
mom is a bad parent. But she's a single mom working two jobs. Sadie's dad lives by himself. He won't
see anybody and refuses to take medication. Sadie
hasn't talked to him in a couple of years. She knows
her family loves her in their own way, but it hasn't
felt like enough for a long time.

She has a lot of plans. To go to college on a
basketball scholarship, travel, have a career, live in
a nice big house with a picket fence and a husband

who's a lawyer/musician and makes decent money. She'll probably coach her kids' soccer and basketball teams, host sleepovers, and keep working a good job herself. Though to be totally honest, she wonders if she'd feel like a phony in that kind of life, partly because she's never actually known anybody who lives that way. But wherever she ends up, she knows she doesn't want a life like her mom's. Or her dad's. Or her sister's. Lately, and for a long time, to be honest about it, she feels separate from her family, like she's moved past them or something. But no matter where her life takes her, she can't imagine ever going far from her little niece. Missing Lulu is the hardest part about being in juvie.

When Carla dragged Sadie to that party, the one where they got arrested, Sadie would rather have been home having a sleepover with Lulu, making a tent with the covers and getting under it with a flashlight, reading *Goodnight Moon* and *The Runaway Bunny* over and over until Lulu fell asleep, because those are the only books she likes to read. But Sadie knows one of her jobs in life is to steer Carla away from trouble, for Lulu's sake, even though Sadie thinks she'd be a better mom to Lulu than Carla is. But taking the blame for Carla, and going to juvie – that just about killed her: having everybody think she's guilty, losing all her

181 ‖

friends, losing her boyfriend, maybe even losing any chance of a scholarship, and college, and all the rest —

I stop at the bottom of the page, my marker just about dry, and realize how furiously I've been writing. My eyes burn, sweat rolls down my cheeks. I wipe my face on my sleeve but rub my nose too hard. A drop of blood lands in the middle of the page. I try blotting it off but that just smears it, like the bright-red tail of a comet, or a shooting star.

Everybody is staring.

I blink. They blink back.

Slowly I raise my hand.

Mrs. Blanchard clears her throat as if she's going to make a speech.

"Yes, Sadie?"

I push my chair back from the table.

"Permission to use the shredder?"

I have two letters that afternoon at mail call. One is from Julie Juggins. I almost can't believe it. We've been friends for a long time, but she dropped out of sight right before I went to juvie.

Hey, S.,

Hope you're doing OK and sorry I didn't get a chance to see you before you left. Anyways, the team has pretty

much sucked since Coach sent you into early retire-
ment (that's what I'm calling it, anyway). I thought
about quitting, but figured you'll be back next year and
then we'll be so awesome when we're seniors, we will
totally rule. . . .

I get excited about the prospect of that – for about a minute. And then I get depressed about missing most of the fall AAU season, and the high-school season starting in December, and – who knows? – with community service tacked on to my six months in juvie, probably summer ball next year as well. And I'm still waiting to hear if my conviction and my time in juvie is going to make me ineligible for basketball scholarships. Mom asked Vance to look into it for us as a favor, but so far we haven't heard anything. Julie might as well be writing about a dream she had, for as likely as that future seems right now.

The other letter is from Mom, with a picture from Lulu. Mom says the reason the tenants at Granny's house haven't been taking care of the place is because they moved out without telling her, so now she's going to have to find some new tenants, only who will want to live that close to Dad and all his junk?

I can't believe I'm saying this, but I'm thinking about
moving us out to your grandmother's – all of us: me,
Carla, and Lulu. If Carla goes back to school, she's
not going to be able to keep paying her rent, and since

there's no mortgage out at your grandmother's we would all get a break. I could try to keep an eye on her if the three of us were living together, and it'd be easier helping take care of Lulu. That's a big IF, of course. Carla says she's been looking at the course catalog and plans to call the registrar at the community college. And she says she'll see about going part-time somewhere if she does start taking classes. But she's never been too good at following through. And then there's the question about whether she and I could actually survive under the same roof. We'll see. It would be strange living right next to your dad, of course, but I don't expect we'd see him much more than now, the way he keeps so much to himself. Anyway, I'm thinking about it. I guess I could have told you all this over the phone, but I'm never sure when you're going to call and I thought you might like some actual news in a letter.

I read the letter twice, to make sure I'm not hallucinating. Mom and Carla living together. Yeah, right.

I fold it up and open Lulu's picture, which I'm pretty sure is supposed to be of me. Anyway, it's a girl with a giant head, spiky hair, stick arms and legs, enormous fingers and toes, big fat body, big fat butt, tiny little motorcycle, and a frowny bird sitting behind her that might or might not be Lulu.

I trace the outlines of the picture over and over with

my finger, imagining her at Mom's kitchen table with her big crayons and a frozen waffle.

C. Miller hands me a manila folder with my name on it.

I look up at her and hold her gaze, which I know I shouldn't do but I can't help it. "Please, just this once? It's a picture of me, from my niece." I know I sound pathetic, and I know there's no point, but I can't bear to give it up.

"How old is she?" C. Miller asks.

"Three," I say. "Her name is Lulu."

C. Miller nods sympathetically, and for just a second I think there's a chance. But then she says, "Sorry, Sadie. They told you that at Intake. In here, you don't get to keep anything."

Dear Lulu,

You draw the best pictures of anybody. I have the one you sent me hanging up over my bed, right next to my pictures of you and Carla and Moo-Moo. I hope you're taking good care of that rock you gave me the day I left. You can wear my basketball shoes if you want, around the house or whatever, but you probably shouldn't sleep with them anymore. Too stinky. Ask Moo-Moo if you can have one of my basketball jerseys to sleep in instead. I already told her it's OK. You can have whichever one you want and you can keep it, too. I wish I was there with you now. We could eat frozen waffles for breakfast.

Dear Julie,

Thanks for your letter, and glad you didn't quit the team. If Coach lets me back on next year, I'm betting we can win States. Hey, do you ever run into Kevin? I accidentally called him last night and he sounded weird. I mean, it's hard to know what a normal person would sound like if they got a call from their ex-girlfriend who's in juvie, but it kind of sounded like maybe he was seeing somebody else and didn't want me to know it. Weird, right? Why would I care if he had another girlfriend? . . .

They clean out Middle-School Karen's cell late that afternoon without telling us what happened to her, but I'm guessing she must have gotten released just like she predicted. An hour later, they bring in a new girl. Everybody else is watching TV; I'm trying to read a book, thinking about going to my cell early and disturbed that I'm actually considering it. She's an angry-looking white girl with a puffy face and a shock of purple hair and empty holes in her eyebrow and nose and lip and tongue. The hole from her nose ring looks infected.

Officer Killduff introduces her to her cell. She balks at the door, and he practically has to shove her inside. She comes back out a minute later and paces around the common area, seemingly unable to stand still. The other girls watch her for a while, but nobody speaks, and pretty soon they turn their attention back to the TV. There's just something about the new girl that makes everybody want to stay away. Maybe it's that nervousness. Maybe it's something else, some vibe she gives off. Even the guards keep their distance, practically ignoring her, even though she keeps pacing and pacing.

And then, just my luck, she lurches over and throws herself in a chair right next to me. The table I have my book propped on starts shaking, and I realize it's because her leg is bouncing wildly underneath. Her hands shake, too.

"Hey," she says. "I'm Summer, like the season. What's your name? What are you in for? What are you reading?"

She talks too fast for me to respond, as if she's high on meth or something.

"Never mind," she says without waiting for an answer. "You're busy. Sorry to disturb you. I'll go sit over there."

She stalks over to an empty chair under the TV next to Weeze, sits for a minute, fires off questions to Weeze, appears to wait for answers this time – but doesn't appear to get them – then gets up again. She keeps doing that for the next hour. Sitting, snapping off a few questions to whoever happens to be nearby, standing abruptly, crossing the room to another chair, wandering in and out of her cell, approaching the guard table but thinking better of it as soon as she gets there and quickly heading somewhere else, bouncing around like a pinball.

But there are only so many places to go, and Summer ends up next to me again, rubbing her hands together, glancing at me, but mostly looking down, studying patterns on the linoleum floor. "What'd you say your name was again?" she asks. "I forgot."

"It's Sadie," I say.

"Sadie, Sadie, Sadie. OK. Thanks. I'm bad with people's names." She laughs. "Ha! What I'm bad with is people, you know?" She gets up again but then sits back down.

"Here's the thing, Sadie," she says, leaning close. "My mom. Something might have happened to her, you know? They found her. They said they found her in the bedroom. They won't tell me anything. They keep asking me all these questions, you know? But I don't know anything."

She's wringing her hands now, and tapping her foot so fast and so hard that her knee bangs into the underside of the table. "They said there was a gun. I can't talk about it. My dad's so mad at me. He won't talk to me. But I was at work when it happened. I was at the Tropical Smoothie. You ever go there? To the Tropical Smoothie?"

"The one at the mall?" I ask.

She nods. "They brought me to the police station. They said to tell them what happened, but I told them I was at work. They wanted to know about my boyfriend. His name's Andy. He didn't have anything to do with it. I don't even know where he is."

She stops talking as abruptly as she started but keeps sitting, keeps tapping her foot.

"So what happened?" I ask.

She shakes her head. "I'm not supposed to talk about

it. They said I would see a lawyer. They would send one to talk to me." She jerks her head up to glare at me. "You better not say anything, either. I didn't tell you anything." She pounds on her knees with her fists. "I swear to God. What was your name again? I forgot. I don't care. You just better not repeat anything I said."

I edge my chair back. "Calm down, all right? You didn't tell me anything, and I'm not going to say anything."

"Damn right," she says. "Damn right. OK. I'm gonna go lie down. That's my cell over there. You think they'll give me something to help me sleep? They ever do that in here? You think I can ask the guards?"

I say I doubt it but she can try if she wants.

She shakes her head, still acting methed out. "Never mind. I'm going. OK. See you later. Bye. Thanks for talking."

Summer goes back to her cell, which is just ten feet away, sits on the bunk for a minute, then gets up and bangs her face against the wall. Blood sprouts from her forehead and nose. It's all so sudden, I don't react at first. She staggers backward into the opposite wall and then slumps to the floor, at first cradling her face in her hands, then pulling them away and staring at the blood.

I call over to C. Miller and Officer Killduff.

They put Summer on suicide watch – take away her juvie-issue clothes and make her wear the suicide blanket. She protests. She only hit her face on the wall that once, she says, and it was an accident. She *swears* it was an accident.

"Ask that girl I was talking to," she says from inside her cell. "The one that called you all. She saw it."

C. Miller, standing at Summer's door, looks at me sitting at a nearby table in the common room and raises her eyebrows. *Well?*

Summer can't see me. I shake my head and mouth no.

C. Miller has to sit watch after that, staying near Summer for the rest of the shift, walking her to the interview room down the hall to see a lawyer, taking her to Nurse Batch when she bleeds through her bandage.

Bad Gina gives me grief about it the next morning at breakfast. "I saw you rat that girl out," she says. Weeze nods in agreement, but I don't think her heart's really into giving me a hard time. It's just what Bad Gina expects of her.

"That's so messed up," Bad Gina says. "Getting her in trouble like that when she just came on the unit."

I'm planning to ignore her, but suddenly Fefu grabs Bad Gina's potato patty and squeezes it into a ball.

Bad Gina curses and grabs Fefu's hand. "Let go, you little Mexican," she growls. "I was going to eat that."

Fefu squeezes out a thin stream of grease, then drops the potato ball into Bad Gina's Styrofoam box. The Jelly Sisters laugh so hard they both spit out food.

Bad Gina scoots her chair as far away from me and Fefu as she can, muttering, until she's almost sitting in Weeze's lap.

I hand Fefu a napkin.

"Gracias," I say.

She grins. *"De nada."*

Carla comes on Sunday afternoon for visiting hour.

"Hey, Sadie," she says, sounding almost shy on the other side of the Plexiglas. "Mom says hi and she'll come next week. Lulu says to give you a giant hug and a kiss. And an Eskimo kiss and a butterfly kiss."

She puts her hand up on the glass the same way Mom did when she visited. I put mine up there, too.

"Tell her you did, anyway," I say.

"Yeah." She taps the glass. "This sucks. Mom didn't tell me."

"She tell you about my nose?" I ask.

She nods. "You OK? It doesn't look bad at all. Really. Not even swollen or anything. Just kind of bruised a little bit."

"Thanks," I say. "It's been more than a week. Anyway, *you* look good. Did you cut your hair or something?"

Carla smiles at the compliment, which isn't totally sincere, but not a complete lie, either. She's way too thin, her cheekbones practically cutting through the skin – not heroin-chic thin but not far enough away from it, either. Her hair does look nice, though, cut shoulder length with a braid down the side. I'm pretty sure I've never seen her shirt before, one of those French-looking T-shirts with horizontal black and white stripes. All she needs is a beret.

"I've been working on things," she says. "I even went jogging one day."

I say I think I see a little color in her face.

"Nah," she says. "It was cloudy. Lulu rode her tricycle so we didn't get too far. This is just some blush."

"How'd you get off work today?" I ask. "I thought they had you on the schedule for Sundays."

"I told the new manager I would quit if he didn't let me off. He's such a jerk. He said, did I mean if he didn't *get* me off? So I threatened to report him for sexual harassment and he just laughed and said, Yeah, right, like anybody would believe me. Anyway, he actually even asked me out on a date after, if you can believe that."

"So what did you tell him?"

Her face reddens some more, but it isn't the blush. "We're sort of going out Tuesday night. But it'll be after my AA meeting, and yes, I said after my AA meeting. It will be my third one. Mom's been watching Lulu. She had to cut back on her Target shifts, but she said she thought she could manage OK."

Carla quickly changes the subject before I can give her grief about dating her boss. She says she told Lulu that if she'll start wiping herself when she uses the potty, she can have ice cream for breakfast once a week for the rest of her life.

Lulu is holding out for twice a week.

And Carla tells me about Mom's crazy scheme about moving into Granny's house.

"As if," she says. "God. Mom needs to get out or something. She needs to meet a guy, somebody who can pitch in for rent or move her to a bigger place. She'll go crazy living next door to Dad and all his junk."

"Maybe," I say. It's typical Carla to dismiss Mom's concerns about money, but I have to admit, she does seem to be making an effort, at least a little: jogging with Lulu, AA meetings, changing her look. Though she still hasn't said anything about going back to school or finding a new job.

"So tell me more about Lulu," I say. "Has she been asking about me?"

Carla rolls her eyes. "Oh, no, not much. Only starting when she wakes up in the morning, and ending about when she falls asleep at night. And she won't wear anything to bed but that basketball jersey of yours, either. 'Mommy, where's Aunt Sadie? Mommy, is Aunt Sadie coming over today? Mommy, why can't Aunt Sadie come over today? Mommy, can we go over to Moo-Moo's house and see Aunt Sadie?'"

I laugh but can't help tearing up when she says that.

Carla frowns. "It's probably not healthy, her asking about you all the time."

I quit smiling. "I'm sure she'll get over it soon. She's probably still adjusting to not having me around."

"She's three, Sadie. She just doesn't understand."

I tighten my grip on the phone, fighting the urge to snarl at Carla, to ask her who she thinks she is, lecturing me about Lulu. Lulu is practically as much my daughter as Carla's in a lot of ways – and it kills me to be away from her. And screw Carla, anyway. I wouldn't even be in this mess if it wasn't for her. And I wouldn't be so far away from Lulu.

I keep glaring at Carla in silence. She tries to glare back, but it's no contest. She blinks and looks down.

"My bad," she says finally.

"Maybe we should talk about something else," I suggest. She agrees.

"Hey," she says, brightening. "You haven't seen that girl in here, have you? The one in the newspaper? They said she was in juvie."

"I don't know," I say, though I suspect I know who she's talking about. "They don't let us read the newspaper."

"She killed her mom," Carla says. "It was terrible. Shot her in the face and then just went to work like it was no big deal. That's where they arrested her. They said her boyfriend was involved somehow, like talked her into doing it or whatever. He wasn't there when she shot her mom, but they texted about it. She texted him right after she did it. Her name is Summer. I can't remember her last name, but they got it from the neighbors. The police wouldn't give it because she's a juvenile, but it wasn't hard to figure out, I guess."

I nod. "Yeah, she's in here. She's on my unit."

"No way!" she says. "Did you talk to her?"

"A little. She's pretty messed up and wasn't making a

whole lot of sense. They have her on suicide watch."

Carla's eyes widen. "She tried to kill herself?"

"Not exactly."

Carla says they figure she was high when she shot her mom – with her dad's shotgun. That her parents didn't want her seeing the boyfriend, that he was bad news, into a lot of nasty drugs, that she'd been this nice girl when she was in middle school, until she got with the guy.

"She went all Columbine, I guess. That's what everybody said. You should stay away from her, Sadie," she says, trying to sound like the big sister she hasn't been to me in years.

"I don't think that's going to be a problem," I say. "She spends all her time in her cell. And if she does try anything, they'll put her on lockdown."

"Good," Carla says. "Some people need to be locked up."

She catches herself, realizing what she's just said.

I'm already grinding my teeth in anticipation of the apology. But of course that doesn't stop it from coming.

They let Summer have her clothes back and come out of her cell after a couple of days. Nobody will talk to her, though. Whenever she tries to sit next to anybody, they move. Me included. She corners Fefu once – she must know a little Spanish – but the Jelly Sisters walk over and pull Fefu away. I can't hear what they say to Summer, but she doesn't approach Fefu or anybody else after that.

I don't say anything about what Carla told me, so I'm not sure how the other girls know about Summer, but they all seem to. Maybe they heard something when they called home or maybe there's some kind of secret juvie news channel that I'm not privy to. Nobody talks about her, and after the incident with Fefu, nobody even acknowledges her when she's around.

She's different from everyone else in juvie, or that's how it seems. She reminds me of those dead zones in the Chesapeake Bay I read about, where the red algae grow out of control from all the runoff and fertilizers and pollution and poisons. Dead fish float to the surface. Nothing can live there except the algae. And those dead zones are spreading, merging into one another, threatening to take over the entire bay.

Summer is like that: using up too much of the available oxygen, not leaving enough for the rest of us to breathe. Maybe anybody who kills somebody is like that, especially if it's their own mother.

A couple of days later, Summer disappears somewhere off the unit. Maybe another conference with her lawyer. Or maybe she's gone to court. Or been transferred to adult jail and charged as an adult for the murder. Or escaped. I don't give it much thought. Nobody does. She could be a ghost for all we know or care.

Summer never comes back – not that night or the next day. A janitor comes down on Saturday and mops and scrubs and disinfects her cell, the same as they did when Middle-School Karen left, and soon there's nothing left to confirm the fact that she was ever even here. Nobody tells us anything, of course, and we don't talk about it, though I see all the girls at one time or another staring at her cell door – more interested in Summer now that she's gone than they were during the week she was here. I catch myself doing it, too, though I can't say why. It's as if we're all wondering if she left something behind, some trace, some *aspect*. A blood splatter. A clump of hair. A message carved into the wall. A coded confession. Or maybe it's that darkness she brought in with her, which has mostly lifted but still won't all go away.

CHAPTER 14

In which word gets out

I knew it Monday morning, the third week after the arrest, the minute I walked into school. Kids were staring at me at the lockers.

"What?" I said to this one boy, a little sophomore with floppy blond hair. I recognized him from the junior varsity basketball team. He blinked at me but couldn't hide his grin.

"Nothing," he said nervously. "I was just getting my books."

Maybe I was being paranoid.

But then I ran into Julie Juggins on my way to homeroom and she confirmed it.

"What are people saying exactly?" I asked.

She shook her head. "It's pretty bad."

"Julie . . ."

"They're saying you were dealing drugs. You and your sister. That those guys in your car were your suppliers or something."

I punched the wall outside homeroom. "Shit, shit, shit. Did you tell anybody?" I demanded. "How did people hear about it?"

Julie looked offended and drew back. "You know I didn't. I would never do that."

"Then how did people hear about it?" My phone was practically buzzing itself free from my backpack. I checked, and there were four texts. Five. A couple were from teammates. Two were from Kevin. The one that had just come in was from Coach.

Mrs. Tomzcak came out of homeroom to shut the door. "In or out, girls?" she said.

"In," said Julie.

"Out," I said, turning and running down the hall to the restroom. I was pretty sure I was going to be sick.

I had to work at the car wash after school, so couldn't meet with Coach until later that afternoon. He didn't have an office. The AAU team just had use of the gym at my high school. We sat on the bleachers. The other girls were in the locker room getting dressed for practice.

"You want to explain?" he said, clearly pissed. I hadn't

seen him since the game where I got ejected. He yelled at me a lot for that. I couldn't imagine what he was going to do now.

I didn't want to look at him – I knew I looked guilty, and there was no way he was going to believe me. Plus, since I'd confessed for Carla, I couldn't tell him the truth, anyway. Or not the whole truth. "I messed up," I whispered. "I should have said something, but it's just been this big mess, with lawyers and my mom, and going to court."

"So it's true, then," he said, keeping his voice low, which was the one good thing.

I nodded. "I'm not sure what you heard, but, Coach, the drugs weren't mine. There were just these guys, they had them, and I gave them a ride somewhere. The drugs – it was just pot – it was theirs. They got out of the car and left the pot there for somebody to pick up."

Coach sighed. "So you were just in the wrong place at the wrong time. Is that what you're saying?"

"Sort of like that," I said, desperately wishing I could explain.

"That's it, then," he said, still with the low voice. "You're off the team. First there's what you did to that girl in the game last week, which was inexcusable. Now this. I want you out of here and I mean right now. You can give your uniform to one of the other girls to turn in."

"But, Coach," I said, blinking back a flood of tears, stunned. "I haven't even gone to court yet." As if that mattered. "It's not until Thursday."

Coach just shook his head, letting me know how stupid I sounded, and how pathetic.

Kevin came looking for me a couple of hours later. I was sitting on that limestone outcropping on Government Island, staring out over Aquia Creek at what was left of the sunset. I heard him a good ten minutes before he got there – calling for me and crashing through the underbrush when he lost the trail.

And then, finally, after he'd frightened off all the birds and squirrels and deer and muskrats and beaver and herons and anything else that lived on the island, he found me.

"Hey, Sadie."

I didn't turn around. "Hey."

"Mind if I sit down?"

I scooted over to make room for him on the rock.

"You're all wet," I said. "And muddy."

He pulled off his boots and banged them on the rock. "Yeah. I don't exactly know the dry way to get here through all that swamp. I brought a blanket, though." He held it out to me.

"Did you think I'd want to fool around?" I asked, annoyed. "Is that what you had in mind?"

"No," he said. "God, Sadie. I just thought you might be cold. It's getting dark, you know. Jesus."

"Sorry."

"It's OK." He opened the blanket and tucked it around both of our shoulders. "There."

I'd expected him to be mad at me – for getting arrested, for keeping it a secret, for running off without telling anyone where I was going, for not answering when he kept calling my name just now – but the way he was acting left me feeling helpless suddenly. It felt good to lean against him, and we sat there for half an hour without saying anything else. The last traces of sunset melted out of the sky. There was an early moon, though, and soon everything in the world turned black and silver.

"You want to talk about it?" Kevin asked finally.

I waited until I thought I could speak without choking on the words. "I thought I could just make it all go away," I said, "if I didn't tell anybody, if I did everything exactly right. Like it never even happened. Like I would do my community service but just tell everybody it was for National Honor Society or something. I even thought about going down to the food bank so you and I could work there together. Driving forklifts, loading trucks, all that stuff."

Kevin actually laughed. "They don't let us drive the forklifts. You just stock shelves and go through the donations and organize them and do inventory and help customers."

"Yeah," I said, sagging against him more, leaning my head on his shoulder. "I figured."

He put his arm around me and pulled the blanket tighter around us. "You could have told me," he said. "I mean, I love you, Sadie. I would have been there for you no matter what. Look at me. I'm all wet and everything. I probably have leeches and ticks all over me from wading through that swamp and trying to find my way across your island."

I sat up and stared into his eyes. "Wait. You *love* me?"

He'd never said it before. Not in that way. It had always been just "Love you." Or *lv u* in his stupid texts. But never with the "I."

He got this dumb, quizzical look on his face and shrugged, and smiled. "Of course I do."

I kissed him for a minute, pulled back to study that dumb look some more, to make sure it was for real, then kissed him again, this time deeper, and this time longer.

Mom was mad when I got home late, after curfew, but I didn't care. I was happy and hopeful for the first time in weeks. So I didn't tell her about getting kicked off the team, or about hiding out on Government Island, or about Kevin finding me there and telling me he loved me. I didn't tell her the rest of what he said, either – that he'd skip school on Thursday to come with me to court, even though it meant he'd have to sit out his soccer game that afternoon, and that he'd always, always, always be there for me no matter what. I told myself it wasn't any of her business, but I think really I just didn't want to see her get that look that said, "I'll believe it when I see it."

CHAPTER 15

In which a sleepless Saturday night turns into Sunday morning and there's still no damn coffee

The Saturday night after Summer disappears from Unit Three, I stay up late reading *Holes* in my cell. I feel pretty bad for the hero, Stanley Yelnats, who is a sweet kid, just in the wrong place at the wrong time. I'm surprised they allow the book in the juvie library, since it makes all the kids out to be decent people, while the warden and the guards are the creeps and the criminals. But maybe no one bothers to vet the kids' books.

I still can't sleep after I finish, so I'm awake when they bring in somebody else to Summer's cell. The unit door buzzes open just beyond my cell door, followed by shuffling footsteps and the sound of shackles dropping to the floor. I hear a girl's voice, maybe drunk, protesting: "I'm not going in there. Forget it. I want to go home. Let me go home, damn it. *I mean now!*"

A guard barks at her, and her protests stop. I hear whimpering, then a cell door slamming, then the predictable crying, then nothing.

I get an old song stuck in my head after that for no good reason: "Just Like U Said It Would B," by Sinéad O'Connor, this Irish singer Mom used to listen to. Not that juvie has turned out to be anything like they said it would be – or like I thought it would be.

It keeps on being that kind of night: jangly and disruptive and void of sleep. When they wake us up Sunday morning, I feel pissed off at the world – even more when I remember there won't be any coffee, just as there hasn't been any since I got here. I have a headache before I even crawl off my bunk, and the breakfast doesn't help any, either. It's the same as the day before and the day before that: runny eggs, cold potato patty, dry white toast, grape jelly, fruit cup circa 1980.

At least Bad Gina leaves me alone. So does everybody else. They're too busy sitting around the new girl, who looks hungover but answers their questions anyway. It's the opposite of how they all were with Summer. I try to shut out the chatter but can't help overhearing. There seems to be no getting away from anything in juvie.

Her name is Nikki. She says she goes to River Bend. "Go, Bears."

She says she got into a fight the night before with a girl whose full name seems to be "That Bitch Rhoda."

That Bitch Rhoda showed up at a party where she wasn't invited.

That Bitch Rhoda had her hands all over New Nikki's boyfriend.

That Bitch Rhoda might have got cut, but New Nikki didn't have a knife, so it must have been somebody else who did it, even though New Nikki got charged.

That Bitch Rhoda got what she deserved, whoever might have did it.

That Bitch Rhoda better pray they never let New Nikki out of juvie, swear to God.

For some reason we're given a choice that morning: church or nothing. So we go to church, or rather church comes to us. His name is Reverend Chilton, and he shuffles onto the unit so slowly that I wonder if he came straight from the hospital and will be returning there as soon as we're done. He has a gaunt, angular face, tufts of hair around his ears but none on top of his head, kind eyes, and a rumpled suit that practically swallows him, or what there is of him. He also has a dry cough and keeps apologizing for it.

"Might we make a circle with the chairs?" he asks the Sunday guards. So we sit in a small circle with Reverend Chilton and his worn leather Bible and his fumbling hands, one guard parked at the desk by the door, the other hovering nearby, behind us.

"I should start by offering an apology," Reverend Chilton says, nodding as he speaks. "This is my first time coming out here —"

"Mine too!" chirps New Nikki.

Reverend Chilton nods softly, sympathetically even. The Jelly Sisters glare at New Nikki. New Nikki looks at the floor. Bad Gina rolls her eyes.

Reverend Chilton coughs and smiles. "Anyway, thank you for allowing me to sit and talk with you all this morning. Driving over here – actually while my wife, Glory, was driving me over – I was thinking about a passage from the Gospel of Matthew, which I expect you've all heard, but I'd like to read it if I may."

He fumbles through his Bible until he finds a ribbon marking his page, pauses a little longer to adjust his glasses on the bridge of his nose, then begins.

"When the Son of Man comes in his glory, and all the angels with him, he will sit on his glorious throne."

Reverend Chilton's voice, already soft, drops even lower as he reads, so we have to lean forward to hear.

"All the nations will be gathered before him, and he will separate the people one from another as a shepherd separates the sheep from the goats. He will put the sheep on his right and the goats on his left."

Reverend Chilton glances up to see if we are able to follow along OK. He keeps nodding. I find myself nodding back. He looks for his place, tracing lines with his index finger, and smiles when he finds it.

"Then the Lord will say to those on his right, 'Come, you who are blessed by my Father; take your inheritance, the kingdom prepared for you since the creation of the world. For I was hungry and you gave me something to eat, I was thirsty and you gave me something to drink, I was a stranger and you invited me in, I needed clothes and you clothed me, I was sick and you looked after me, I was in prison and you came to visit me.'"

He pauses again to cough into his handkerchief and apologize.

Then he continues: "The righteous will answer him, 'Lord, when did we see you hungry and feed you, or thirsty and give you something to drink? When did we see you a stranger and invite you in, or needing clothes and clothe you? When did we see you sick or in prison and go to visit you?'

"The Lord will reply, 'Truly I tell you, whatever you did for one of the least of my brothers and sisters, you did for me.'"

Reverend Chilton stops there, though I know there's more to the passage – the part where Jesus condemns the people on his left, the ones that are supposed to be the goats. But Reverend Chilton doesn't seem all that interested in hell, or in eternal damnation, or in scaring anybody.

"I expect I know what you all are thinking," he says. "That this old preacher is coming in here because of that verse, or that one line, really: 'I was in prison and you came to visit me.' You're likely thinking I am suggesting that you all are the least of these, the ones Jesus was talking about, who the righteous felt called to help, because of where you are and why you're here. And certainly many people will view you in that way, and certainly that's understandable. But it's important to also understand that there are others who are, well *leaster*. . . ."

He stops and smiles. "I guess that's not really a word, but maybe it says what I mean.

"I believe that the challenge to care for others, to care for those who have less than we do, to care for those who suffer, is a challenge to all of us. And that includes you all, even in here. Maybe especially in here. Jesus doesn't distinguish. Jesus says it's your responsibility, each and every one of you sitting with me today. And my responsibility. And your guards'. And everyone's in this" – he looks around, maybe to remind himself where he is – "in this *facility*."

"Praise Jesus," New Nikki says, pretty obviously mocking what he's just said.

"Yeah," adds Bad Gina drily. "Praise Jesus."

The Jelly Sisters glare at them both.

Fefu crosses herself, her lip quivering. Reverend Chilton looks slowly around the circle at all of us, not responding to anyone's sarcasm, not even seeming to recognize it in their voices, then ends with his gaze on me. It strikes me in that moment that he might have

Parkinson's disease, because his nodding hasn't stopped the whole time he's been on Unit Three. That's probably why his wife – Glory, I remember – has to drive him over. I wonder what else is wrong with him, what's behind his cough and his frailty.

"Could we bow our heads?" Reverend Chilton asks, and I do. Then he says the Prayer of Saint Francis, which my mom taught Carla and me when we were little and used to go to church.

"Lord, make me an instrument of your peace.
Where there is hatred, let me sow love;
where there is injury, pardon;
where there is doubt, faith;
where there is despair, hope;
where there is darkness, light;
and where there is sadness, joy.

Grant that I may not so much seek
to be consoled as to console,
to be understood as to understand,
to be loved as to love.
For it is in giving that we receive,
it is in pardoning that we are pardoned . . ."

I open my eyes before he finishes. Fefu is crying, quietly at first, then harder. I don't know how much she understands of what Reverend Chilton has said, and maybe she isn't crying about that at all. Maybe it's just having him here, this sweet old man, speaking to us in a warm voice. Reverend Chilton gets up slowly from his chair and shuffles over next to her. Good Gina rouses herself and gives him her seat. He thanks her and puts his arm around Fefu, patting her gently and whispering some things while she buries her face against his coat.

One of the Sunday guards, the one who's been hovering, taps him on the shoulder. "You're not allowed to touch the inmates," she says.

Reverend Chilton tells her it's OK, he'll just be a moment, and lowers his head to whisper some more things to little Fefu.

The Sunday guard taps him again. "It's not OK, sir. You're not allowed. And you won't be allowed back."

"Very well," Reverend Chilton says, straightening himself and patting Fefu one last time. She wipes her eyes but can't stop the tears. Reverend Chilton brushes her wet hair out of her face and tucks it behind her ears and smiles the kindest smile I've ever seen.

I wish it had been me crying.

At lunch that day, New Nikki asks Bad Gina why she's in juvie. "What did you do to end up in here?"

Bad Gina doesn't seem to mind talking about it. "I'd just met this guy, it was the stupidest thing. He said he was going to run in and buy some booze at this liquor store, and would I drive him there in my car, but I guess he had a gun and tried to rob the place. But the manager had a gun, too, so the guy ran off and left me in the car. So I was just sitting there like an idiot when the police came. Plus it turned out it wasn't even his car. They said I had to tell them who the guy was or else I was the one going to jail. I gave them his name but they couldn't find him. They said I'd made it all up and I was protecting him. So here I am. My parents are so pissed off. As if I care. Anyway, I'm out of here soon."

She turns to me with that reptile smile of hers. The story sounds too close to mine to be a coincidence, and I wonder who blabbed to her.

Mom comes again during visiting hour. We've been talking on the phone pretty regularly, so there's not much news for her to share, and not much I want her to know about how things really are in juvie. I can tell something's bothering her, though, and I ask what it is, thinking it's going to be about Carla or Lulu or Dad.

But it's not. "You remember my cousin Becky?" she asks.

"No," I say. "I don't think so."

Mom frowns. "You have to remember her. We visited her that one time, up in Delaware."

I shrug. "If you say so."

Mom gives me a look. "Well, she has breast cancer. They just diagnosed it. She called me yesterday. I might go up there."

Now I feel bad. "Sorry, Mom." I press my hand on the glass. She does, too. We're both silent for a minute.

"And something else," she says, not looking at me now.

"What? Is somebody else sick? Is Dad OK?"

"Yeah, yeah," she says. "Everybody's fine. It's just – I got a call from Dave the other day – that's all."

I blink. Several times. "Dave the magistrate?"

Mom nods. I can see she's worried about my reaction, but I don't really know how I feel about it.

"So are you going out with him?"

Mom's hand slides down the glass divider and ends up lying flat on top of her other hand. "Probably not."

I don't know why she's telling me this. She never discussed it with me before when she used to go out with guys. I want to tell her she deserves to be happy – everybody deserves to be happy – and she should just go out with this Dave already. She shouldn't sit around the house all lonely.

But the truth is I don't want Mom dating anybody. I don't want anything to change on the outside – except for Carla to get her shit together.

"Don't do it," I blurt.

This catches Mom by surprise.

"Don't," I say again. "Guys suck, anyway."

Mom frowns. "Watch your language." She straightens in her visitor's chair. "Anyway, I just wanted to let you know. We don't really need to discuss it any further. I'm not sure why I even brought it up."

* * *

I still have Reverend Chilton on my mind, and I'm feeling guilty about what I said to Mom, so that night I decide to do something for the least of these, who I figure has to be little Fefu. I find an old Chutes and Ladders game on the bookshelf and ask if she wants to play, even though it says "Recommended for ages 3–7." How a little-kid game like that ended up in juvie I have no idea.

Fefu grins as I pull out the board and the little game pieces and the number wheel. I spin first to show her how to do it and walk my guy a couple of spaces. Fefu goes next and lands on the first ladder. I show her how it allows her to move up and ahead, and she gets so excited she actually claps her hands. A couple of turns later, I land on a chute and have to slide down to a lower square. She nods appreciatively and says some things in Spanish, I guess dissecting the finer points of Chutes and Ladders play. She bounces in her chair after each turn as she pulls farther ahead of me, climbing ladders and counting her little guy forward as I keep landing on every chute on the board.

Pretty soon she's a couple of spins away from winning. She keeps bouncing in her chair, as excited as if the guards have just informed her that they're letting her go home.

And then she lands on the longest chute of all, the one that drops from the top of the board all the way back down to the bottom.

She freezes. She stares at the board, looking as if

she might cry or worse. She can't bring herself to move her guy.

"Come on, Fefu," I say cheerfully. "It's just a game."

She shakes her head.

"You have to move your guy," I say, pointing, as if she can't see it for herself.

She refuses.

I reach for it. "Come on," I say. "Don't be a sore loser."

She pouts as I slide her man down the long chute and I think we're done. But we aren't. She curses in Spanish and knocks both our game pieces to the floor. Then she picks up the board, breaks it over her knee, and flings it across the room.

The Sunday guards grab her and drag her to her cell, and that's the end of the game.

The divisions in Unit Three are getting more and more entrenched as the days drag into November. Bad Gina mostly hangs out with New Nikki her first week in juvie, with Weeze sort of hovering at the edge. The Jelly Sisters stick with each other, except when they're raiding other girls' meal boxes. Every day there's some sort of incident between the Jelly Sisters and those other girls, especially Bad Gina. The rest of us try to stay out of the way.

I try checkers with Fefu, and things go well as long as I let her win. I get tired of intentionally losing the games after a while, though, and when I take her last checker, she starts cursing in Spanish and dumps the board, which gets her sent to her cell again. Good Gina and Chantrelle take over the game and play for a while, until one of the Jelly Sisters walks by and "accidentally" bumps their table, knocking over all the pieces. There's some sudden shouting back and forth until the guards intervene, and the next thing I know, the rest of us are being ordered to our cells as well.

Cell Seven has only been crying every other night for a couple of weeks and no longer has to wear her suicide blanket. But she still keeps mostly to herself in her cell. I have no idea what she does in there. She doesn't read. She must just sit there. I guess probably she's on some heavy meds. Lithium, maybe. That's what Bad Gina says, anyway.

One day I happen to be sitting at a table with Bad Gina, something I generally try to avoid. We're playing chess, though I'm distracted, keeping a wary eye on the Jelly Sisters across the room. I'm pretty sure Bad Gina keeps cheating, swiping pawns and nudging her men into different positions when I'm not looking, not that I really care all that much.

Cell Seven wanders out of her cell and sits with us. I think she'll say something, but she doesn't. She just sits.

Bad Gina breaks the silence. "So, yeah, when I get out of here, I'm going to Mexico. Did I mention that before?"

I shake my head. "What's in Mexico?"

She takes my rook with her knight, though I'm pretty

sure she moves an extra space to do it. "You mean besides Mexicans?" she asks. "Me and my boyfriend – we're going to open a café at one of those little beach towns and live down there. Or maybe a shop where you rent scooters and snorkels and stuff. Once I'm out."

"I thought you didn't have a boyfriend," I say, remembering her story about how she ended up in juvie.

She waggles my rook. "I never said that."

I castle with my bishop to protect my queen. "You said you were with some guy who robbed the liquor store."

She clenches her fist around the piece. "I didn't say he was my boyfriend. I didn't even know that guy. I just met him that one time."

I shrug.

Cell Seven scoots her chair close to the table, and close to Bad Gina. "Take me with you?" she whispers.

Bad Gina and I both stare. I've never heard Cell Seven speak before. She's so pale, so washed out, that it's a miracle she doesn't just turn translucent, or vanish altogether, out here in the bright artificial light of the common room.

"I have four hundred dollars," she says. "I can get my mom's bank card, too. I think there's some kind of limit or something, you know, to what you can withdraw or whatever. But still, it's something. I know her code. No kidding."

Bad Gina sighs. "Yeah, yeah. You told me that already."

"I did?" Cell Seven asks. She seems genuinely confused. I'm guessing it's the lithium.

"Yeah," says Bad Gina. "You did. Anyway, can't do it. Sorry."

Cell Seven's eyes rim with tears. "Can't take me with you?"

"No." Bad Gina doesn't look at her anymore.

Cell Seven eases back from the table. "OK, well. I kind of need a nap, anyway."

And just like that she crosses the common room and disappears back into her cell.

"That chick is so messed up," Bad Gina says.

"What's she in for?" I ask. "You never told me."

Bad Gina takes my queen, though there's no way she could have been in position. "Said she killed her friend. Vehicular homicide. Drunk driving. Something like that. But you never know. She could have just made it all up to get sympathy or whatever. People in juvie are all such liars."

A couple of days later, there's a power outage. The electronic doors jam and we're stuck in the gym. Officer Killduff paces nervously, probably going through nicotine withdrawal. He barks at us to grab some floor, which of course we do.

After half an hour, I raise my hand. Officer C. Miller comes over and squats next to me.

"Hey, Sadie."

"Hey," I say. "Any chance I can get up and shoot some baskets?"

C. Miller laughs. "In the dark?"

"There's enough light to see," I say. "Sort of."

She drums her fingers on the hardwood floor and laughs again. "Well, why not? Let me check to see if it's OK."

Seconds later, I hear Officer Killduff: "She wants to *what*?"

I can't hear what C. Miller says back, but I guess it's convincing enough, because she comes back over and says, "Sure."

I'm the only one who gets up at first, the only one who fishes through the bin for a basketball that has the right amount of air, the only one who steps up to the foul line once I find it with just the red emergency exit signs to see by. I launch a couple of clunkers before finding my range, and then hear the most satisfying sound in the world on my next couple of shots: nothing but net. Fefu scoots over closer on the floor so she can watch. She claps every time I make a basket.

Bad Gina comes over then, too, and snatches the ball. Her first shot doesn't even hit the backboard. Neither do the next two. "Too dark in here," she whines.

"Not when I shoot," I say, banking in a twelve-foot jumper.

I toss her the ball. "Let's play one-on-one. Shoot for it from the top of the key."

She misses, and barely touches the ball after that, unless she just happens to graze it with her fingertips while hacking my arm as I keep dribbling past her. When she defends the lane, I go baseline and shoot reverse layups. She tries fouling me, but she's no Jelly Sister and I just shove her off and shoot pull-up jumpers. I can tell she's getting madder and madder, but I don't care, even when she finally gets her hands on the ball – after my last basket – and flings it into the rafters.

Final score: 21–zip. The ball looks stuck for a minute, but then falls. I catch it on one bounce. Fefu cheers.

"God," Bad Gina swears as she stomps off the court. "You're such a basketball dyke."

I keep shooting. Loosened up now and feeling it. Layups, free throws, pull-up jumpers, three-pointers.

C. Miller comes over after another half hour, grabs a rebound, and rims out a shot from the corner. She's so bored I guess she doesn't care what Officer Killduff might say, though I can tell by the way he abruptly stops pacing and crosses his arms that he doesn't like it one bit. I can't actually see his face in the gloomy gym, but know he's glaring at us. I worry that C. Miller will get in trouble later – for fraternizing with inmates or whatever – but don't say anything. I'm happy to have somebody to shoot with who knows what she's doing.

"You still play?" she asks.

"You see it," I say.

"You know what I mean," she says. "Outside. For your school."

I tell her yes, that and AAU ball. "Until I got kicked off the team."

"When did that happen?"

We've been taking turns shooting while we talk, but now I just stand there with the ball. "Guess."

"Right," she says. "Of course." Then she tells me she read my file.

I don't look at her. It's not a conversation I'm interested in having.

"So what happened?" she asks. It's the first time we've really talked in the almost four weeks since the Jelly Sisters broke my nose. "How'd you get mixed up in all that stuff?"

I shoot again – and miss. "Wrong place at the wrong time," I say. "I didn't do anything. It was just this messed-up situation with these guys."

C. Miller has the ball now and dribbles it next to her. "You didn't do anything?" she repeats.

"Yeah," I say. "That's right. I didn't do anything."

She shakes her head. "The guards have a name for girls like you."

"What?" I ask.

"Wrong-Wrong. It's kind of racist. They say it with a fake Chinese accent and make one of those Chinese faces."

"What's it mean?"

"Wrong Place–Wrong Time."

I swipe the ball from her. Not that she's guarding it. "Funny."

"Yeah, well, they call a lot of girls that. I didn't think you'd be one of them, though."

I don't know why I'm letting the conversation even continue.

"Look," she says. "I don't mean to get all preachy. But you went to the party, didn't you?"

"Yeah. So?"

"And they were doing drugs there. Drinking beer and stuff. And you let those boys in your car, didn't you?" She doesn't wait for answers. "So it sounds to me like you didn't listen to that voice in your head that tells you when something's a bad idea, and that you should bail."

I'm getting irritated. "So what's your point?"

She swipes the ball back. "I'm just saying."

"Right," I say, past irritation and all the way into annoyed. "You want to know what's a bad idea?"

She shoots from the top of the key and makes it. "What's that?" she asks.

"This conversation."

I'm about ready to throw the ball across the court and walk away, but C. Miller asks if I want to play Horse, as if we've been talking about something else all this time. The weather. The WNBA. Shoes.

We play three games in quick succession, and I beat her every time, neither of us talking except to call out letters when one of us misses. I think about letting her win one, but I'm still too annoyed. Anyway, it isn't like playing checkers with Fefu. If C. Miller wants to beat me, she's going to have to do what I'd tell anybody who isn't good enough: get better.

Minutes like that – when I feel full of myself – don't last long. Sooner or later, usually sooner, this deadening quality creeps back into juvie and falls over everything, infects everything, smothers everything. Especially when you have somebody like C. Miller reminding you about how bad you screwed up and how you should have known better. But even without that, just when you start to feel good about your life because of some little thing that might go well, there are fifty other reminders about where you are and where you're going to be for a long time, and how you got here and what everybody back home thinks about you now, and will probably think about you for the rest of your life.

There goes that girl Sadie. You know about her, right?

I read in the *Washington Post* this story about the dangers of the Internet. It focused on this girl who was just starting college. Ten years earlier, the *Post* had done an article about her having ADHD and how most of the kids who were diagnosed with it were boys but more and more of the time it was girls, and she was one of them, etc. Now, suddenly, as she was just about to leave for her freshman year, it occurred to her that anytime anybody googled her – like some boy in college who might want to ask her out – the first thing they would find out was about her having ADHD.

At least my juvie record won't go online. It's all supposed to be confidential. But that isn't much consolation.

Not really. In a small town like ours, people don't need the Internet or Google. They just know.

Reverend Chilton doesn't come back on Sunday. I'd been looking forward to seeing him again and feel sadder than I should from missing somebody I've only met once. The guards turn the TV to something called the *Hour of Power*, which is an evangelical megachurch with a smarmy preacher. Carla is supposed to come during visiting hours, since Mom came the Sunday before, but she never shows up. I call that night when we get phone privileges, but she doesn't answer. I hope she's at AA or somewhere with Lulu with her phone off. I pray that she is.

I must still look bummed out the next day, because C. Miller asks me what's up when she comes on duty. I'm sitting alone in the common room, and for some reason I just start talking – about all the druggies Carla works with, about how she's supposed to be cleaning up her act, about Lulu, and how I'm worried Carla's not taking care of her right. It all comes out in a rush, and I feel out of breath when I stop.

C. Miller is quiet for a minute, nods as I guess she thinks about what I just said, then asks if I'd like her to check on Carla.

"You'd do that?" I ask.

She nods. "Yeah. I was kind of a jerk to you last week about you getting busted and everything."

"Nah," I say. "You were probably right. Partly right, anyway."

C. Miller nods again. "So your sister. She's at that Friendly's near the hospital?"

"Yeah."

She gets up from the table. Guards aren't supposed to sit next to inmates for more than a couple of minutes. They're supposed to keep moving, like sharks. I don't know what to make of C. Miller's offer, besides just being grateful. And wondering, as nice as she is – way too nice for juvie – how she ever got to be a guard in the first place.

CHAPTER 16

In which I go to court

I wore a blue sundress and let Mom fix my hair. She did my makeup, too, though when she left the room, I wiped most of it off. Carla was late getting to the house – she had to drop Lulu off at day care, but that wasn't really an excuse and Mom let her know about it.

"Mom, quit yelling at her," I said, handing Carla a tissue. I knew Carla wanted me to console her, but I'd gotten immune to her tears these past few weeks.

"Can we just go already?" I said, grabbing the car keys. "I'm pretty sure you're not supposed to be late for court."

None of us talked on the way. Kevin was supposed to meet us there, but I'd tried calling him a couple of times that morning and he hadn't answered. I kept telling myself not to worry; he'd been so sweet and supportive the day he found me on Government Island – of course he'd be there.

I didn't see his car when we arrived.

"Maybe he parked down the street," Carla said. I'd finally told her and Mom the night before that Kevin was coming.

"Yeah," I said. "This parking lot is really small."

Mom shook her head.

"Come on," Carla said, touching my arm. "He's just running a little late."

A bald, heavyset deputy sat on a stool next to a body scanner just inside the Juvenile and Domestic Relations building. "Anything metal, put in the tray," he said, sliding a small bin across the counter at us. "No cell phones allowed. If you're carrying your cell phone, take it back out and leave it in your car."

Mom and Carla waited while I ran back outside to get rid of our phones. I tried Kevin one more time. His voice mail was full; I couldn't even leave a message.

Mr. Ferrell, my lawyer, had a couple of other clients inside and kept scurrying from one to the other, popping in and out of a small room off to the side of the courtroom doors. We were still waiting in the foyer two hours after my case was scheduled to be heard. Mom read a book, or pretended to. She seemed to be stuck on one page. Carla closed her eyes and sat like that until I thought she'd fallen asleep. I elbowed her. "What?" she said. "I was practicing meditation."

"Since when do you meditate?" I asked.

She closed her eyes again. "I don't know. I read about it somewhere. You should try it."

I actually did for a while – tried deepening my breath, clearing my mind, all that meditation stuff. It didn't work. I looked up nervously every time someone came through the scanner and into the foyer, still hoping it was Kevin.

Mr. Ferrell finally ushered me and Mom and Carla into the consultation room. He seemed flustered. He loosened his badly tied tie and unbuttoned the top button on his dress shirt. I saw sweat stains when he took off his coat.

"OK," he said. "There's been a complication. No big deal. Just a complication. Judge Scott is still out sick, so there's a substitute judge. His name is Judge Cannon, and he's from King George County. He's reviewing the agreement we worked out for community service. That's all. But everything else is the same. We'll go in; we'll sit at the table up front." He indicated himself and me. "Mrs. Windas," he said to Mom, "you and your other daughter here, y'all will sit with the other observers. There won't be any witnesses called. This is all pro forma. Everything's already worked out. Sadie pleads guilty; Judge Cannon says a few words – kind of a lecture is what it is, about being sure Sadie takes advantage of this opportunity, this second chance, et cetera. Then he'll pronounce the sentence. Then we go out to see the clerk of the court and sign some papers. We'll have to wait some more for that. And then Sadie can go on to school and finish up her day. You all can. Any questions?"

Yeah, I wanted to say. *I have a question. Where's Kevin? He said he'd be here. He promised me. And why are you so nervous if you're sure everything's still going to be OK?*

I shook my head instead. "No. I'm good."

He smiled and squeezed my arm. Then he shook hands with Mom. The way he checked out Carla, I thought he might try to get her number. Except for her red eyes, she actually looked nice. She'd taken out her nose ring and most of her earrings, fixed her hair, and put on a short black skirt and a nice blouse.

The kid whose case was before mine had on a Big Johnson T-shirt. Mom and I couldn't get over it. He must have just shaved his head that morning because there was a streak of dried blood just behind his left ear. His parents – I assumed they were his parents – were dressed up, though: gray pantsuit on her; brown coat and tie for him. When the bailiff called them into the courtroom, they zombied across the waiting area and disappeared through the double doors, looking more bored than worried.

I figured the more kids who went in before the judge

looking like him, the better it would be for someone like me, who dressed up. Carla started bunching up her skirt, nervously pinching at the fabric until I stopped her. I didn't want anything wrinkled. I wanted us to be perfect. I even asked Mom in a whisper to straighten Mr. Ferrell's tie for him, but she wouldn't do it.

The Big Johnson kid's parents came back out of the courtroom half an hour later – without him. Their faces were drained and blank. I wanted to grab them and ask what happened. *What is it like in there?* The bailiff called my name just then – "Windas?" – and we followed him inside.

The courtroom was tiny. There were four rows of benches that looked like church pews. Mom and Carla slid into one of those. Mr. Ferrell and I continued past them to the defendant's table in front, below a raised platform with a massive desk and an elevated witness stand. On TV shows, they're always saying, "You may approach the bench." I'd always had this little-kid idea that there would be an actual bench up there somewhere, but there wasn't. A court stenographer sat at a smaller desk next to the judge's. Another lawyer – I assumed he was the prosecutor – had stacks of law books and folders and yellow legal pads spread out on a table next to ours. Mr. Ferrell pointed me to a chair, then stepped over to speak to the other lawyer. They talked about football.

The judge was in his chambers, so we all waited. It was noon; he was probably eating lunch while he reviewed the plea agreement. My stomach growled, which surprised me, since I wasn't the least bit hungry. I glanced back to check on Mom, and she managed to smile, though it looked more like she was grimacing. Carla gave me the thumbs-up, but she was crying again and I was already wishing she hadn't come. A few people who had nothing to do with my case sat in pews in the back. None of them were Kevin. The door cracked open and my heart leaped, but it was just the bailiff.

I stared at my hands. They were dried and cracked, and I could have really used some lotion. I knew Mom would have some, but she was too far away for me to ask.

The judge finally came in, and the bailiff said, "All rise." He called court into session, also just like on TV, and then read my name and case number off a clipboard. The judge adjusted his robe, and then we all sat. He banged his gavel. The courtroom was as quiet as death.

He cleared his throat. "Sadie Windas?"

My lawyer stood and motioned for me to stand, too.

"Yes, sir. Your Honor."

Judge Cannon looked down the slope of his nose at me for a long minute. He had a squarish head, a throw rug of black-and-gray hair, and long, low rectangles of gray mustache.

"You're pleading guilty," he said, "to distribution of a controlled substance?"

I nodded. Mr. Ferrell whispered that I needed to say it out loud.

"Yes, sir. That's correct."

Judge Cannon kept staring. He hadn't blinked once. "There is an agreement here," he said, holding a thin sheaf of papers between his thumb and forefinger. "In consideration of your guilty plea, and your academic record, and your part-time job, and your participation in high-school sports. The agreement calls for a suspended sentence of six months, two hundred hours of community service, drug-counseling class, and random drug testing. Do you understand these conditions?"

"Yes, sir."

"If you violate any of the terms of this plea agreement, you do understand that you will serve the entire six-month sentence in juvenile detention?"

"Yes, sir." My legs were trembling. I wished I could sit. But at least it was almost over.

"Fine," Judge Cannon said. "We'll just need one more thing from you and then we'll proceed to sentencing."

My lawyer dropped his folder on the defendant's table. "Your Honor? I'm sorry? What?"

The prosecutor echoed him: "Your Honor?"

Judge Cannon didn't bother to look at either of them. "I said we'll just need one more thing. We'll need the names of the suppliers. Miss Windas will have to give the court that information. Otherwise I will not approve the plea agreement."

"But Your Honor," Mr. Ferrell stammered, "she's already told the detectives she doesn't know their names.

They were men she met at a party. She made an admittedly foolish decision to drive them to a rendezvous with drug buyers. She compounded that one bad decision when she agreed to wait in the car with the drugs for the buyers. But that was the extent of her involvement."

Judge Cannon scoffed. "That story is not plausible."

"Judge?" the prosecutor interjected. "If I may?"

Judge Cannon said no, he may not. Then he shifted his gaze back to me. "Miss Windas, you have one opportunity to make things right, and this is that opportunity. You will give up the names, or you will spend the next six months in juvenile detention. It's that simple."

I couldn't speak. My heart raced. I opened and closed my hands. I turned to look at Mom and Carla again, but Judge Cannon stopped me.

"You will face the bench, Miss Windas," he snapped. "And you will provide the names. Now."

I waited for Carla to stand up and confess. I waited for Mom to set the judge straight on a few things. I waited for this surreal moment to end. I waited for magic, a miracle, deus ex machina.

"I'm sorry," I said, my throat so dry that it seemed unlikely that the judge even heard me. But he did, and it made him even angrier.

"Would you be sorry if you hadn't been caught, Miss Windas? Are you at all sorry that the two men you refuse to name are still out there selling drugs, jeopardizing futures, ruining lives?"

"Yes, sir," I rasped. "I *am* sorry—"

He cut me off. "No, Miss Windas. I don't think that you are. But I'm going to do you a favor. I'm going to give you ample time to contemplate your actions and to discover at least a modicum of genuine remorse. You don't need to worry about that. Congratulations. You won the sweepstakes. I will give you the weekend to put your affairs in order. You will surrender to the juvenile detention facility in Stafford on Monday. You will serve a sentence of no less than six months, after which you will be on probation, perform your community service, and pay all costs to this court of this proceeding and of your supervision."

He scribbled something on the sheaf of papers, then glared at me once more. "You should be ashamed of yourself, Miss Windas."

He looked past me to where Carla and Mom were sitting. "Your family should also be ashamed."

He slammed his gavel again and told me I was dismissed.

CHAPTER 17

In which everything happens so fast that Mrs. Simper and I need slow-motion video to sort it out

On Thanksgiving they give us processed-turkey sandwiches and cranberry juice for dinner. Nobody talks much, and we're all pretty quiet on the phones that night. Lulu's already asleep by the time I get to call, which makes me sad, and annoyed that Carla and Mom didn't keep her up to at least say hi. I don't talk to them for very long.

That general quiet on the unit, once it takes hold, doesn't let up – through the weekend and into the following week. Everybody seems to be on edge. Maybe it's missing our families over the holiday. Maybe, for some, it's not having a family to miss.

Chantrelle goes to court that next Thursday.

We're all in the common area outside our cells watching afternoon TV when she comes back. It's one of those shows where people are reunited with long-lost family members. The Jelly Sisters are actually tearing up. Bad Gina snorts, and New Nikki giggles; Weeze tries to shush them. I edge my chair as far away as I can.

We all kind of pretend not to notice Chantrelle at first. Nobody likes people seeing them in shackles.

Once the guards let her loose, Chantrelle grabs a chair near mine, drags it ten feet away, slams it down, and throws herself into it. Good Gina carries a chair over next to her.

"I ain't going," Chantrelle says, loud enough for everyone to hear.

Good Gina whispers something back to her.

"I don't give a shit," Chantrelle says back. "I ain't going. They can kiss my black ass. I ain't going to no juvie prison in no Roanoke Rapids or Applemattox or anywhere."

Good Gina keeps whispering. Officer Killduff, who has been writing something in the daily log, fixes his steely gaze on Chantrelle but doesn't say anything.

She stands up and paces. "I told them it wasn't me. I told them it was another Chantrelle. I told them I didn't do it. I *told* them."

Good Gina follows her, laying her hand on her friend's arm. But Chantrelle is too agitated and shrugs her off. "I ain't going, and I want to see somebody try to make me."

Officer Killduff stands up at the guard table, still staring hard at Chantrelle.

She glares back him. "What you looking at, anyway?" she demands.

Good Gina grabs Chantrelle's arm again.

"She's just upset," Good Gina says. "She'll be all right. She doesn't mean anything."

Officer Killduff keeps his gaze fixed hard on Chantrelle.

Chantrelle shrugs off Good Gina's hand. "Hell, I don't," she says. "I mean every word I say. I ain't going to no juvie prison. Y'all can all go to hell."

Officer Emroch, who's on duty today instead of C. Miller, returns from wherever she's been and walks over to the guard desk. Officer Killduff speaks to her quietly, then lifts his walkie-talkie. It squawks, and he mutters something. Then he stands.

Both officers step toward Chantrelle. Officer Killduff points at her chair. "Time to take a seat, Chantelle. You know you're not allowed to raise your voice or curse on this unit. You know that."

Chantrelle stands her ground. "It's Chan*trelle*," she snarls. "It ain't Chan*telle*. It's Chan*trelle*. How many times I got to tell you that?"

Officer Killduff narrows the distance between them without seeming to actually move. "Chan*trelle*, Chan*telle*. I don't care what it is – you sit yourself down and you do it right now or else you're going in the restraint chair. That what you want?"

Chantrelle backs away but keeps talking. "What I want is you can shove a restraint chair up your ass 'cause I ain't sitting for nobody that can't say my name right."

Officer Emroch speaks this time. "Chantrelle. I know your name. We all know your name. We just need you to calm down and sit like Officer Killduff said. That's all."

"Uh-uh," Chantrelle spits back. "He got to say it, not you." She clenches her teeth and returns her glare to Officer Killduff. "Him. He got to say it, and he got to say it right."

Officer Killduff actually seems to smile in response, his mouth a narrow slit, edging up at the corners. He reaches suddenly for Chantrelle's chair – the only thing standing between him and her – but she's quicker. In one motion she snatches it away and lifts it over her head.

Everything and everybody freezes – for a second, an instant, a breath. Chantrelle's eyes flare wider and wider, showing white all the way around her irises. She must already know that she's gone too far and that there is no getting back to where she was before, no taking back what is already done, no changing what is about to happen.

"You want it?" she says, already beginning her swing. "It's yours."

The chair somehow misses Officer Killduff but hits Officer Emroch dead-on, sending her sprawling across the room and into a wall.

Officer Killduff lunges at Chantrelle and tackles her

hard to the floor, but she's stronger than she looks, and angry, and she fights back, thrashing wildly and screaming and cursing.

"Grab some floor!" Killduff shouts at the rest of us as he struggles with Chantrelle. "Grab some God damn floor!"

I drop right away, but there is a flash of something next to me, a sudden movement, a shout, something to do with the Jelly Sisters, and then more bodies crash into one another, more chairs fly, more people yell and scream. I scramble under a table and press against the wall. Little Fefu sits frozen on the floor near me but still in the way, so I crawl out and drag her back under the table. Good Gina curls into a ball next to us, whimpering.

Chantrelle somehow manages to pull away from Officer Killduff and hurls herself toward the door, but he grabs her leg, tackling her again. She goes down hard and cracks her head on the floor near me and Good Gina and Fefu. Somebody knocks a table over on Officer Killduff. He pushes it off, but instead of coming after Chantrelle turns his attention on whoever else is fighting.

I should stay where I am, out of the way, but Chantrelle's lying on the floor, blood pooling behind her head and her eyes rolling back. I slip out from under our table, not sure exactly what my plan is except maybe to at least protect her from getting hurt even worse from the other fighting. Just as I get to her, though, the unit door buzzes open and several more officers storm in with batons drawn.

"Get her!" Officer Killduff yells to them from some other part of the room. "Get her!"

They must think he means me, because the next thing I know, two of them are on top of me and Chantrelle, shouting, twisting my arms behind my back, then lifting me up and slamming me into a restraint chair they brought in with them.

"I was just trying to help!" I yell, but they ignore me. Two of them hold me down, practically sitting on me, as a third fastens belts around my arms and legs and waist and torso and finally my head. I can't move but keep yelling. "Just see if Chantrelle's OK! She hit her head! See if she's OK!"

And then, as quickly as everything started, it stops.

Officer Killduff and a couple of other officers have the Jelly Sisters sitting back-to-back on the floor, their hands bound behind them, scowling and muttering to each other. Another officer has Chantrelle in handcuffs and already sitting up, though obviously woozy. Officer Emroch must be behind me, because I can't see what's happening with her. Somebody else – I can't tell who – is lying on the floor across the room, half-hidden by a pile of tables, moaning. Bad Gina sits in a chair nearby, one eye swollen, blood crawling down her chin from her nose. New Nikki sits next to her, looking freaked out, shifting her gaze from the blood on Bad Gina to whoever is on the floor. Fefu and Good Gina still huddle under the table, where I should have stayed.

And then I see Cell Seven. In the sudden calm, she walks out of her cell, kneels to pick up something small and metal, and slashes her wrist.

Nurse Batch comes right away, the paramedics five minutes after that. They manage to stop Cell Seven's bleeding and whisk her off Unit Three on a stretcher. Another paramedic team comes in as they're leaving and goes immediately to work on Officer Emroch and Chantrelle and Bad Gina – though all Bad Gina needs is an alcohol wipe and an ice pack. Mrs. Simper, the warden, comes onto the unit and confers with Officer Killduff for a while, then she kneels down beside Officer Emroch and says some things to her. She looks carefully around the room at the Jelly Sisters, still sitting in handcuffs back-to-back on the floor; at the fallen girl, who is still unconscious and who I finally realize is Weeze; at a subdued Chantrelle; at the chaos of tables and chairs; at everybody else; at me.

I can wiggle my fingers, but that's about it. The rest of my body is numb, and I shiver with claustrophobia so bad it takes every ounce of self-control I have to keep from screaming.

A couple of officers lead Fefu and Good Gina back to their cells. Officer Killduff and another officer drag the Jelly Sisters to their cells as well and lock them in. Bad Gina, still holding an ice pack, her face cleaned up now, walks over to hers unescorted. She winks at me just before she pulls the cell door shut behind her.

Nurse Batch comes over, I guess to make sure I'm still breathing. She checks my pulse and gives me water from a plastic bottle with a straw, though it sloshes all over me when she pulls it abruptly away. She glares at me.

"And to think I fixed your face," she rasps.

"I didn't do anything," I say, pointlessly I'm sure. The strap across my chest is so tight it's hard drawing enough breath to speak.

She shakes her head. "Like I haven't heard that before."

Chantrelle has a concussion. The paramedics put on a bandage and wrap a lot of gauze around her head. After a while, they stuff her into a second restraint chair and wheel her somewhere off the unit. All the fight has long since gone out of her and she never looks around again and she never says another word.

They take Officer Emroch and Weeze off the unit on stretchers.

Other officers I haven't seen before are milling around, talking to Officer Killduff. C. Miller even shows up, I guess working a late shift or called in for the emergency. After another half an hour, she comes over and lets me out of the restraint chair. I'm surprised at how badly I tremble when I stand up. I can barely walk to my own cell, not that I'm in any hurry to be there.

"Don't get too comfortable," C. Miller says after I stagger over to my bunk. "They might not be done with you yet."

I'm too tired to be outraged by the unfairness of it all.

I didn't do anything except try to help somebody. I slump against the cell wall and pull up my blanket. As much as I want to lie all the way down, I don't want to fall asleep if they're just going to wake me up again in a little while for whatever is coming next. Plus my head is still reeling from the suddenness of the violence and, just as quickly, the end. How could everything have happened so fast? Chantrelle I understand. She'd been sentenced to long-term detention in a juvie prison in another part of the state. The Jelly Sisters must have used the chaos of Chantrelle's meltdown as an opportunity to attack Bad Gina and Weeze, though I didn't exactly see it. And then there was Cell Seven. I blanch, horrified all over again as I remember her, standing just outside her cell, expressionless, cutting into her wrist as calmly as if she were blowing seeds off a dandelion.

C. Miller comes to get me an hour later. "Come on," she says. "They want to talk to you."

"Where?" I ask, pushing myself up cautiously, stiff and sore from the restraint chair and from being roughed up by the guards.

She looks over her shoulder, then back at me. Then she shrugs. "It's to the warden's. She wants to see you. I'm taking you to her office."

She puts me in handcuffs but not shackles, and I'm not sure what to make of that. One minute they're slamming me into a restraint chair, and the next I'm practically walking free out of the unit.

I want to ask C. Miller but am still feeling too cowed

by all that's happened to test the limits of my relationship with her. She probably has a million questions about what-all happened on the unit, and why I was in the restraint chair, but she doesn't ask, either.

Mrs. Simper is alone in her office and has her back to us, studying a video monitor. She doesn't turn around, so C. Miller and I just stand there for a good five minutes.

Finally, without looking at us, Mrs. Simper says, "Officer, can you pull a chair over next to me for Miss Windas to sit in? Thanks. And you can just wait over there by the door, in that other chair over there."

C. Miller pulls a chair over as instructed, but I'm not about to sit down until Mrs. Simper directly tells me to.

She presses a button that freezes a grainy image of our unit on her video monitor and then pats the chair seat next to her. "It's OK, Sadie. Go ahead and sit. You have permission."

She still hasn't looked at me.

"Now let's watch this together," she says. She hits PLAY, and everything that happened that afternoon happens again on the monitor, only from the vantage point of a camera mounted to the opposite wall from where I'd been sitting: the officers closing in on Chantrelle, everybody crowding away, Officer Killduff trying to grab the chair, Chantrelle throwing it, Officer Emroch going down. And then pandemonium. Too much happens too fast, though, and I can't follow it at all. Mrs. Simper slows it down, and some things are clearer this time: Officer

Killduff tackling Chantrelle, then tables and chairs and bodies flying, and a body lunging away from Killduff, and then hitting the floor, and another body crawling out from a pile of tables. Most of what's going on is still a blur, though.

Mrs. Simper backs it up and slows it down even more. "There," she says, pointing. "You see that? The two black girls, they're attacking the two white girls." She means the Jelly Sisters and Bad Gina and Weeze. She takes the video backward and forward a couple more times and finally I see it: one of the Jelly Sisters taking a swing at Bad Gina, the other slamming Weeze against a wall and hitting her over and over in the face until Weeze drops to the floor. Bad Gina gets hit a few times but manages to slip away; Weeze doesn't.

Mrs. Simper stops the video, then starts it up again on the slowest setting. "Now look at this part. That's the girl who started everything. Chantrelle Jones. She hits the floor there. That must have been where she got a concussion. And that's you. I had the hardest time figuring out what you were doing. The officers said you attacked her when she was down and they had to pull you off. But what it looks like to me is you were trying to help her. Is that accurate?"

I nod. "Yes, ma'am."

"I see," says Mrs. Simper.

Not "Thanks," or "Now I understand," or "So sorry the officers put you in restraints."

Just "I see."

Mrs. Simper isn't through with the videos. There are two others, shot from other angles in the unit, and she studies them over and over as well. I just sit there next to her as she hits PLAY and REWIND, PLAY and REWIND, jotting notes on a legal pad, and only occasionally stopping to ask me questions.

"What's going on right there?" she asks at one point, tapping her pen on the monitor at Fefu, sitting on the floor as the fights rage around her, and then being dragged by me under the table.

I tell her.

"I see," she says again.

Someone calls. Mrs. Simper pauses the video to answer the phone, but her side of the conversation doesn't reveal much, and neither does her face.

"I see," she says to whoever called.

"And the officer's husband?"

"And the prisoners?"

"No arterial damage?"

"Good."

"And the other one?"

"I see."

"We'll fax over the orders in the morning."

"Yes, that's procedure."

"Yes, shackles and van."

"Yes, Snowden."

That reference I do understand. Snowden is where they put mental patients, next to the hospital. I assume they're talking about Cell Seven.

When Mrs. Simper hangs up, I ask if everybody is OK.

She looks at me as if I've spoken in an unfamiliar language. "Do you know why any of these other girls are in here, Sadie?" she asks.

I shrug. "I know what some of them told me. Chantrelle said they had the wrong Chantrelle for grand-theft auto. She said Good Gina shot her boyfriend in the hand, and the Jelly Sisters stole some checks."

It occurs to me that Mrs. Simper might not know the nicknames, but if she's confused she doesn't let on. "Nothing is ever what it seems to be in here," she says. "No one is ever who they present themselves to be. That's a given. So the first thing you give up when you walk through these doors is trust. I know your story, or the version of it in your file. But that's not the full story, is it?"

"No, ma'am," I say.

Mrs. Simper nods. "Do you know why we make things so severe in here, Sadie?"

I shrug. "To scare kids so they don't screw up again?"

"No," she says. "The young people we see in here – most of those you'll meet – they've been here before, and we expect to see them again."

"Then, why?" I ask, though I suppose I already know the answer. Didn't I just see why, in the explosion of violence with Chantrelle, and what followed with the Jelly Sisters, and then Cell Seven, all of it happening in a minute, a couple of minutes, followed by hours studying the security tapes to try to figure everything out?

"There is a little girl," Mrs. Simper says, "the youngest we have at the moment, who is ten years old. She's here because she wanted a bicycle and so she took one from a young man who happened to be riding by. She beat him with a metal pipe. He was in a coma for three days."

This knocks the air out of me. "You mean Fefu? The Hispanic girl on our unit? You mean her?"

"I mean," Mrs. Simper says, articulating her words carefully, "that as noble as your *instincts* may be to help, it is not your job to help. It is your job to follow orders. For you, for everyone incarcerated, there is nothing else. You were ordered to get down on the floor. That is what you should have done, and that is *all* you should have done. That is all you will do in the future. You will not rescue, or help, or save." She pauses. "You will do what you are told to do."

My face burns with anger and embarrassment.

"Is that clear?" she asks quietly.

I can't speak, afraid that the voice that comes out of my throat won't be mine.

"Is that clear?"

On the way back to my cell, C. Miller tells me she went by Friendly's to see Carla.

"Was she high?" I ask, almost weak with gratitude to have C. Miller be nice again.

"No," C. Miller says. "Just busy. I was only planning on checking her out, but we started talking and I told her I knew you. She was pretty suspicious. Kept looking around like she thought I was there to arrest her."

"Sounds like Carla," I say.

We stop so C. Miller can radio to have a set of doors opened.

"We got past it," she says. "She said to tell you she has an application in at Victoria's Secret."

I laugh. "She can clean up pretty well if she puts her mind to it," I say, remembering how nice she looked in court and the first time she visited me in juvie.

We're standing outside the door to Unit Three, but C. Miller doesn't radio for the door just yet. "I probably shouldn't have done it," she says, "but we're having a play-date on Saturday, just going to the park."

"You and Carla?"

She laughs again. "No, stupid. Me and Carla and her little girl and my little girl. LaNisha."

"You have a kid?" I say. "You never told me that."

She sniffs. "You think you're the only one with a life? Anyway, like I said, I probably shouldn't have, but we just got talking about our daughters and they're both the same age and everything and then we made the playdate. I don't know too many moms my age. It was kind of nice to talk to somebody else that's a single parent."

"Huh," I say, taking it all in.

C. Miller gets on her walkie-talkie, and the door buzzes and clicks. She holds it open, but pauses before ushering me through.

"She asked me if you're still mad at her. She didn't say about what. Anyway, I didn't know what to tell her about that."

"Yeah," I say. "Me neither."

I'm exhausted but can't fall asleep. I lie on my bunk, staring up at the ceiling and that stuttering fluorescent light. My stomach rumbles – I haven't eaten since lunch, and not very much then – and I have my own videos playing over and over in my head: of Chantrelle, the chair, the officers, the violence and the blood, the Jelly Sisters, the way one kept hitting a defenseless Weeze, the unshakable feeling I have that Bad Gina was responsible for what happened. When I close my eyes, I see her winking at me, as if I'm somehow responsible, too – only how can that be? I didn't do anything except try to help Chantrelle, and only for a few seconds, before they pulled me away from her and put me in the restraint chair.

I sit up on my bunk and bang the back of my head on the wall, though nowhere near as hard as Summer did the day she came onto Unit Three. I do it again, as if just like that I can banish all these thoughts. I expect it to make a noise, but the thick wall absorbs the sound. And that's when I realize something is different: I no longer hear Cell Seven's crying, that terrible lullaby she's sung half the nights since I've been in juvie.

Now that it's gone, I almost miss it.

CHAPTER 18

In which Mom wants the truth and I want Kevin, but it's too late for either one

Mom didn't even wait until we got to the car before she started in on Carla. "What have you done? God damn it! This was not supposed to happen!"

Carla was already bawling so hard that she couldn't have answered if she wanted to.

Mom had already chewed out the lawyer, Mr. Ferrell, who couldn't stop apologizing and blaming the substitute judge and backing away until he was trapped against a wall and the bailiff had to come over and pull Mom away.

I didn't say a word. Just signed something they gave me to sign at the clerk's window. Mom stuffed a copy in her purse and stormed out the door past the deputy on his stool, past the metal detector. I thought I was going to have to stop her from storming into traffic.

Mom kept raging at Carla. Carla kept sobbing. I wanted to jump out of the car. *Six months!* It felt like somebody had just died. Like when Dad moved out. Like when we buried Granny.

The streets blurred past. Mom kept yelling. Carla kept crying. I kept thinking about Kevin, about why he hadn't come like he'd promised. The car felt claustrophobic, so I rolled down the window, but it still wasn't enough air. I panicked at the thought of being locked up in a cell. *Six months . . .*

"Shut up!" I screamed suddenly, startling us all. "Carla, stop your stupid crying! And Mom, leave Carla alone! We told you what happened! Blame the judge! Blame me! Just shut up, both of you!"

Mom turned in the driver's seat and slapped me, swerving onto the shoulder of the road.

"Great!" I yelled as she righted the car. "Thanks. That felt great. Want to do it again? Huh?" I slapped myself. "There! Saved you the trouble." I slapped myself again, hard. Mom grabbed my arm and held it, but at least she shut up. And Carla stopped crying. A powerful silence took over the car. I couldn't see. I couldn't speak. I couldn't feel anything.

Mom drove us home, one hand on my arm the entire way.

* * *

I was the first one out of the car, and practically sprinted inside, into my room. I tore off my blue sundress and threw it on the bed. Pulled on jeans and boots and a sweatshirt. Grabbed my helmet and key and tore out of the side door so I wouldn't have to see Mom and Carla in the kitchen. I threw the blue tarp off my bike, jammed on my helmet, and jumped up to bring my full weight onto the kick-starter. It caught the first time. Seconds later, I roared out onto Clearview – a gray sedan had to hit the brakes – and took off in the direction of Route 1.

My rear tire fishtailed through gravel a couple of miles later when I turned off Route 1 onto Mountain View Parkway. I nearly lost the road but managed to straighten out by the time I hit the first curve. I knew exactly where I was going: to the soccer field behind the high school.

I spotted Kevin's car in student parking and squealed to a stop, then hopped off my bike and kicked the driver's-side door of his stupid, smelly Fiesta until it was good and dented.

I didn't bother to turn off my motorcycle when I got to the soccer field. I just sat on the sideline and watched Kevin trying to pretend he was so totally into their practice that he didn't know I was there. He was distracted and kept screwing up. His coach kept yelling at him. Even his teammates got on him. I couldn't hear what they were saying over the engine, but I could guess.

Finally he just stopped playing. He stood in the

middle of the field, arms dropped by his sides, with that dumb, helpless look on his face that was supposed to be so endearing but now just pissed me off.

I sat and waited. Kevin walked off the field slowly, toward me – his coach yelling the whole time from the other sideline – until he was close enough that I could see his eyes were red. As if that made all the difference.

"Where were you," I said. It wasn't a question, because I knew he didn't have an answer – not one that would do.

He started to say he was sorry – I saw it coming – so I revved the engine to drown out the words.

He tried again: "Sadie—" But I revved the engine again, and every time after that if I thought the words were about to come out of his mouth.

"Where were you," I said again.

His eyes got redder. "My parents found out," he said. "They wouldn't let me."

"You said you'd be there."

"I know, I know." He was practically whimpering. "But what happened? You got probation, right? Everything's OK? This will just blow over with my folks. I'm—"

I revved the engine yet again before he got to the "sorry."

Then I squeezed the clutch, tapped the Kawasaki into gear, and took off. Kevin didn't try to stop me or anything. He just stood there, looking sad. I almost felt sorry for him. Almost.

Five minutes later, my cell phone vibrated in my

pocket. I knew it was him. I was well on my way to Government Island by then. I didn't stop to answer or see what he might be texting. I just kept riding until I got to Coal Landing Road, and that copse of trees where I always hid my bike. I stashed everything, left Mom a message that I'd be home before dark, then tossed the phone as far as I could, deep into the swamp, and went to find that outcropping of freestone where I always sat overlooking Aquia Creek. Last time with Kevin.

Now just me.

CHAPTER 19

In which they come for the Jelly Sisters, we get work release, and C. Miller has news about Carla

It's just me, Fefu, New Nikki, and the Ginas at breakfast the morning after the fight. I can't eat. Good Gina can't seem to, either. The others don't seem to have any problem. Nobody talks.

Guards I've never seen before come onto the unit with restraints. They go in the Jelly Sisters' cells, and five minutes later lead both girls off in shackles. Wanda stares straight ahead the whole time. Nell keeps her head down. Neither of them says anything, the same as Chantrelle the evening before when they came for her in the restraint chair. I wonder if we'll ever see any of them again – the Jelly Sisters, Chantrelle, Cell Seven, Weeze. Officer Emroch.

Bad Gina is the first to speak.

"They're probably going to get, like, felony assault," she says.

Good Gina blinks at her. "What about Chantrelle?"

Bad Gina blinks back. "What about her? She attacked two guards and put one in the hospital. That's a whole lot of felonies. They'll probably charge her as an adult. Wouldn't surprise me if they already hauled her over to the regional jail last night to be with the real criminals."

Good Gina starts crying. It's a silent, shuddering sort of cry. She doesn't bother to cover her eyes, so tears splash onto her breakfast.

Bad Gina turns her attention to the rest of us.

"I bet they give us reduced sentences for what happened," she says. "Or maybe at least work release. I just hope they don't send us to work at the homeless shelter. They don't make people take showers or anything, and the whole place stinks from their BO. That's what I heard."

I've had about enough of Bad Gina already this morning, and we've only been out of our cells for an hour.

"Aren't you just a little concerned about your friend?" I ask.

She frowns as if having a hard time figuring out who I mean.

"Weeze," I say. "Remember her?"

Bad Gina's face sags, but it almost looks willful, as

if she's doing it for effect. "Yeah, I know, right? Those bitches. I don't think Weeze even knew how to fight or anything, or knew how to defend herself. But she was conscious and all when she left. I tried to get close to her, when they had her on the stretcher, but the guards wouldn't let me. I was going to tell her to milk it for all she can at the hospital, and they'll probably reduce her sentence, too, all the way down to probation or community service or something. The worse you get hurt in juvie, the lighter they make your sentence. It's practically a law."

"And you know this how?" I ask.

She lifts a clot of gray eggs on her spork, waggles it at me, then chews it thoughtfully. "Because it just makes sense. What they don't want in juvie, more than anything, is trouble. If there's trouble, they make it go away, whatever it takes. Mrs. Simper, she's like a genius at it. I've seen them come and go like you wouldn't believe."

I close the lid on my Styrofoam box, wishing I could make Bad Gina go away.

She picks the conversation back up again during first class that morning, which is GED prep.

"Hey, Sadie," she whispers, her face half-hidden behind her workbook from Mr. Pettigrew. "Look. About Weeze. It's not like I don't care about what happened to her and all of that. It's just that I'm happy for her that she's probably out of here. And she kind of had a girl-crush on me or something, so I was a little uncomfortable with that. That's all. I just didn't want you to think that I was being insensitive earlier. I mean, Weeze was my friend and all, but you have to get kind of hard in here about stuff like that."

"You said you've only been here a couple of weeks longer than me," I say.

"Yeah. Only I wouldn't call it *only* since it doesn't feel like *only* so much as it feels like I've been in here since about the time I was *born*."

She is actually tearing up, which surprises me. New Nikki, sitting on the other side of Bad Gina, doesn't bother to hide the fact that she's listening in.

"OK," I say. "Sorry."

Bad Gina sniffs. "Thanks. Anyway, I'm kind of jealous of her, if you want to know the truth."

"Jealous of Weeze?"

"Yeah. Her and Cell Seven."

"Why?"

"Well, they're out of here, aren't they?"

"Yeah," I say. "But Weeze got beaten unconscious, and who knows how bad she might be hurt. And Cell Seven slashed her wrist again. How messed up is that?"

Bad Gina leans closer to me and lowers her voice, I guess so New Nikki can't hear. "If I tell you something, you swear you won't repeat it?"

"What?" I ask warily.

"I told Cell Seven to do that."

"You told her to cut her wrist?"

Bad Gina nods. "She was freaking out from the minute she came on the unit. Sobbing and carrying on every night, keeping everybody awake. Girls were threatening her and everything. But I told her to keep doing it. Keep crying and stuff. And I told her how if she really, really wanted out of here, she might try cutting herself. Only I showed her how you do it if you don't really want to hit a vein, but just freak everybody out and make them think you're suicidal."

I recoil. "I don't think I want to hear any more."

She ignores me. "But see, it didn't work the first time. They sent her off to Snowden or wherever, but then they sent her back. I didn't think she'd do it again. I mean, I thought she might, but I wasn't sure."

"Why'd you tell her that?"

Bad Gina shrugs. "I know you're not going to believe me, but here's the truth: I did it to help her. I felt bad for her, for how much she hated it in here. I mean, it's not like the rest of us love it or something. But Cell Seven was going crazy in here. So I found this loose metal piece on one of the chairs in the gym that I kept bending until it came off, and I gave it to her. But I was very specific about where to cut. I didn't want her to really hurt herself. Just convince them she was suicidal so they'd let her out, let her go home or whatever. I don't know what she used that second time. That didn't have anything to do with me, anyway."

I think about my conversation with Mrs. Simper the

whole time Bad Gina tells me this. *Nothing is ever what it seems to be in here. No one is ever who they present themselves to be. The first thing you give up when you walk through these doors is trust.*

I realize it's not simply that I don't believe what Bad Gina is saying, but that whatever comes out of her mouth is just as likely to be a lie as it is to be the truth.

Once again I can't sleep that night, and I forget to bring a book, so after an hour of yoga and just sitting, I decide to work on my running wall flips. This girl Allie Hoffman and I used to do them in the gym after basketball practice until Allie broke her arm one time even though we did it over wrestling mats.

I don't have any wrestling mats in my cell, of course, so my mattress has to do. I drag it over next to the wall, but don't get my first step high enough and land so hard on my butt that it feels like I bruise my tailbone. I bail out of my next couple of tries when I'm too tentative and don't get horizontal. Finally, though, I nail it – everything but the landing, that is, since I land on all fours instead of my feet.

That jams both my wrists and bruises my knees, but not too bad. I limp around the cell a few times, shaking out my arms, mad at myself for being such a wuss. Then I attack the wall with everything I have, and this time I stick the landing.

I do a bunch more before I stop for a break, and I'm

hunched over, hands on my knees, trying to catch my breath, when I realize somebody's watching me – one of the night guards, staring through the narrow mail-slot window in my door.

I nod, but he just shakes his head and wanders off. I guess no matter what trick you're doing, no matter how amazing, it gets boring to watch after a while.

At least all those running wall flips wear me out enough that I can finally fall asleep.

I dream about running. It isn't one of those frustrating dreams, either, where the harder you try to run from something, the slower you get, like you're stuck in molasses or mud or your legs are too thick or your feet are too heavy or you're just too tired. My dream is just the opposite: I'm flying down the streets I grew up on, along paths by the river, through wide-open meadows I've never seen before that seem to go on and on forever.

There's another new girl in the unit. They must have brought her in sometime during the night. I'm surprised I slept through it. Her name is Kerry – maybe fourteen, white, quiet, mousy even, with limp brown hair that hangs in front of her face like half-closed curtains. She sits next to me at breakfast. I say, "Hey," and she says, "Hey" back, and we sit in silence after that until her spork breaks.

"Raise your hand and tell the guard," I say.

"It's OK," she says. "I wasn't gonna eat any more anyway. It's gross."

"Doesn't matter. You have to tell them or they'll think you broke it on purpose. You'll get everybody in trouble and we'll all lose our sporks."

She looks frightened but raises her hand. The night guards are still on duty, and the one who watched me do wall flips snatches the spork away.

"Is it always like this?" Kerry whispers.

"Like what?" I ask, bothered that she thinks I'm some kind of expert on juvie.

Her voice is so soft I can barely hear. "You get in trouble if your spork breaks. And that way they search you at the intake room. And they make you look down when you walk, and keep your arms behind you."

"Yeah," I say through a mouthful of potato patty. "It is."

When Officer Killduff and C. Miller come on duty Monday morning, they're carrying armloads of shackles.

"Everybody line up," Officer Killduff orders.

C. Miller is assigned to me, Fefu, and the new girl, Kerry. I'm last. "What's going on?" I ask.

"Work release," she says, cinching everything tight. I want to ask where. And I want to ask what happened to the girls they took off the unit. Most of all, though, I want to ask how things went on the playdate with Carla and Lulu and C. Miller's daughter. She's too busy, though, and Officer Killduff is standing too close with the Ginas and New Nikki.

As soon as they have us all shackled, Officer Killduff and C. Miller walk us off the unit, a ten-minute procession down a couple of corridors and through a couple of automatic doors, all the way past Intake and through a wide set of double doors.

And suddenly we're outside – or mostly outside, in a giant loading cage with a big juvie transport van. I drink in as much of the fresh air as I can swallow. It's the first time I've been out since that afternoon in the rain.

It's a crisp December day with a high blue sky – we could use visors and sunglasses. Before our eyes can adjust, though, and almost before I even have time for another breath, they herd us into the back of the van. I can still see outside, but everything looks artificially green through the tinted windows. Officer Killduff and C. Miller get in with us and off we go – first around the outside of juvie and through the parking lot where I left my motorcycle seven weeks ago, then down the access road to the highway.

We stop an hour later at Lake Anna State Park, which is south of juvie and about as deserted a place as I've ever seen.

"Hell, yeah," Bad Gina says as we climb out of the van. "Sweet *ass*."

If anybody is alive at Lake Anna, we don't see evidence of it – just an empty boat dock, and an empty food pavilion, and an empty boat-rental shack, with canoes and Jet Skis lined up near the water like so many big dead fish. A wide expanse of white sandy beach opens out in front of us, and the lake seems to go on and on, ringed by a thick forest of trees and, mostly hidden but still looming high above the tree line, the two massive cooling towers of the Lake Anna nuclear power plant.

I remember now why I never come down this way. They use river water to cool the reactors, then dump it into the lake. They say there's no danger of exposure to radioactivity, but I'm not convinced.

Officer Killduff and C. Miller unlock our shackles and hand us enormous canvas bags that we sling over our shoulders. Then they give us grabber tools with claw ends for picking up trash.

"These Spotsyltuckians that live around here left a serious mess over the weekend," Officer Killduff says. We're in Spotsylvania County, but I guess he thinks saying "Spotsyltucky" makes it sound more redneck. "You're picking it up. Once your bag is full, Officer Miller or I will escort you to a Dumpster to empty it. If you need a break, if you need to go to the bathroom, if you so much as need to stop working for a second so you can sneeze, you will ask permission."

The beach is disgusting. Cigarette butts, beer cans, broken soda bottles, soggy disposable diapers, uneaten or half-eaten or half-chewed and then spit-out hamburgers and chicken and coleslaw and hot dogs and chips and other unidentifiable food are scattered everywhere. And there's more garbage besides: wrappers, bags, tissues, busted Styrofoam coolers, bent Frisbees, popped balloons, cups and straws and lids, ripped towels, and piles of dog poop.

After an hour, we've barely cleared twenty feet of beach, and haven't even started on the stuff bobbing in the water or sunk to the bottom, but nobody seems to care. It's nice to be outside. As we move into the second hour on trash duty, Good Gina starts singing. First it's one of those sappy teen-girl ballads. The new girl, Kerry, grins and sings along softly. Fefu shakes her head. Bad Gina and New Nikki are far enough away that they probably don't hear, but when Good Gina starts in on a dance song we all know, I join in. Kerry and Fefu, too, though Fefu doesn't know all the words in English.

By the end of that second hour, we're all sweaty. It's warm for a December day – hot as the sun climbs directly overhead – but I'm still happy to be outside and singing with Good Gina and Kerry and Fefu. Fefu seems happier than anybody and can't seem to stop giggling, and I decide she can't be the girl Mrs. Simper was talking about who put the guy in a coma to steal his bike.

Kerry and I start talking after a while, during a lull in the singing. She asks me about visitors and phone calls. "I wasn't really paying attention when they told me all this last night," she says.

I explain how it all works. "Anybody in particular you want to see or call?" I ask.

She shakes her head. "Can't call. Don't have any money in the phone account."

I tell her she can call collect, but she shrugs off my suggestion.

"They don't want to talk to me anyway."

"Who?" I ask. "Your parents?"

She shakes her head again. "Anybody. And my parents don't even live here anymore."

"Where are they?"

She looks down at her trash bag. "I don't know. Nowhere. Or nowhere I know, anyway."

"So where do you live?"

"Foster family. And they definitely don't want to talk to me."

"Because?"

"I sort of tried to burn down their house."

"Jesus," I say.

"Yeah," she says. "Well, it was just the bedroom that caught fire and they put it out before it did too much damage. I've never lived anywhere where they had so many fire extinguishers. They keep one in every room. Smoke alarms, too. They even have a sprinkler system. You'd think they had pyromaniacs living with them all the time or something."

"Yeah, you'd think," I say, though I'm not sure Kerry picks up on the intended irony, since she just shrugs.

"I just like fire," she says. "It's fun. I don't usually set them indoors, but it'd been raining a bunch and everything outside was too wet. It was supposed to just be some paper in the trash can, but they had these long curtains that kind of caught fire, too."

"So it was an accident?"

"Yeah, I guess. Sort of. They didn't think so, though. Probably because I already burned down some other stuff since I'd been there. Their wooden swing set for their kids, and this little shed they had in their backyard. Stuff like that."

I wander away on my own for a while, and it's not until later that it occurs to me to wonder why Kerry wanted to find out about visitation and phone privileges. I guess it's important just knowing there's a way to have contact with the world, even if there's nobody out there to take your call.

We finally get a lunch break. Everybody ducks out of the sun under the pavilion. C. Miller hauls out boxes from the van – limp sandwiches, warm fruit cups, bags of chips, and Wal-Mart–brand orange sodas.

"I know we're not supposed to ask questions," Good Gina says when we finish, "but would it be all right to lie down on the picnic tables while we digest our food?" Officer Killduff grunts, which we all take to mean yes.

The park is deathly still. Not a bird in the sky, not a fish jumping in the lake. And still no people. Officer Killduff lights a cigarette, and I can't believe it but Bad Gina sits up and asks if she can have one, too.

That's as close as I've ever seen Officer Killduff come to laughing. He takes a long, satisfying drag, then blows out the smoke slowly in Bad Gina's direction. "It's not allowed," he says.

I ask Officer Killduff if I can go to the restroom, and he says OK. Before I even get up off the picnic table, Bad Gina says she has to go, too. He thinks about it for a while – I have no idea why it takes so long – then says, yeah, sure. "Be sure to flush," he says. "And wash your hands." Nobody laughs except C. Miller, probably because she thinks she has to.

Bad Gina and I sit in adjacent stalls, and she starts chattering right away.

"Wouldn't it be so cool to ride those Jet Skis?" she asks. "I haven't done that in forever. You ever ride a Jet Ski? I'd like to try this thing I've seen people do where you push the nose down and you actually go underwater and then pop out, like a whale or something."

I've actually been thinking about those Jet Skis myself – that if Lake Anna wasn't so junky and polluted, and if it wasn't for those nuclear reactors, this might be a fun place to come back to sometime. Kevin would love doing something like that. Carla used to love doing stuff like that, too. I think I might tell her about it if I get the chance to call tonight. I bet Lulu would like it, too.

Bad Gina finishes before I do. I hear water running but don't hear her leave.

When I finally come out of my stall, she's still there, leaning against her sink.

"Hey, Sadie," she says. "Check this out." She points to a second door out of the back of the restroom, on the opposite side from the pavilion. "We could walk right out

269 ||

of here. Cut through those woods."

"And go where?" We're miles from the nearest highway.

She grins. "Mexico. I told you I'm going."

"Right," I say. "And how are we getting there?"

She keeps grinning. "There are ways."

I wash my hands. "No, thanks. I like it in juvie too much. I'd hate to miss out on any of my time there."

"Whatever," she says, still leaning on her sink.

"Why don't you bring New Nikki?" I say. "You guys seem to get along pretty well."

"She's all right," Bad Gina says. "Just kind of young."

"She doesn't sound too young. Didn't she say she stabbed a girl?"

Bad Gina rolls her eyes. "Yeah, well, who hasn't?"

We work in silence the rest of the afternoon, except for Good Gina, who whistles a lot even though she can't carry a tune. As the afternoon wears on, we wander farther apart on the beach, each of us carving our separate, meandering little paths through all the garbage.

C. Miller comes down to join me at the water's edge.

"Pretty warm out for December," she says, squinting up into that high blue sky.

"It's not too bad once you've been out in it for a while," I say. "You're just coming from the shade. Cooler up there."

"Yeah, I guess," she says. "Anyway, you doing OK?"

"Sure," I say. "It's nice to be outside." I lean on my

trash grabber and survey the quiet lake and the verdant tree line. I always liked that word – *verdant.* Dad is the only person I've ever heard actually say it. He was always a good one for using uncommon words.

"So," C. Miller says. "That sister of yours."

"Yeah?" My throat closes up a little. I both want to hear this and don't.

"We got together like I told you, with Lulu and LaNisha. We met at that park in town, with the tennis courts."

"And?" I press, gripping my trash grabber. "How did it go? How'd she look? How was Lulu?"

C. Miller laughs. "Lulu was great. She and LaNisha decided they were best friends after about a minute. And Carla seemed OK, too. I don't really know her that well, but she was different from how I'd seen her at Friendly's. She was dressed a whole lot better. And she didn't look so tired or so skinny, either. Maybe because of what she was wearing. Or maybe she's taking better care of herself lately."

I let go of the breath I hadn't known I was holding and stare out at the water. "Thank you," I say, glancing back at C. Miller. "Really, I can't tell you how much I appreciate you checking up on her for me."

C. Miller smiles. "Like I said, it was nice to meet another single mom my age." She hesitates, and I tense up again. I knew this sounded too good to be true.

"She asked if she could use me for a reference at

Victoria's Secret. She knows somebody who works there, but they aren't sure about hiring her because of her record. She thought it might help to have me, since I work corrections."

"What did you say?"

"Told her I couldn't."

"Oh."

C. Miller kicks at something buried in the sand. It turns out to be a beer bottle. Heineken. "It's not my job to save your sister," she says. "That's not anybody's job but Carla's. I can maybe be her friend, but that's all."

I pick up the Heineken and stuff it in my trash bag. "So she's stuck at Friendly's. With all her druggie pals that work there."

"At least she's trying," C. Miller says. "You have to give her some credit for that."

"Yeah," I say. "Maybe."

I thank her again for checking on Carla. C. Miller says don't mention it.

Officer Killduff yells down to her to line us up and head back to the juvie van. It's time to go. C. Miller and I survey the beach, which is still covered with trash.

I hate the thought of leaving. Probably everybody else does, too. Bad Gina curses and empties her trash bag into the Dumpster.

C. Miller tells me not to worry, we're supposed to come back tomorrow.

* * *

I call Mom that evening. Lulu gets on the phone first and tells me she's painting Moo-Moo's toenails.

"She's letting you use nail polish?" I'm afraid I'll break down, it's so sweet to hear her voice – the same as it's always been.

"No," she says. "Not with polish. With a paintbrush."

"And paint?"

"Uh-huh."

"What color?"

"Blue."

"Just her toenails?"

"Her whole feet, too."

"So Moo-Moo has blue feet now?"

"Uh-huh."

"That sounds really pretty," I say, swallowing hard.

"Aunt Sadie?"

"Yeah?"

"When you coming home?"

Mom takes the phone from her then. I can hear her tell Lulu that that's enough for one night, and she needs to go on and wash her hands real good in the sink. I want to ask Mom how Carla is doing, if it's as good as C. Miller made it out to be. But then I decide if it's not, I don't want to know about it. Not tonight, anyway. It's been too nice a day to risk ruining with bad news about Carla. So instead I ask Mom about her cousin, since she'd told me she was planning to drive up to Delaware for a quick visit. Mom says they think they caught the cancer early, so her cousin is pretty optimistic.

"And what about Dave?" I ask. "Did you go out with Dave?"

She sighs. "I don't know why I told you about that."

"So?"

"So I'm not saying one way or the other."

I laugh, surprised that I'm relaxed about this. "That means yes, right?"

She laughs, too. It's nice to hear. "It means I'm not saying."

I hang up, still feeling good about things. Then I hear Good Gina, at the next phone, once again pretending to talk to her boyfriend who she shot, loud enough so I can hear: "Oh, I miss you, baby. I can't wait to see you. I can't wait until we're together again. I'm going to be the best girlfriend ever once I get out of here, and I mean that."

New Nikki is on the third phone, and by the looks of things, she's having phone sex or something close to it, whispering in a low, raspy bedroom voice, practically humping the wall until one of the guards sees what's going on and makes her hang up. Her face is still flushed when she sits down at one of the tables. Bad Gina asks if she needs a cigarette, and New Nikki blushes an even deeper shade of red.

I sit with Fefu and Kerry.

"Wow," says Kerry, nodding at New Nikki. "Did you see that?"

I nod. "Yeah. Quite a show."

Bad Gina stands up to use one of the free phones, and we all watch her for some reason, as if we think she might pick up where New Nikki left off. She doesn't. She gets into a heated conversation with somebody instead, though I can't make out what they're saying. She never takes her eyes off the guards and stops talking anytime one of them wanders over close enough to hear the conversation.

Fefu, too, gets into an argument with somebody over the phone, not bothering to keep it quiet, but since it's in Spanish I don't know what it's about. She's still worked up when we get back to Unit Three. She opens a Candy Land board and stacks the cards facedown and sets up the spinner and the game pieces. She must have played before, and judging from the defiant look she has – teeth bared, eyebrows knitted together – she's clearly ready to kick my butt or anybody else's.

I make sure to let her.

CHAPTER 20

In which it's the day before going to juvie,
and I visit Granny one last time

I stayed in bed all day Friday, Saturday, and most of
Sunday the weekend before turning myself in to juvie. I
probably should have made better use of my last days of
freedom – spent the night on Government Island, taken
Lulu to the zoo in DC, stuff like that – but I couldn't
seem to make myself get out of bed no matter how hard
I tried.

Carla came over, and I let her in long enough to tell
her to just keep her mouth shut. "If you confess now,
nobody's going to believe you," I said. "Or if they do, you
go to jail, and where does that leave Lulu? And I'll still be

in juvie because I already confessed and they won't let me take it back."

"How do you know?" she asked. It sounded like she was begging for something.

"Any idiot can see it," I said, my jaw clenched so tight I thought I might break some teeth. Carla started crying, and I told her to leave.

Sunday afternoon Mom made me open the door. She brought in a grilled-cheese sandwich and some tomato soup on a TV tray. "Sit up. Here. You have to eat."

I took a few slow, careful bites. I wasn't even a little hungry, though I hadn't eaten since breakfast on Thursday, before the sentencing. I worried that if I ate too much or too fast, I might throw up.

Mom sat on the floor and leaned against the wall and watched me. "Last time I'm asking," she said.

"What?"

"Did it happen the way you said, or not?"

I didn't know what she wanted me to say. She must have known everything was Carla's fault, but what good would come from changing my story now? All it would do was confirm Mom's reason for being furious at Carla. And if my going to juvie was going to mean anything, I needed Mom to be there for Carla, not to punish her.

I didn't answer her question and she didn't ask it again. We just sat there together for a while until she told me to get up and come on — we were going to the cemetery.

* * *

Eternal Rest sits on rolling hills west of town. It's kind of a dumpy cemetery, but I suppose in the end those things don't really matter.

Something was happening when we arrived. There were four sheriff's cruisers and an ambulance parked by what looked like a bulldozer lying on its side next to a fresh grave.

Mom parked as far away as she could. A groundskeeper walked past.

"Accident?" Mom asked.

He shook his head. "Fellow come out here little while ago, tried to dig up where his little boy just been buried. Stole that bulldozer out of the shed over there. Turned it over in a ditch."

"That's terrible," Mom said.

"Terrible to lose your child," the groundskeeper said.

Mom and I just looked at each other.

We hadn't been to the cemetery since Granny's funeral, nearly three years ago, but Mom was acting like it was an old habit, something we did on Sunday afternoons. She got down on her knees and pulled out some weeds from around Granny's headstone. I knelt down to help her, brushing off dried bird poop and tracing Granny's name with my finger. I still couldn't figure out why we were there. Mom and Granny had always gotten along well, but Granny was Dad's mother, not Mom's.

When all the weeds were gone, and the bird poop, Mom wandered off and left me alone. I sat on the brown grass and leaned against the headstone.

The last time I'd seen Granny was at the hospital when she was in respiratory failure. She had already said good-bye to Mom and Carla, and now it was my turn. I was alone with her in the room, and she pulled me so close I was practically lying next to her on the bed. She said there was something important I needed to know. She said I should always remember that life is hard for people like my dad, but that for people like her and me, it's pretty simple.

She pulled me even closer so she could whisper, like it was a big secret between just the two of us.

"You wake up every morning," she said, "no matter what happened the day before, and you tell yourself you're going to do good."

I waited for more.

"That's it, Granny?"

She nodded. "That's it."

I didn't know what to say, so I told her how much I loved her and she told me how much she loved me, too.

"Can you send your daddy in here now, sweetheart?" she whispered slowly, her voice fading.

I hesitated a second, and then said, "I will, Granny. I'll go get him right now." Only I couldn't. She'd forgotten that Dad wasn't at the hospital. Even with his mom dying, he couldn't make himself leave her house and come.

I went out in the hall with Mom and Carla and Lulu, who was just a baby then. I told Mom about Granny's request, but when she went back in to explain, Granny was gone.

Mom patted Granny's thin, frail hand, then left to find the nurse. Carla sat in a chair and cried and gave Lulu a bottle. I lay in bed next to Granny again and closed my eyes and held on to her until Mom and the nurse came back and said it was time to let her go.

After half an hour or so, I left Granny's grave to find Mom. She was sitting under an elm near where the guy wrecked the bulldozer, and she was talking to somebody who I quickly realized was the guy. The sheriffs were gone, but the bulldozer still sat on its side in the ditch. They were going to need a couple of tow trucks to haul it out.

I stood and watched for a while, Mom saying some things, I guess trying to help, the guy staring off at nothing. It broke my heart to see him like that, so obviously devastated, knowing his little boy was buried not far away, knowing there wasn't anything anybody could do to bring him back. Even God couldn't build a bulldozer big enough.

I sat under another elm tree and waited. Mom was with the guy for a long time, until the shadows grew so long that they melted away into dusk. I wondered how long she would sit there, but I didn't mind the waiting. We were supposed to meet Carla and Lulu back at the house for dinner, but I had a feeling that this was where Mom and I were supposed to be.

Granny was three years gone, but I felt her in that moment. It was the same as if she'd been sitting next to me, cradling me in her warm arms, telling me to take what I was seeing along with me into juvie, telling me to keep it in my heart and not feel sorry for myself, not for one minute, and telling me to remember:

You wake up every morning, no matter what happened the day before . . .

CHAPTER 21

*In which be careful what you ask
for because you just might get it*

The guards tell us it's raining, so we can't go back out on
work release right away. If we'd never been allowed outside in the first place, we'd probably have been all right
– our usual complacent juvie selves – but now everybody
seems to be on edge again.

Bad Gina takes it even harder than the rest of us,
though her mood brightens considerably that afternoon
when she gets a letter from Weeze. She reads it out loud
to New Nikki and Good Gina – loud enough so Fefu,
Kerry, and I can hear it as well, though we're a couple of
tables away playing Chutes and Ladders. Somebody had

duct-taped the board back together.

"Listen to this part," Bad Gina says. "'So since my jaw's wired shut, I can't eat anything except through a straw, so they have to puree everything, even meat and stuff. I think I already lost ten pounds.'"

Bad Gina laughs. "Liquid meat. Probably the best thing ever happened to her blubber-butt self, getting her jaw broken."

Good Gina doesn't say anything, but I can tell from the stricken look on her face that she wishes she wasn't sitting with them.

"There's more," Bad Gina chirps. "This is good. Check this out. 'They said I don't have to go back to juvie. They're going to send me to a halfway house for the rest of my sentence after I get out of the hospital. But I hope I get to see you again. I hope we can still be friends.'"

"You think she's in love with you or something?" New Nikki asks.

"Yeah, probably," Bad Gina says. "God, what a homo."

I glare at her. Weeze was her friend, got hurt on account of being her friend. And this is how she gets repaid? No wonder the Jelly Sisters attacked Bad Gina. I'd like to hurt her, too, and catch myself thinking of ways I might do it without getting caught.

Kerry touches my arm and tells me it's my turn. It takes me a second to remember we're playing Chutes and Ladders. It takes longer to shake the thought out of my head about hurting Bad Gina.

In the real world, you can walk away from somebody who gets on your nerves, ignore them, get lost in a crowd, hang out with other people, do other things. In here, though, the world shrinks so much that there's no getting away from people, no separating yourself from their crap. Little things become big things because there isn't anything else.

It keeps raining for the next couple of days, or so Officer Killduff says. He could be making up phony weather reports for all we know. There's one bit of good news, though – from Carla. She doesn't get the Victoria's Secret job, but the Friendly's manager puts her on the breakfast shift, so at least she won't be hanging out so much with the afternoon drug crowd. Plus she can get Lulu at a decent time from day care. The news makes me so happy I don't care about the rain, or the fact that we haven't been able to go back to Lake Anna.

Fefu and Kerry and I keep hanging out together in the days that follow, sometimes with Good Gina, too – playing cards, board games, kid stuff. They act like I'm their big sister; it's a role I've been in most of my life with Carla, so I'm kind of used to it, and with the good news about Carla's work, I don't really mind. Kerry decides we should teach Fefu how to read, so there's a lot of Dr. Seuss going on for a while.

Some things don't change. Good Gina keeps pretending to talk to her boyfriend. New Nikki loses phone privileges for humping the wall again. Bad Gina keeps having these agitated conversations with somebody every night, shutting up when the guards come close, keeping her voice low so none of the rest of us can hear what she's saying. And Carla doesn't pick up when I call her cell phone. But instead of freaking out, I decide to have a little faith in her. When I do finally catch up with her, she tells me she's been at AA. Twice in a week.

Friday morning they bring in the shackles and everybody gets excited. Officer Killduff orders us into line, and five minutes later we're climbing into the back of the juvie van, me and Fefu and Kerry on one side, the Ginas and New Nikki on the other. Bad Gina, opposite from me, licks her lips nervously and grins, though not exactly at me.

No one tells us we're going back to Lake Anna, but once we get to the interstate and head south, everybody knows. New Nikki says she wishes the van was going the other direction, up to DC, where her cousins live, and there are all these clubs they could take us to, where we could get in underage if we dressed slutty and guys would buy us drinks.

New Nikki starts up about this one guy she hooked up with one time, and Good Gina shrinks away on their bench seat. She might have shot her boyfriend and all, but I know hard talk like that still makes her uncomfortable. It's kind of weird to say, but seeing that gives me hope that maybe we won't be *so* changed once they let us out.

Fefu has been teaching Kerry how to sing "Itsy-Bitsy

Spider" in Spanish – "*La araña pequeñita*" – and pretty soon they get me singing it, too. The hand motions are the same, though Kerry has difficulty climbing the spider up the water spout, thumb-forefinger, thumb-forefinger.

Bad Gina scowls but doesn't say anything, which is a nice change.

We hum down the interstate for another half hour until we get to the Lake Anna exit, then wind through two-lane roads in thick forest. For some reason I start thinking about the girls who aren't on Unit Three anymore. It still feels strange to me that they're all gone – the Jelly Sisters, Cell Seven, Weeze, Chantrelle, Middle-School Karen, even Summer. And not just gone, but so suddenly, and absolutely. Nobody talks about them, except that day when Bad Gina got a letter from Weeze and made fun of her. I guess that's just the way it is in juvie. One minute they're stripping away everything you own, down to your last underwear; the next minute they're sending you home to your parents, or shipping you off to a long-term facility south of Richmond, or carrying you to the hospital to wire your jaw, or locking you up on another unit with the violent offenders.

They start erasing you when you enter; they keep erasing you after you leave.

The rain has turned the garbage soggy at Lake Anna, even more disgusting than before, if that's possible. You go for a diaper with your trash grabber, and half of it stays on the ground. Usually the grossest half. But you still have to pick it up. Same with the food. Same with everything.

Fefu and Kerry keep singing the Spanish "Itsy-Bitsy Spider," like a broken record, but I don't mind. I'm happy that they actually seem to be enjoying themselves. It takes me forever to get all the words right, but then we sing it over and over until Bad Gina throws a wet bag of chips and tells us to knock it off already.

"God!" she snarls. "I'd like to crush that itty-bitty spider under my shoe."

"Yeah," echoes New Nikki. "Same here."

I'm in too good a mood to let them spoil it. "I think you mean 'itsy-bitsy.' "

Bad Gina glares. "Yeah," she says evenly. "Whatever. Itsy-God-damn-bitsy."

I smile, though I'm already on dangerous ground with Bad Gina. "Except it's Spanish," I add. *"La araña pequeñita."*

Bad Gina throws a busted flip-flop this time. "Just shut up, Sadie."

Fefu snares the flip-flop and stuffs it in her trash bag. She and Kerry giggle.

Then they start singing again. Bad Gina and New Nikki huff and work their way up the slope of the beach as far away as they can go without getting barked at by Officer Killduff, who's standing at the top of the sandy slope in the speckled shade of a gnarly dogwood.

C. Miller stays down with us on the beach. She

doesn't sing along with Fefu and Kerry and me but asks us to repeat the words. She says she wants to teach it to LaNisha when she gets home.

After an hour, C. Miller tells us we can take a break for water. There's a cooler under the tree next to Officer Killduff, and everybody troops up the hill for some. I stay by the edge of the lake, though, and inhale deeply and look around at the silver water and the lush green tree line and the clear azure sky. Of course there's also the nuclear power plant with its massive, ghost-white cooling towers, but I try not to focus on that right now. There's always going to be something — a fly in the ointment or whatever. I mean, look at me. It's nearly Christmas, and I'm two months into a six-month sentence in juvie, picking up other people's soggy nastiness and singing "Itsy-Bitsy Spider" in Spanish with a pyromaniac and a girl who shot her boyfriend and a ten-year-old who clubbed a guy with a metal pipe so she could have his bike. And they're the nice ones.

But it could have been a whole lot worse. It could have been Carla in prison for four years instead of me in juvie for half of one. And it could be Lulu without a mom instead of just missing her aunt.

I dig unsuccessfully for something with my trash grabber before realizing it's dog poop and not a brown paper bag. Fefu and Kerry come back from getting water just in time to see what I'm doing and practically fall down laughing.

I kick wet sand over it and move on.

Shortly before noon – the sun directly overhead, though it still isn't too hot – Bad Gina tells Officer Killduff she has to go to the restroom.

He nods to C. Miller. "Take her."

"It's OK," Bad Gina says, a little too quickly. "I'll just run up and run back."

Officer Killduff stares at her. "She goes or you don't."

Bad Gina flashes him her girliest smile. "Just trying to be helpful."

C. Miller rolls her eyes. I want to warn her about Bad Gina. I can't say why exactly. It's just a feeling I can't shake as I watch them trudge together up the beach. Everybody else stops working to watch, too, as if it's the last time we'll ever see them.

Officer Killduff yells at us. "Back to work or back to juvie."

We lower our heads and continue picking up trash in the opposite direction from the pavilion. Officer Killduff barks about stuff we missed and we keep having to go back and get it.

I look up the beach again, but C. Miller and Bad Gina aren't back yet. I try to focus on my job, but something still doesn't feel right. Finally I ask Officer Killduff if I can go to the restroom, too.

He looks exasperated. "You couldn't ask me that before, when they went up?"

"Sorry." I shrug.

He nods. "Hurry."

I'm halfway up the beach when a strange wind picks up. It catches a rivulet of sweat on my neck and leaves an icy chill. I walk faster.

There's nobody at the pavilion or the Dumpster, nobody outside the restroom or at the boat-rental office or anywhere else that I can see. Lake Anna is as deserted as it was when we came before.

I push open the restroom door and step inside. It takes a minute for my eyes to adjust to the dark, and when I walk in farther and turn the corner I freeze.

C. Miller lies sprawled on the floor, blood covering one side of her face. Bad Gina's nowhere in sight, but I look immediately at the back door, remembering what she said last time we were here – about making a break.

C. Miller moans. I rush over and lift her head gently. "Are you OK?" I ask, my stomach twisting at the sight of all that blood. "What happened? Are you all right?" She opens her eyes, stares blankly for a minute, then lifts herself onto her elbows and scrambles away from me into the corner.

"It's OK," I say. "You got hurt. It was Bad Gina."

C. Miller looks scared and confused. She throws her arms up in front of her as if trying to ward me off.

"No," I say. "It's not me. It's just her. I'm going to help you."

She scrambles farther away, eyes wide with fear.

This is no good. She won't let me anywhere near her. "I'm going for help," I say. "Just don't move."

I push myself up and out the front door of the rest-room and scream down the beach to Officer Killduff. He takes a few running steps in my direction but then stops and looks at the other girls.

"Help!" I scream again. "God damn it! Help!"

I slam back inside the restroom, where C. Miller is wiping blood from her face, shaking her head as if trying to clear her thoughts. I grab a wad of paper towels and kneel next to her even though she tries to crawl farther away. "I'm not going to hurt you," I say. "Just take this and hold it." I press the paper towels against the cut and push her hand down over the towels to keep the pressure on.

She moans in pain, and her eyes are still full of fear. It makes me sick that she thinks this was my fault, that I did this to her.

I think about what Mrs. Simper said, about only doing what I'm told. But I look again at the fear in C. Miller's eyes, and in that instant I decide: no way am I taking the blame for something else I didn't do. Not this time. Not ever again.

I open the back door and take off after Bad Gina. She might have outrun me that day in the gym, but there is no way in hell she's getting away from me today.

Everything that's happened can't have taken much more than a couple of minutes. That's already enough for a pretty good lead, but there's only one road heading off from the restroom, more of a dirt track really, and Bad Gina has to be on it. I take off sprinting, all out, as hard as I can go, drawing on every ounce of conditioning from years of basketball, throwing myself down that road after Bad Gina the way I've always thrown myself after every loose ball and into every fast break my whole life. I don't slow down for a quarter of a mile, not even when I finally spot her up ahead, maybe two hundred yards away, disappearing around a curve. My sides ache, my lungs burn, but I pick up the pace even more and keep it there, running crazy under a dark tunnel of trees. A minute later, I catch sight of her again.

I keep pushing, gaining on her with every step, until I'm close enough to hear her labored breathing. We're on a straight section of the trail, and there's a clearing up ahead. A black car. A guy standing next to it, smoking a cigarette.

Bad Gina starts yelling, "Start the fucking car! Start the fucking car!" But the guy looks uncertain about what to do. We're a hundred yards away. He just stands there. I pull even with Bad Gina.

She swings an elbow at my face but I duck away easily and keep going. I know I should be afraid. It's stupid, what I'm doing. The guy could have a gun. But I'm too far in now to quit. She swings at me again.

"Hey, Gina," I say, as if we're just out for a friendly jog. "Holding up OK?"

She doesn't answer. We're fifty yards from the car.

Bad Gina yells at the guy again, but he panics. Jumps in and slams the door shut. The engine roars to life, and the tires spit gravel as the car lurches forward.

Bad Gina wails. "No!"

"Well," I say, "this sure has been fun."

Then I grab her ponytail and yank hard, just like during that AAU game. She doesn't have time to get her hands out to break the fall, just lands straight down on her back. I'm sure it knocks the wind out of her because she just lies there gasping, flailing her arms and legs, eyes so wide I think her capillaries will burst.

The black car vanishes.

"Don't worry," I say, standing over her. "You'll live."

Once she gets her breath back, I roll her over onto her stomach and sit on her. She struggles to free herself. "Get off me, bitch!"

I push her face into the dirt. Not too hard, just hard enough to make my point. She wails some more but doesn't fight after that, just lies there cursing and spitting for the next ten minutes until Officer Killduff shows up, gun drawn, and puts us both in restraints.

CHAPTER 22

In which I tell Lulu a story

I was the one who put Lulu to bed the night before I turned myself in to juvie. Mom had already retreated to her bedroom; Carla needed something from the store.

First I read the *Everyone Poops* book, and Lulu and I spent a lot of time discussing it. I quizzed her afterward.

"Does toothpaste poop?"

"No."

"Does a Chia Pet poop?"

"What's a Chia Pet?"

"Never mind. Does poop poop?"

"Maybe."

"Close enough."

After I turned the lights out, we took turns drawing on each other's backs. I couldn't guess what she was drawing on mine because her pictures lacked all sense of proportion: heads that covered both shoulder blades, bodies an inch high. She couldn't guess what I drew on her because she was just a little kid and thought everything was either a house or a monkey.

We snuggled together under the covers after that. I deliberately slowed my breathing down, the way I used to do when she was a baby, and hers gradually slowed along with mine until I thought for sure she was asleep. She wasn't, though, and when I tried to ease myself out of bed, she opened her eyes.

"Tell me a story, Aunt Sadie?"

I was happy for the excuse to stay, so I settled back in. "What about?"

"About you and Mommy. And Moo-Moo and Granpa."

"You don't even know Granpa."

"I went to his house," she said, as if that was the same thing.

So I told her a story about this time we all went camping in the mountains – me and Mom and Dad and Carla. I was probably eight, so Carla would have been eleven.

"We hadn't ever done much camping before," I said. "It was Moo-Moo's idea. I was the only one excited about it. Your mom didn't want to go. She wanted to stay home and watch TV. Granpa didn't like to be in the car with all of us so much. But Moo-Moo wanted us to do something together, a family thing, so we went, anyway."

Lulu wanted to know if we cooked marshmallows.

"Of course," I said. "And I ate about fifty. And we wrapped potatoes in aluminum foil and cooked them under the coals in the fire, and we cooked hot dogs on sticks, and when we were finished eating, we tied our food bag to a rope and hung it really high off the ground from a tree limb."

Lulu wanted to know how come, and I told her that it was to keep it safe from bears, and so a bear wouldn't come inside our tent looking for the food if we kept it with us in there.

"I don't want a bear to eat you or Mommy or Moo-Moo," Lulu said, snuggling closer. "Or Granpa."

"Me neither. And it didn't happen, so that was good."

"Yeah."

I lowered my voice to a whisper. "Only something else *did* get in the tent."

Lulu looked worried. "Was it a bad monkey?"

"No," I said. "Worse. It was a skunk. Your mommy got up to pee in the middle of the night, and when she came back, she must not have pulled the zipper all the way down on the tent flap, so a skunk got in."

"Did the skunk spray you guys? Did it spray Mommy?"

"No. But your mommy saw it, and she got so scared that she ran away into the woods to hide. She told us later that she was afraid if she yelled, it would spray everybody.

But the problem was that she ran too far and got lost."

Lulu sat straight up in bed. "Did she have a flashlight?"

"Uh-uh," I said. "And she got really lost because instead of stopping and waiting for us to come look for her, she kept walking, thinking she could find her way back to the campsite. Only she couldn't."

"So what happened?" Lulu asked, obviously frightened. I wondered if she was too little for this story. I'd chosen it because it had a happy ending and it was one of the few stories about the four of us that did. But now I was worried that I was scarring her for life or something.

"Everything turned out OK," I reassured her. "Granpa woke up before too long. Somehow he knew something was wrong. And when he saw Carla wasn't there, but the skunk was, he just quietly opened the tent flap and let the skunk out. Then he woke up me and Moo-Moo and gave us all flashlights and said we had to go find your mommy. So that's what we did."

"How?"

"Well, we stayed close together so we could see one another's flashlights but search kind of a wider space. And we took turns yelling for Carla. It took us about a whole hour. Maybe even longer. Maybe almost all night. I just remember I kept tripping over things and nearly falling down, and I was so mad at Carla for running off like that. But Dad – Granpa – he kept us going until we finally heard Carla's voice."

"What was she saying?"

"She was saying 'Help me! Help me!' because she had fallen down off some slick rocks and hurt her leg. Granpa had to climb down and get her and carry her back up the side of the mountain, and he even carried her all the way back to our camp."

"Was Mommy OK?"

"She had to wear this kind of boot thing while her ankle got better, but that wasn't until we got back home and she went to the doctor. But that night, when we got back to our camp, there was a big problem, because we hadn't closed the tent flap and the skunk was in there again, curled up on one of the sleeping bags. Only this time your mommy wouldn't let Granpa kick him out. So we ended up sitting under a big tree the whole rest of the night with a poncho over us. Your mommy and I were shivering because we got kind of wet and cold and so Moo-Moo and Granpa held us in their laps until me and your mommy fell asleep."

"What happened to the skunk?"

"He woke up after a while and went back to his own family. Granpa and Moo-Moo carried us into the tent while we were sleeping and tucked us in our sleeping bags, and everybody slept until really late the next morning."

Lulu smiled. "I like that story."

"Yeah," I said. "Me too. We used to be a great family." As soon as I said it, I wished I hadn't.

Lulu looked worried again. "Can we still?"

I felt bad. "Still be a great family?" I was stalling for time.

Lulu nodded.

I thought about how I was going away to juvie for the next six months, and how I was afraid Lulu would think I'd abandoned her. I thought about Dad hiding out at Granny's and not seeing anybody for years, and Mom tired all the time from working two jobs, and Carla promising over and over that she was finally getting straight.

But then I thought some more about what I was about to do the next day. Really thought about it. I had to believe it was the right thing to do, and I had to believe that it would matter, that it would make a difference in Carla's life. In all our lives.

"Can we?" Lulu asked again, still wanting to know whether we could be a great family again. As if it was all up to me.

I hugged her tight. "You bet."

CHAPTER 23

In which Mrs. Simper pays me a visit

It's long after midnight when I finally get back to juvie from Lake Anna. They make me go back through Intake, since I've been unsupervised on the outside, and it's still the same old drill: strip search, oral inspection, body-cavity search, shower. I'm just putting on my juvie-issue underwear when Mrs. Simper walks in, looking very, very tired. She waits while I pull on my orange jumpsuit and black sandals, then tells the guards they don't have to put me back in shackles.

"Just this once," she says to me. "Don't get any ideas."

I nod.

"Officer Miller should be all right," she says before I can ask. "She's in the hospital overnight for observation."

The paramedics who checked all of us out at Lake Anna had told me pretty much the same thing, but it's a relief hearing it again. I want desperately to ask if anyone told C. Miller that it wasn't me who attacked her but decide to wait to see if Mrs. Simper mentions anything.

"What about Bad Gina?" I ask.

Mrs. Simper gestures at the door, and the guard calls down to the control center to have it unlocked. "She's somewhere else. There's an APB out for her boyfriend, the man you reported seeing."

"Did she confess and everything?"

Mrs. Simper shakes her head. "First she said it was you who attacked Officer Miller. Then she said Officer Miller attacked her and it was self-defense. Then she said she didn't know who the man with the car was. Then she said the man with the car robbed the liquor store that she was convicted of robbing, and he threatened to hurt her family if she didn't escape and go away with him."

"So that's a no, then?"

"Right."

We amble down the halls without speaking. It seems like months, not hours, since I last heard the click and buzz of each set of locked doors.

The night guards let us onto Unit Three and unlock my cell. Mrs. Simper follows me in there, too.

I sit on the bunk. She looks around as if it's the first

time she's ever been in such a place. I scoot over and offer her a seat, but she doesn't take it. I wait for another lecture like the one she gave me the day Chantrelle freaked out and the Jelly Sisters put Weeze in the hospital: how I should have waited for Officer Killduff; how I shouldn't have gone after Bad Gina; how in juvie you do what you're told, no matter what.

Mrs. Simper finishes her inspection of my cell and studies me for a long minute. "What am I going to do with you, Sadie?" she asks.

"A reduced sentence?" I ask, only half joking. After all, I did keep Bad Gina from getting away. That's got to be worth something.

"A reduced sentence?" Mrs. Simper repeats.

"Yes, ma'am."

"I see," she says.

Mrs. Simper finally takes me up on my offer to sit. She presses down on the mattress. "These really aren't very comfortable, are they?" she asks.

I shrug. "I guess they're all right. I've slept on worse."

"Really?" She seems genuinely interested, so I tell her about Government Island and camping out there and sleeping on the ground a lot of nights.

"It's not far from here," I say. "I could take you there when I get out." I don't know why I'm being so friendly with Mrs. Simper, except that she's being so friendly to me, walking me here without shackles, sitting with me on my bunk, hanging out in the middle of the night as if it's the most natural thing in the world.

She stands abruptly.

"Well, good night, Sadie," she says, turning to leave. Then she pauses and faces me again. For just a second she reminds me of my mom – I'm not sure why. I think she might even try to hug me.

She doesn't.

"I wouldn't pin my hopes on an early release," she says. "That's not how it works in here."

I slump against the wall. "But I'm not even guilty in the first place," I say, though I know it sounds lame.

Mrs. Simper shakes her head. "Just because you're not guilty," she says, "doesn't mean you're innocent."

The cell door locks behind her, leaving me just sitting there. Gravity takes over after a while, and I slide down the wall until I lie on my bunk under the stuttering light, exhausted, ready to collapse into one of those dead sleeps I used to fall into after two-a-day practices plus weight training.

It's not that easy shutting off my brain, though. I mull over what Mrs. Simper just said. I remember C. Miller telling me pretty much the same thing that day the power went out and we were stuck in the gym shooting baskets.

I shouldn't have gone to that party the night Carla and I got arrested. I shouldn't have let Dreadlocks and Scuzzy in the car, or waited in the 7-Eleven parking lot. But I let those other voices get too loud in my head – convincing me that I was sick of chasing after Carla and it shouldn't be my job, anyway, or it was OK to drink just a little that night, or it wasn't worth the hassle of saying no to the guys, or we'd just have to wait in that parking lot five minutes, that's all, five lousy minutes, and then we could go home. What could possibly go wrong?

So, yeah. Maybe they were right. Maybe not being guilty wasn't the same as being innocent.

EPILOGUE

In which I do the math

We never go back to Lake Anna – work release is canceled forever, according to Officer Killduff – and C. Miller never comes back to juvie. Her injuries aren't too serious, though Carla tells me she has headaches for a couple of weeks after the attack. Carla also says C. Miller can't remember anything that happened after walking into the bathroom, which I guess is a good thing, though part of me worries that she'll always wonder if I had anything to do with it, no matter what she's been told.

I'm sad at first that she's gone, but it's mostly for myself. C. Miller's definitely too nice for a place like juvie.

I call her one night – Carla gives me the number – but we don't talk about the attack. She tells me she's taking classes at the community college, which was something Carla suggested, of all people. And she's playing some recreation-league basketball. She says she and Carla hang out some, and LaNisha and Lulu started a Saturday gymnastics class called Tumbling Tots for three-year-olds.

I hear LaNisha in the background, singing, and realize I have no idea what she looks like. That makes me sad at first, but only for a minute, since I'm pretty sure when I get out, Lulu and C. Miller will both be happy to introduce us. "Take care of yourself, Sadie," C. Miller says. I tell her I will.

The next time Carla visits, I almost don't recognize her. She's chopped her hair even shorter than before, to her chin, and it's bouncy and healthy-looking in a way I barely remember. Her face has filled out a little, too. It's almost like looking at a picture of Carla when she was my age, before the drugs and Lulu's dad and the drinking.

She tells me the assistant manager just quit at Friendly's and they're considering her for the job, which would mean more money, and if she's management, Friendly's would pay for business classes at the community college if she wanted to take them. She also tells me Mom's definitely decided to move into Granny's. It's too good a deal: no rent, and she can look after Dad, *and* there's tons of room for Lulu to run around and play when she's over.

Mom comes to visit the next week and confirms that she's moving out to Granny's. She tells me that Carla's thinking about moving in, too. Carla somehow managed to leave that part out. "I explained everything to your dad," she says. "Through the door, anyway. But I just have a feeling he's going to be OK with it. It'll be a lot better than having strangers living there."

Mom also tells me she and Mr. Ferrell finally heard from the school board. They said there wouldn't be anything on my permanent record about being in juvie if I want to come back and finish my senior year. "Plus you can play basketball again," she says. "So long as you stay out of trouble." It takes a minute for me to register what she's just said. But once I do, I'm so happy that I drop the receiver. It makes so much noise hitting the wall that I lose phone privileges again, but I don't even care.

The next time I call Carla, Lulu answers. I grin when I hear her voice. I can't believe I ever thought the wind through the leaves was my favorite sound in the world. It's got nothing on Lulu.

It's a couple of days before Christmas, and she asks if I want to hear her sing a Christmas carol. I'm so thrilled I can hardly stand it, only instead of "Silent Night," she sings "All I Want for Christmas Is You," which totally cracks me up.

She tells me, as if I didn't know, that it's about a

girlfriend and her boyfriend and they want to be together for Christmas.

"Just like I want you to be here for Christmas, too, Aunt Sadie," she adds.

When I ask what she's been doing lately, she tells me about all the great things she and Carla have been up to – Christmas shopping, going to see Santa, going to Washington to see all the Christmas trees from all fifty states they have decorated near the White House. It's hard to hear at first – all that I've been missing out on, all the sorts of things Lulu and I used to do, but that she's doing now with Carla. But it's also kind of wonderful, too – everything I had hoped for.

Then, without missing a beat, Lulu starts in on the family gossip, surprising me with how much older she suddenly sounds, even at three and a half. She says Moo-Moo has been going out with this guy Dave, but Carla doesn't think it's serious. Then she tells me Carla dated her new boss a couple of times, but that Moo-Moo doesn't think *that's* serious, either.

I ask Lulu what "serious" means, and she whispers into the phone: "It means you kiss them."

"Ew," I say. "Gross." I tell her I think Carla and Mom should both join a convent, and Lulu asks what that is.

"It's a place where there are only girls," I say. "And they dress funny. Like in *The Sound of Music*."

Lulu wants to know if they would take her there, too, and I say, "Of course."

"And you, too, Aunt Sadie?" She sounds worried.

"Sure," I say. "It's not like I have a boyfriend or anything."

Lulu is quiet on the phone for a minute, then says, "If you wanted, you could."

Christmas is hard. We don't get any visitors since it falls it the middle of the week. The same with New Year's. But then I get another letter from Dad, another envelope from him, anyway, with that faint, spidery script of his. There's a poem inside, an old Indian prayer that I recognize. Granny used to have it tacked to the wall next to the desk where she paid all her bills and wrote letters and stuff.

Hold on to what is good
even if it is a handful of earth.
Hold on to what you believe
even if it is a tree which stands by itself.
Hold on to what you must do
even if it is a long way from here.
Hold on to life
even when it is easier
letting go.
Hold on to my hand
even when I have gone
away from you.

Like everything else, I have to give this back to the guards to keep until I'm let out. But I already have it memorized by the time they come to collect the mail.

Not long after that, I get a letter from Kevin.

I don't open it at first, just stare at the handwriting, which is big and loopy like a girl's. I must look weird or upset or something, because Kerry, Fefu, and Good Gina come over to see if I'm OK. I nod and wave the envelope.

"From my old boyfriend."

Good Gina gives me a hug. Kerry pats me on my shoulder. Fefu just wants to get back to playing checkers.

I finally open it.

He says he hopes I don't mind him writing.

He says he's been thinking about me a lot lately.

He says he ran into Carla and she cussed him out in the middle of a sidewalk downtown. He told her about a hundred times that he was sorry, and then she told him about me rescuing C. Miller and chasing down Bad Gina.

He says he's told everybody at school.

He says he started playing indoor soccer at a place called the Field House, and he went with his dad to visit colleges last weekend, and his youth group went on a mission trip to Louisiana to build houses for hurricane victims.

He says he hopes I'll write him back, and he hopes we can keep writing to each other.

It's a sweet letter – in a way it's almost as sweet as the one from Dad with Granny's poem.

* * *

I lie in bed that night for a long time, thinking about Kevin's letter and his request that I write him back, not so much about whether I'll do it – I'm sure I will – but about what I'll say, and how I'll say it. How do you put into words all the ways in which you've changed? The language I spoke before juvie doesn't seem adequate anymore. It's probably time I learned a new one.

I close my eyes. I haven't figured it all out yet, but I'm not worried. There's plenty of time. Even drifting off to sleep, I can still do the math: three months down, three to go.

ACKNOWLEDGMENTS

My deepest thanks to Kaylan Adair, who saw better than I did – and, thank God, let me know it – the book *Juvie* had the potential to be. Thanks to Janet Watkins, who really should be on the Candlewick payroll for her careful reading and insightful editing and all-around support. And thanks to Kelly Sonnack, who continues to be such a wonderful advocate for me and all the writers and illustrators fortunate to have her as their agent and friend. Thanks also to the many people who helped during the writing of *Juvie* in all kinds of ways, whether they know it or not: Jill Payne and my CASA family; Ainsley Brown; Anne and Carl Little and my UU family; everyone in my yoga family; Stacey Strentz McLaughlin; Patrick Neustatter; Neva Trenis; Wayne Watkins; Johanna Branch; Clyde Watkins; Nora Lea Watkins; Ted and Anita Marshall; a certain DEA friend who is undercover so I can't say his name; the amazing Rabe family, who bring great light into the world wherever they are; everyone who fought to save Government Island; plus our book and library friends – Paul Cymrot, Emily Simpson, Sydney Simpson, and Sean Bonney (and Jack and Cable and Quinn and Ellie and little Maple). Special thanks to Maggie and Eva and Claire and Lili and Marty and Pete. And more special thanks to our Circle friends, Marylise and Damian Cobey, Chris and Beatrice Kerr, Steve and Becky Slominski, and all the kids, who fill our house and our hearts with love and a whole lot more.

IF YOU ENJOYED ----------

WOULD YOU DO TIME FOR YOUR SISTER'S CRIME?

STEVE WATKINS

WHY NOT TRY... ----------

Blink is on the run. He was just trying to steal some
breakfast; now he's stumbled on a fake kidnapping.

Enter Caution. As in "Caution: Toxic". Also on the
run, she sees Blink as an easy mark. But there's
something about him that tugs at her heart.

Together, they devise a blackmail scam which
is at best foolhardy ... at worst, disastrous.

NEVER ENDING
MARTYN BEDFORD

"The greatest teen
novel ever to come my
way and I don't expect
to find a better."
Robert Swindells

It happened during a family holiday in Greece, and
now Shiv is tormented by guilt. Nothing her parents
have tried has helped her move on.

With its unconventional therapy, the Korsakoff
Clinic is her last hope. It is there she must confront
the events that have torn their lives apart.

"A gripping, original
and stylish novel."
The Times

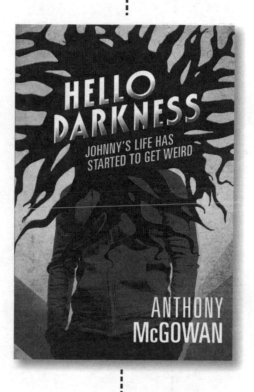

Someone is on a killing spree – slaughtering the school pets
with a cold-blooded savagery. The number-one suspect:
Johnny Middleton.

Johnny's had problems in the past, but they're behind him
now. So what if he still sees the world a little differently?
He's not crazy and he's not a killer.

And he's going to prove it.

WONDERLAND

JOANNA NADIN

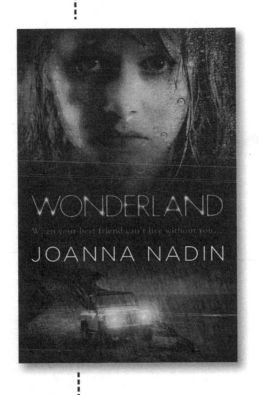

I wasn't always like this.

Once I was as bright as she was.

People took notice because she
was with me. Stella.

A BOY.
A GIRL.
A BUMP.

TROUBLE

A NOVEL BY
NON PRATT

Hannah is smart and funny.
She's also fifteen and pregnant.

Aaron is the new boy at school.
He doesn't want to attract attention.

So why does Aaron offer to be the
pretend dad to Hannah's unborn baby?

Growing up can be trouble but that's
how you find out what really matters.

Ink Slingers
STORIES SET FREE

BOOK TALK (AND OTHER THINGS WE LOVE)

PREVIEWS

INTERVIEWS

COVER REVEALS

TRAILERS

WRITING TIPS

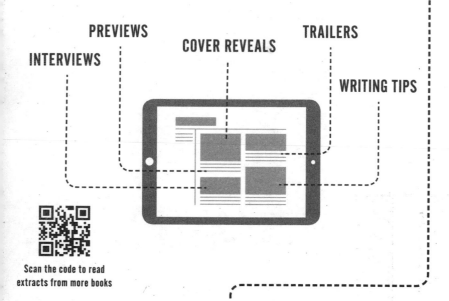

Scan the code to read
extracts from more books

For a chance to win other great reads visit

www.INK-SLINGERS.co.uk/WIN

Enjoyed this book? Tweet us your thoughts @WalkerBooksUK